# LINERS OF TIME

A new edition of John Russell Fearn's classic pre-war time travel novel, together with an early novelette *Invaders From Time,* both of which introduced new concepts to science fiction!

"My very real regret in these crud new days of Earth-in-peril pix is that authors who pioneered—Hamilton, Cummings, Williamson, Starzl, even John Russell Fearn—are not reaping the yellow harvests of Hollywood gold rather than the Odd Johnnies-Come-Lately who do the 'original' stories. It's only a shame that one of the oldtimers didn't collect a little pelf when Hollywood lifted another of their ideas off the shelf and filmed it."

—FORREST J ACKERMAN

# THE GOLDEN AMAZON SAGA

# LINERS OF TIME

## JOHN RUSSELL FEARN

*Edited by Philip Harbottle*

**WILDSIDE PRESS**

Published by Wildside Press LLC
www.wildsidepress.com

# Contents

# Contents

# INTRODUCING "LINERS OF TIME" by Philip Harbottle

In 1931, when English tyro author John Russell Fearn discovered a remaindered copy of the U.S. pulp *Amazing Stories* in a Woolworth's store (the standard introduction to the genre in England, where no home-produced science fiction magazines existed) it changed his life. Here, at last, was a market!

As I have recorded in my introduction to *The Intelligence Gigantic* (also now available from Wildside Press) Fearn had already been working on that first novel for some time. It had been written and conceived in the traditions of the English scientific romance popularised by Wells, and traditional English boys' adventure stories.

Whilst he was awaiting the results of his first submission, as any good aspiring author should do, he studied this new market—by the simple expedient of taking out a subscription and obtaining all the back issues he could find, and reading the stories printed in the magazine.

They made an immediate and lasting impression, resulting in Fearn writing a long "fan" letter to the editor. His letter was published in full, leading off *Amazing*'s "Discussions" column in the March 1932 issue.

He revealed that "I consider that Dr. David Keller and Edward Elmer Smith, Ph.D., rank as your finest authors." After analyzing (not uncritically) the science in Smith's *The Skylark of Space*, he wrote: "Anyhow, though, it was a rattling fine story, the finest I have ever read, and I am now eagerly reading the sequel. It certainly beats its predecessor, and that's saying something!"

Like many others at that time, he had fallen under the spell of E. E. 'Doc' Smith.

When Fearn eventually heard from *Amazing*'s octogenarian editor, Doc Sloane, that his first story had been accepted, it positively galvanized him into creative action:

"All my submerged ambitions shot to the surface. Since England didn't want science fiction I would write for America... Promptly I wrote *Liners of Time* in exactly one month and sold it just as promptly to *Amazing*." (*Science Fiction Fan*, 1936).

In this story, written in the white heat of enthusiasm, Fearn set out to emulate Smith—if not to surpass him. Plausibility was sacrificed for sheer imagination, and Fearn departed considerably from his original "English" style.

In later years, this would be seen as detrimental to Fearn's reputation as a writer, but at that time Fearn was quite understandably only concerned with building up a career as a published author after years of frustration in England.

The novel's swift acceptance prompted Fearn to write a direct sequel, *Zagribut*, in the same style, and featuring the same characters, but endeavouring to go even further in sheer imagination and wondrous events. This was also accepted—before his original novel *The Intelligence Gigantic* had even appeared! Few SF authors can have made a more impressive debut than Fearn—I can think of no other author who entered the field by selling three novels in a row!

*Liners of Time*, although written and accepted in 1932, was eventually published as a 4-part serial, beginning in May 1935. Despite this delay, the serial still went down well with most readers—the magazine's letter columns were full of approbation, by both readers and fellow writers, notably Joseph Skidmore:

"John Russell Fearn has a wonder story in his serial *Liners of Time*. The story theme is a great idea; it's clever, thought stimulating, and amazing…Two or three points of science appearing in *Liners of Time* tempted me to write in with a critical, controversial pen; but the points I dispute are trivial compared to the grand aggregate worth of the story. So I refuse to look for flaws in a valuable gem with a hyper-critical microscope. As an author, I know how that goes… American authors will do well to note the splendid literary style of this English writing chap, Fearn. *Liners of Time* is one of the best-written Mss. that have appeared in *Amazing Stories*. The punctuation in this story is a high academic standard. Fearn inspires one to do better writing." (*Discussions*, October 1935).

There was one notable exception to the paeans of praise. This came in the same issue from regular correspondent "Wild Bill" Hoskins, who specialised in strongly criticizing authors and stories that roused his ire. His opening remarks were quite uncompromising:

"John Russell Fearn doesn't write science fiction. He writes science FICTION, with the accent definitely on the fiction, and the science practically non-existent…"

"Wild Bill" went on in his long letter to berate the author for his dubious science and the time paradoxes implicit in the theories expressed in the story, and even his use of the English language, for which he "deserved the razzberry for not saying what he meant." He concluded:

"In short, Mr. Fearn, for *not* using your knowledge and training to write *real* science fiction; for doing what (nearly) all other authors do and what has made science fiction the (Censored—Bill) literature it is today; for writing *Liners of Time* and other things to drive me crazier; for all that, Mr. Fearn, nuts to you."

The editor invited Fearn to respond, and his good tempered and equally long reply, printed in the April 1936 issue, was both witty and urbane. He contested some points, conceded others:

"I freely admit I do not strive for scientific accuracy by any means; indeed I ignore possibility altogether if I can get a thrill by being particularly fantastic. It is a fact, in case Mr. Wild Bill is not already conversant with it, that those who break every known rule, in any walk of life, usually get the biggest following. I don't break *every* rule of science, but I certainly shelve facts many a time—and, Mr. Bill or otherwise, I shall continue to do so where I think it is necessary...

"...Lastly Mr. Bill has consigned to me a razzberry and some nuts. At least I may take fresh hope from these small but nevertheless edible morsels. Until Wild Bill has solved the cause of the English language and completely solved how to place himself in seventy different times at once, I shall remain here to make him crazier (his own words, I believe.)"

However, paradoxically, it is the very deficiencies of the novel that make it of interest today. The reason for this is best exemplified by a wonderfully perceptive piece by scientist-author "Hal Clement" (Harry Stubbs) entitled "Physical Sciences" appearing as a thematic essay in *The New Encyclopaedia of Science Fiction* (1988) edited by James Gunn. Describing the work of the early sf magazine writers, Clement pointed out that:

"Writers drew on the physical sciences not only for ideas but to make plausible their romantic or epic stories of distant places or the future. In any kind of story authors must convince their readers that the events *could* happen: plausibility is the means by which readers are sufficiently convinced of the validity of the fictional experience that they can suspend their disbelief for as long as the experience lasts...

"...In the magazine stories of the 1920s and 1930s, the physical sciences were king. Hugo Gernsback, founder of *Amazing Stories*, published many kinds of stories... His greatest discovery was Doc Smith, whose Skylark serials have spaceships gallivanting around the Solar System (and eventually the galaxy)...

"...In many tales of this time, physics was replacing magic as a storytelling device. Authors and readers shared the opinion of the general public: anything was possible; sooner or later science would learn how. In some instances authors used scientific information as a source of plot ideas; in others they invented a plot and then sought scientific justification for the things that were to happen…

"…John Russell Fearn's *Liners of Time* (1935' 1947) exemplifies this use of physical sciences; its justifications of time travel, invisibility, and the hurling around of planets were just gobbledygook…"

Clement labelled Smith's and Fearn's type of story as "wishful SF" but went on to further point out that:

"In all these cases, criticism of the author's scientific knowledge must be tempered by consideration of artistic problems… Scientific plausibility is important to an SF story, but a reasonably fast pace is essential to *any* story."

However, as early as 1938, Fearn had, in fact, *completely abandoned* this type of science fiction. He wrote: "I have felt for a long time that the day of the unwieldy science novel has gone, unless it was done by a master such as Edward E. Smith. In the past I have been guilty of several massive efforts, which though they may have contained the germ of some new idea were swamped entirely of all hopes of characterization." (*Amazing Stories*, January 1939). Thereafter Fearn wrote in an entirely different style—indeed, *several* different styles, and under several different names. But that is another story…

In 1947, Fearn's serial was published as a hardcover book in England, by World's Work. It was again packaged by the publisher—as had been *The Intelligence Gigantic* four years earlier—as "A Master-Thriller Science Fiction Novel." The novel was never again reprinted during the author's lifetime, although, as with *The Intelligence Gigantic* in the late 1940s, an overseas paperback publisher (in this case Fireside Publications of Canada) contracted to publish the book only to fold before it could be scheduled.

Inside the book's dust jacket, World's Work promoted their 1947 edition as an unashamed pure entertainment:

"If you are one of the growing army of science-fiction fans, you will find this novel entirely to your liking. As science it is super-super, giving one, as it does, intimate details of future amazing inventions, machines which bridge not only eras of time millions and billions of years apart, but which also traverse space and land one upon worlds yet unborn, or, perhaps, on Jupiter whence comes the villain.

"For those who like their thrillers melodramatic, *Liners of Time* will be no disappointment. For amid the noise of weird machines, through the navigation of ships which not only treat time as space but space as sport, there is still a brave hero who navigates the lustrous liners and a charming heroine, who supports and aids him, as well as a most obnoxious villain who is, as he should be, thwarted in the end."

As with the novels of 'Doc' Smith that inspired it, *Liners of Time* can certainly be read and appreciated by ordinary readers at this level—on which level it can also of course be *deprecated* and condemned by the *literati* who see no merit whatsoever in pulp fiction. Their loss, our gain!

Whatever its literary shortcomings (and these have been grossly exaggerated—page Joseph Skidmore!) *Liners of Time* has frequently been alluded to in various SF history and reference books that identified notable stories that shaped the subject of fictional time travel. And rightly so, because at the time of first publication, it was highly influential. *Had it in fact been published when it was first submitted, in 1932, its impact would have been even greater.*

As it was, by 1935, three years later, a few other writers had independently anticipated some of Fearn's ideas, most notably Nat Schachner in "Ancestral Voices" and Murray Leinster in "Sidewise in Time."

These two stories are generally awarded the laurels as the pioneer seminal stories respecting the theory of "alternate worlds"—parallel time tracks caused by the action of a time traveller—and published in *Astounding Stories* in October 1933 and June 1934 respectively/

Fearn also anticipated the "time loop" paradox whereby someone returning to the past to meet himself would, in effect, become immortal—a theme most memorably used by Robert Heinlein in "By His Bootstraps" (*Astounding*, 1941).

The earliest pulp classic on time travel was probably *The Legion of Time* (1938/1952) by Jack Williamson. Others followed where Fearn, Schachner, Leinster and Williamson had led.

Science fiction's leading historian, the late Sam Moskowitz, was of the opinion that Isaac Asimov's classic time travel novel *The End of Eternity* (1955) was "obviously inspired by John Russell Fearn's action epic" (*Seekers of Tomorrow*, 1966). Now new readers have the chance to judge his bold claim for themselves!

Fearn's central idea in this novel is that there are various "branches" of time, and that a malign time traveller could seek to "change" time by manipulating events, thereby creating a new time track. The theme has since became universal and is central to many of the Hollywood SF films and television series appearing today. It is one of the core concepts of modern science fiction, and Fearn was one of the first SF writers to explore the theme.

In preparing this new edition for publication, I have discovered that many of the most audacious cosmic concepts were later to be revisited by Fearn in his much later Golden Amazon novels (currently available in new Wildside editions).

In my essay on Fearn appearing in the reference work *Twentieth-Century Science-Fiction Writers* (St. James, third edition, 1991), describing *Liners of Time* and its sequel *Zagribud* (as it was retitled on publication in 1937) I said:

"In these stories, Fearn went the limit with imagination, the results of his exposure to the "super science" stories of Smith and Campbell. Wonderful events abound: time travel on a cosmic scale, invisible cities, entire planets being destroyed. All is explained away in a welter of pseudo-science. Buried in the hodge-podge was the core of an interesting idea—that of differing time-lines capable of being altered and manipulated by an unscrupulous time traveller. Fearn's ideas were subsequently properly developed by other writers…"

Schachner's story, "Ancestral Voices," whilst poorly written, was important and influential, and set the pattern for countless other stories by those writers who followed. The author's protagonist is a time traveller, who goes back to the fifth century A.D., and kills a man who turns out to have been his ancestor. As a result, the time traveller and all of his predecessors cease to exist, are wiped out clear back to the fifth century as though they had never existed. Their direct ancestor had been killed before he could father any children. The main significance of the story at that time was that it showed that the ancestral line was carried across several races and continents, and was an elegant refutation of the then-rising Aryan myth of racial supremacy.

The new *Astounding Stories* reached the U.K., where it was eagerly read by British author John Russell Fearn. His first novel, "The Intelligence Gigantic," had been published in *Amazing Stories* in 1933, and two other novels accepted but not yet published (nor would they be, until 1935 and 1937).

"I still felt I had not expressed myself exactly as I wanted," Fearn later wrote. "… Then came the day when *Astounding Stories* was revived, and 'thought variant' stories were introduced, full of new audacious ideas. Here, I thought, was my big chance."

Thereafter Fearn wrote a string of short stories and novelettes for *Astounding's* new editor. F. Orlin Tremaine, and during his editorship became a leading contributor. And it was at that time that the first UK SF magazine, *Scoops*, suddenly appeared in England, opening up another market.

Fearn made his British debut with "Invaders from Time," in the 14th, May 12th, 1934 issue *of Scoops*. The paper was a juvenile weekly, and Fearn's story was tailored to the market with its young protagonists and relatively simple plot development. However, it possesses a refreshing naivety and definite storytelling zest. Apart from Conan Doyle's reprinted minor classic, "The Poison Belt," it was probably the best story appearing in *Scoops* during its short life. Interestingly, buried in the welter of pseudo-science, there is an astonishingly scientifically accurate prediction of the use of tasers! Notwithstanding, it has been completely overlooked by SF historians because of its obscure publication. But the fact remains that this was the first time this particular time travel plot had ever been used in a British publication.

Accordingly, it seemed the ideal choice to accompany this new edition of *Liners of Time* as a bonus for collectors.

It seems likely that Fearn took his inspiration from Schachner, but it is quite possible that it was conceived independently. Certainly, in *Liners of Time*, (written in 1932) Fearn had himself speculated on time travel theory long before Schachner's story had appeared. This expertise was on display in Fearn's elegant and urbane reply to a reader's letter in a later edition *of Scoops* (June 16th, 1934):

"… I agree with Mr. Lorenz in that the perfect Time story has never been written, and probably never will, because the science of it is interwoven with complexities that outrage our trained senses. An author must take dramatic license to create a story of Time, and I certainly am no exception. When a story of Time is in hand to be written there always crops up the famous bugbear of all science fiction writers, namely, "what happens to a man's life if he goes back in Time and shoots his grandfather before he—the man who shoots—is even born?

"One could argue forever upon the flaws in a Time story, and for myself at least, I hope the external pleasure of it was ample compensation for my critic in "Invaders from Time." The whole science of Time can be summed up in one word—'paradox'."

Philip Harbottle,
Wallsend,
England,
March 2015

# LINERS OF TIME

## INTRODUCTION

This manuscript, sent to you via the Time-Line from 2000 A.D., will, I know, present many bizarre aspects and situations, but I have at least the consolation of knowing two indisputable facts. One is that I have spoken the truth and related to the best of my ability the history of an adventure; and the other is that my work will be read and analysed by broad minds that are capable of seeing further than the first street corner they are coming to. For this latter reason, knowing the Intense criticism the most intelligent of the readers will direct upon this history of an adventure, I feel it my duty to make clear, before I commence the real narrative, one or two points about Time, from the viewpoint of a Pilot of Time—for such I am.

One fact about Time is that, although you can equally move to past or future, you cannot possibly, in either of the two states, do anything but what you did or will do in one of the states of Time. And further, it is *impossible* to live in any of the Times States, after your birth, without doing exactly what you had already done. Tune cannot be altered. But it *is* possible, I have found, to go any distance *before* your birth and live in the past. Should you return to that same point in the past, once again you would, as I have said, perform the same actions, because a man or woman cannot do two different things in the same period of time…

The sharply critical amongst you will ask many questions as you read my history. At the point where my companion, Elna Folson and I, are flung back into pre-history, you might ask (upon our return) why not go back again to the same place and see once more the wondrous Intelligences we discovered there. The reason why not is because we would only live over again the same experiences… Hence my little explanation.

Another point. In my struggles with Elnek Jelfel, of which you will read, you will ask why I always arrived *late enough* in the passage of events to take up the thread of my experiences and make them continuous. I have merely put this for simplicity. Several times in actuality I overshot the period and came back to the beginning of my experiences, only to do the same actions all over again; but since the repetition is of no interest, I have deleted it, of course...

I have found in Time that Time is always as writ. You cannot alter it. You will do in your lifetime what Time has planned you shall do, and no matter how far you may reach ahead, or delve backwards, you will inevitably be brought to obey immutable law closely.

And now, my friends of the past, I leave you to criticize and dissect my history of an actual experience... Thank you.

SANDFORD LEE,
(Master Pilot of Liner 48),
New York,
2000 A.D.

# CHAPTER I

## *2000 A.D.*

"The President of the Time-Liner Corporation requests your presence in the Debating Room at the eleventh hour."

The cold, implacable, mechanical voice ceased to speak from my Recorder, and was followed by the metallic twang that pronounced the breaking of the electric contact between my flat and Headquarters.

With a puzzled frown I sat for a while looking at the orifice of the instrument, then with a shrug I rose to my feet. In the days of 2000 it is the duty of any employee of the Time-Liner Corporation to obey commands without question. The organization controlling the great company was ruthless and commercial, demanding absolute compliance with all orders, from the highest to the lowest. Even I, Sandford Lee, Master Pilot of Time-Liner 48, was permitted no variance from law, despite my relatively high position.

I glanced at the impulse-clock upon the wall; it was ten minutes to eleven. Still a trifle puzzled by the order, I buttoned up my uniform and slowly ascended the stairs to the glider-room of my flat. I pulled forth my glider from its little shelter, clambered in, and in another moment was sweeping down the tilting chute, lunging into the full depth of the glider atmosphere. For those of you who may not understand this, I had better mention that in 1978 a genius named Carelli discovered that charging certain layers of the upper atmosphere with a gas named tonium—several times lighter than hydrogen—made flying absolutely safe, whether it be glider or flying machine. A fall to earth was impossible except by actual collapse of the machine being flown, which of course was an unheard-of occurrence.

Headquarters—the mighty building of the Time-Liner Corporation—lay perhaps two miles to the south, and despite the hour the glider ways were not particularly busy. I alighted on the Headquarters' roof-landing about ten minutes later, and Hensen, a sentry whom I knew very well, saluted smartly. I returned it, and made my way downstairs to the lower floors via elevator and percussion staircase—a system of suspended gravitation by which one is gently lowered down slopes of great slant, thereby obviating staircases. In the gleaming passage-way of the main entrance to the Debating Room I was met by two guards, bearing the official insignia of the T.L.C. embroidered in gold upon their uniforms.

In silence I was ushered into the Debating Room, and, as I saluted and stood respectfully at attention, I noted the details already familiar to me—the horse-shoe table with the Directors of the Corporation seated at it, and the walls lined with instruments. The bright morning sunlight slanted across upon me from the vast glass windows and picked me out like a solitary figure.

"Commander Sandford, Lee?" Templeton, the President asked, merely as a matter of routine.

"At your service, sir," I replied quietly, and waited for the next.

"We have summoned you this morning, Commander Lee, for a very special purpose. As our most experienced engineer and pilot we feel that you—and you alone—will be able to bring to an end an alarming state of affairs existing with our Time-Liners."

I waited in silence, though I had an idea of what he was hinting at.

"Recently, Lee—commencing I believe about four months ago, our liners began to disappear—and all our efforts to locate them or the passengers and crew have completely failed! There are only two alternatives to be admitted. Either those liners have been turned aside from the time line by some colossal and unsuspected power, or else they have been flung beyond the Limited Stop—the year Ten Million and Two Thousand. If that be so, if the latter is the case, those liners are marooned in far futurity and lost!" Templeton's jaw set and his eyes turned to me interrogatively.

I took a step forward. "Of course, sir, I have heard of these happenings, but I never suspected matters were so serious. Three of our liners have gone, I know. That means nearly fifteen hundred lives...."

"Exactly," Templeton nodded grimly. "Of course, we have had the vibration detectors at work; we have used the time radio-tester; we have even sent out scout time machines, but they have never returned."

Templeton paused and then thumped his fist down on the shining table top. "Lee, it is up to you! Tomorrow Liner 16 should leave New York for the year 40,000. Instead, you will take Liner 48, your own ship. It is more fully equipped than any other ship in our fleet, and is therefore more able to cope with danger than one of the earlier types. At all costs, Lee, you are either to rout this unknown menace, or else find the cause of it, when plans can be made for its removal... That is all."

"Very good, sir." I saluted, and left the vast room. In the passage I paused and considered: fortunately, I was accustomed to receiving imperative orders at very short notice. Accordingly, I decided not to return to my flat immediately, but to settle my affairs in the city before departure. With this in my mind, I turned and descended to the lower levels, finally along the moving passage-way, and so into the street.

I suppose the street, of the year 2000, would appear to you of the past a bizarre and very grotesque affair. To me it was commonplace. The petrol car, for instance, went out of existence in the year 1970, and in its place came the remote-controlled car. The driver, of course, guided and braked his own conveyance, but the motive power came from a centrally situated power-station. This station used solar energy, converted into electricity, which in turn was transmitted on invisible beams to the magnetic propulsion motor in the car's interior. Each car owner, therefore, paid a yearly subscription—or tax—to the Solar Energy Company for his power, and his engine was immediately linked up.

Buildings in 2000 were not so greatly altered, save for the fact that all roofs were sheathed in lead of four-foot thickness. This, be it understood, was to block the very short wave cosmic ray. Petard, as far back as 1948, discovered that this emanation was the main cause of human life becoming shorter, and the only effective blocking to the rays is, of course, lead. The results, it appears, have been very beneficial... But, however, I digress from my narrative.

I was turning into the main street when I almost collided with Elna Folson. It may seem strange to you, but Elna was approximately eighteen thousand years older than I, and yet, by the same paradoxical situation, was about my own age—thirty. Those of you who might expect Elna to be some astounding-looking creature, due to the time of her birth, will be disappointed by my description. For she looked very much as the earlier beings have done.

About five feet eight inches tall, she was dressed, not in some bizarre outfit, but a neat cream-coloured costume, cream stockings, fairly flat black shoes, and a wide-brimmed hat. If you had met her in the twentieth century you would have noticed little difference in her attire, from that to which you were already accustomed. The only change lay in her features. They were a trifle more regular than the earlier types, and the teeth were far more perfect than any of her twentieth-century sisters. There was, too, a keen and brilliant intelligence in the grey eyes, and an air of independence and resolution, entirely lacking in the prototypes.

Elna and I were just very good friends. Such a thing as love was unknown in 2000, or in any of the Ages coming after it. A man and a woman could be good friends without infringing any laws, so closely equal had the sexes become.

As Elna was the daughter of the President of the Time-Liner Corporation in the year 20,000 (her own year), she was a girl of more than average intellect and considerable wealth. I would make it clear here that the Time-Liner Corporation had branches in all Ages. The one in 2000 was the acknowledged head office, but none the less important was the one in 20,000, over which President Folson held sway. The two Presidents—Templeton and Folson—were indeed the only men in the whole time-line who knew the real secret of a time-liner and how it operated. They alone could construct a time-liner from the original plans.

"Why, Sandy!" Elna exclaimed in delight, using my nickname, "I was just wondering whether I would call at your flat or not. You see, I'm leaving tomorrow for home, on Liner 16. I'm not quite sure of the formalities, despite the times I've had vacations from my own Age, and I was thinking of looking you up to get matters in order."

I smiled and took her arm. Together we walked along the street.

"I don't think that you're going to leave by Liner 16," I said quietly.

"Oh, why not?" Her grey eyes were looking at me in pleasing enquiry.

"Because, Elna, Liner 16 isn't leaving tomorrow. I've just come from Headquarters now. I'm taking tomorrow's load, on Liner 48."

"You are! Taking that luxury liner! Oh, I shall feel so—confident."

"That's sweet of you, Elna, but I'm afraid this trip is to be more a matter of grim business than any trip before. There's dirty work going on somewhere in the Time Line, and I've been assigned to locate it. Frankly, I don't half like you coming on this trip. There's going to be trouble, I'm afraid."

"Rubbish!" she pouted. "Who cares for a few mysteries in your old Time-Lines? The trip will be as safe as any other—"

"Safe!" I laughed a trifle harshly, and then proceeded to explain to her all the President had told me. Even then she seemed only a trifle abashed. It takes a lot to upset the courage of a strong-minded young woman of 20,000.

"You tell me that either these precious liners of yours have gone so far into the future that they can't get back—or else they are perhaps marooned in some hyperspace, in some other dimension. You expect me to understand it! Sandy, I haven't the slighest conception of what you're talking about."

"And to think you are eighteen thousand years older than I!" I said solemnly.

She laughed and revealed those magnificent even rows of snow-white teeth.

"It isn't altogether that I don't understand," she amended. "It's more, shall I say, lack of the necessary imagination—or instruction. Nobody has ever yet made the system of time-travel clear to me, perhaps because they don't understand it. It is very wonderful, I know, this travelling between time stations like one used to do in an old railway tram, but still I do not fully comprehend it."

I paused as we passed an automatic dinner-service. With a nod she assented to my enquiring look and we passed inside. A courteous robot ushered us to our tables and placed the electric menu before us. We surveyed it, chose our requirements, and then pressed the corresponding buttons arranged at the side of the menu. Instantly the table top turned over and there was our meal upon metal plates. This "turnover" was effected by tremendous centrifugal force, which naturally prevented the viands from hurtling off. I would mention here that the idea of tabloid food had never really attracted anybody, and the food of 2000 was about the same as it had always been, save for the fact that there were many cultured, delicious dishes from future ages.

"Now," Elna said, when we were comfortably seated, "be a good sort and tell me all about this awfully difficult time business you specialize in."

"If I specialized in it I wouldn't merely be a pilot," I grunted. "I'm not genius enough to fully comprehend it, but I can outline it enough to make the idea clear to you. Listen carefully."

"All right; carry on," she invited brightly, and ate silently as I explained.

"The method of time-travel was discovered after years of research by that wonderful electrical analyst, Ino Carreno, in the year 1980—only twenty years ago. He tried every conceivable method of solving time, having a fortune to do it with and more than his share of brains and ingenuity. He tried everything from a cinematograph film (which he decided was time in analogy) to radio waves. It was, however, his researches in the field of radio that finally enabled him to solve the problem of time-travel. As you will be aware, in olden days when radio was in its infancy, radio waves were subjected to extreme distortion and fading, particularly below the 500 metre band. On very-short waves the trouble was even more apparent. Several well-thought out theories were advanced as to the cause—such as the deflecting of radio waves from the earth; or the 'throw-back' from the Kennely Heaviside Layer. All this, however, failed to satisfy Carreno, and he explored the problem thoroughly, taking radio waves alone, as distinct from television waves..."

"Are you discussing time or wireless?" Elna asked me, with a sly smile, bisecting a bun very neatly.

"I'm coming to the point," I answered patiently. "Carreno's experiments were numerous, but they eventually brought to light the fact that a tenuous, invisible gas, entirely unknown before, existed in bands about the earth—and probably embraced the whole universe; he had no means of testing the latter possibility. Now, this gas, he discovered, was denser in some places than in others, and was very highly ionized, probably by cosmic rays. This instantly accounted for the fading in radio-waves, and occasional spells of static, that made radio impossible. Plainly then, contrary to old-time theory, the Kennely Heaviside Layer was not responsible. You understand, Elna, that static is caused by the free movement of protons and electrons, impinging upon one another, the atoms having been wrenched loose in their components."

"I'll take your word for it, Sandy," she replied, a trifle discouragingly.

"Well, this gas fascinated Carreno. He called it carrenium. At length he managed to construct a small model made of what he called his carrenium alloy. This metal was lighter than the gas, and floated upon it—apparently in mid-air. Carreno, it is reported, only saw the model for a second, then it vanished from sight."

Elna laid down her knife. "And to think intoxicants went out before Carreno was born!" she said irrelevantly. Then with a laugh. "But go on. I'm only joking."

"Puzzled, Carreno buried himself for months in calculations and at last found that the strange gas had two distinct properties. One was that it promoted growth in living organisms by speeding up the action of the cells. This he discovered by 'bottling' some of the gas and testing its effects upon animals. The second property was that it moved with a stupendous velocity parallel to our three-dimensional plane. The gas, in truth, was allied to, but was not actually, the fourth-dimension."

"It was not really the fourth dimension?" Elna repeated thoughtfully. "It was allied to it?"

"Exactly. It lay, to be exact, diagonal to the three-dimensioned plane that we understand. But to resume: Carreno finally projected himself into the gas in a life-size machine. He utilized the gas itself for propulsion—which system, by the way, I'll show you some day on a time-liner. Instantly, Carreno found himself the astounded observer of a four-dimensional universe, with all the ages of time from dawn to infinity unrolling before his gaze, like some mad jig-saw puzzle, as the vastly accelerated speed of the gas—in proportion to normal time—bore him onwards. He came back and summed up his conclusions, which he published, and which you may see in the museum any time you wish. It was once his workshop.

"His conclusions were that the general distribution of the gas throughout the ages had caused Man's gradual evolution, and evolution is, of course, time. Normally, the gas would evolve man further and further into future time, by degrees—but Carreno's discovery revealed that time is purely a mental construction, caused by Man's undeveloped senses. Projection into the actual gas of evolution made it possible for Man to race far ahead of his own Age, into the distant future, or force his way back along the time-line to the past. So the thing went on. For a further test he built a life-sized machine and sent it back into the far past, empty. Of course it never returned—but unhappily he made the mistake of his life when he did that. That time-machine had an accelerator attached to it, which possessed the power of speeding-up a time-machine's speed to five times what we can get now. An average time-liner today moves at a speed of six years to the minute. If only that accelerator could be discovered again it would increase our speed tremendously."

"But surely Carreno took notes of his work?" Elna asked in surprise.

"Yes, but unfortunately the details of his wonderful accelerator were never recorded, for the simple reason that two hours after he sent that machine into the past—the only machine ever made with an accelerator—he collapsed from heart-failure and died without leaving a single workable detail. All that remained was the secret of time-travel, and out of that was born that mighty Time-Liner Corporation. Carreno's workshop in the centre of the city, as you know, stands now as it stood then, and has become a museum in his memory."

Elna had lost her flippancy as I concluded.

"A wonderful man," she said thoughtfully.

"A genius," said I. "Perhaps, if you insist coming on this trip tomorrow, you will be interested to see some of the inner workings of a time-liner."

"I should love it!" she answered eagerly; then pensively again, "Sandy, why do different Ages have different names? For instance, my own Age is called The Age of Security. Then there is the Age of Danger, and so forth. Why? Do you know?"

"Yes. For instance, if a man of 2000 desires important information, he takes the Liner to the Age of Intelligence. If, on the other hand, a man of the Age of Intelligence desires a relaxation, he goes to the Age of Contentment. Or, if a man of Contentment desires excitement, he goes to the Age of Danger, and so on. Time has become utilized merely for the extension of achievement, and the different ages of advancement or in some case retrogression—are defined as Ages. You might as well ask why a train used to travel between New York and California in the old days."

"I see. Thanks, Sandy."

We turned back again to our meal, which had been neglected during my lengthy, and I fear a trifle faulty exposition on Carreno's time-travelling method—but had barely commenced when a slim, pale-skinned man, attired in a close-fitting, black, one-piece suit and flowing cape entered, black hat in hand. As he came by our table he paused and bowed to Elna. She returned the salutation and I rose to my feet.

"Oh—er—Master Jelfel," she said, detaining him. "Just a moment."

He came back again, and somehow I took an instant dislike to his pale, cruel face and deeply-set, startlingly green eyes. His teeth shone in a smile of welcome.

"A request from you, Miss Folson, the daughter of the Time Corporation President, is tantamount to a command," he murmured, and bowed his coal-black head towards me.

Elna was not in the least embarrassed by his silvery effusions. As usual, she rose in almost regal grandeur to her feet, collected and practical.

"Sandy, I want you to meet Elnek Jelfel, Master of the Age of Problems," she said quietly. "Elnek Jelfel, meet Commander Sandford Lee, chief pilot of Liner 48."

"And so one honour is merged into two," Jelfel said, in his strange, faintly metallic voice, and shook my hand with one that was strangely bony and ice-cold. "Indeed, it is an honour to meet the pilot of so wonderful a contrivance as a time-liner!"

I fancied I detected a slight sarcasm in that remark, and bowed stiffly.

Jelfel hesitated before saying something; then he turned to Elna again.

"Perhaps I may have the pleasure of seeing you once more upon your return to your own Age tomorrow?" he asked smoothly.

Elna's eyes indicated her mystification. "How did you know I was going?" she asked in surprise.

The Master laughed, half to himself. "There are many things in the Age of Problems that others know nothing of," he answered enigmatically. "For the time being, Miss Folson—and, of course, my dear Commander Lee—I will say farewell."

He bowed again and then retired to a distant table to commence a meal.

As we resumed our seats I cocked an eye on Elna and she looked at me doubtfully.

"I met him on the liner whilst coming here from my own Age," she explained. "He was very pleasant, and naturally I saw nothing wrong in talking to him. He even took a photograph of me. I've seen him twice, since I've been in 2000, purely by chance I suppose. He told me that this was his first trip from his own Age, and he was finding it very instructive."

I granted. "I don't like the look of him, Elna. His green eyes are fishy, and his manner is altogether too polished to be genuine. He's up to something, and I don't like you being involved in it, either. So he belongs to the Age of Problems, does he? That's—let me see—about the year 22,000, two thousand years after your own Age, and nearly at the end of the trip to 40,000. The Age of Problems...." I mused for a moment, odd thoughts in my mind. Elna watched me intently.

"Well, what's the trouble?" she asked presently, as I remained silent.

"A mystery of decided proportions," I answered her. "The Age of Problems is the Age we always miss on the time-journey. It's shielded by something peculiar which nothing can penetrate. That is why we call it the Age of Problems; it contains a deep and peculiar mystery. A view of the closing chapters of the Age of Problems reveals a charred and blackened landscape from which all life has been burnt out and blistered, as though by a colossal fire. The one Age we never stop at, because it is unexplainable—and yet, Elna, here is Elnek Jelfel, from that very Age! How did he ever get aboard a time-liner?"

Her grey eyes became frankly puzzled. She pulled down her lower lip reflectively.

"Do you know, Sandy, I never thought of that," she admitted presently. "It *is* a mystery, isn't it?"

"More of a mystery than I care to admit. True, he might have gone forward or backward in time far enough to get to another age and board a liner—But no! That cannot be the explanation. He would have to take a liner to do that, and they never stop at the Age of Problems... Elna, I don't like it."

"It *is* peculiar," she said thoughtfully, watching the distant Jelfel from under the shield of her hat brim. "He's a queer-looking man, too."

"Well, we can't do anything by conjecture," I said with sudden philosophy. "We had better be getting away; the dinner rush is on."

She nodded and rose to her feet. I paid the electric menu, then we strolled to the door and out into the street. Here Elna paused and turned to me.

"Well, Sandy, I've my passport to get arranged," she said, "and then I've all my packing to supervise, so I think we'd better call it tomorrow at nine a.m., eh? That's when we start, isn't it?"

I nodded. "All right then, Elna—see you in the morning, and then I'll show you 'round if I can get the opportunity. Good-bye."

We took leave of each other, and left to myself I thought deeply as I walked along the busy pedestrian-ways. I could not for the life of me understand the curious acquaintanceship between Elna and the suave, cruelly-disposed Master of the Age of Problems. Elna, as a rule, was a sensible and discerning girl—a perfect product of her advanced age— so naturally I felt a trifle perturbed at the easy manner in which Jelfel seemed to have won over her feelings towards him.

The more I thought, the more perplexed I became; but presently I had to shelve my thoughts and theories as I became involved in the business problems of the last rushed hours.

## CHAPTER II

### *Into Time*

At eight-thirty the following morning I arrived with my usual equipment at the Time-Liner base. As was customary, everything was bustle and activity along the entry platforms. Loud-voiced officials were shouting instructions and directions through high-powered amplifiers; automatic chutes were conveying luggage and personal belongings into the liner's storage chambers; technicians were busy with the almost incomprehensible mass of complication that was necessary to project the mighty eight-hundred-foot-long liner into the time-line.

At the bottom of the main entry platform I met Elna. She took my arm and we went aboard together. At the door of her suite I paused.

"I'll see you in about half an hour," I promised her. "Then I'll show you around a little." She nodded acquiescence, and I turned to go. Then I hesitated and frowned as I beheld the slim, immobile figure of Jelfel a little way along the main deck. He was leaning against the open airlock, gazing out at the seething activity outside. My course to the control-room took me past him, and as I did so he turned leisurely and recognizing me, bowed.

"Good morning, Commander," he said calmly, his deep green eyes upon me.

"I regret my salutations are brief, Master Jelfel, but urgency demands that I leave you," I returned shortly, and, with a curt salute, I strode on toward my own domain, oddly irritated by the fellow's presence. I felt that he was a bad omen.

As I entered the main control-room Sub-Engineer Aldbury saluted and advanced.

"All set, sir," he said. "We've ten minutes to pass before leaving. We've got those Vibrators fixed up as you requested."

"Did they show anything?" I asked shortly.

"Yes, sir. The readings show that the time line is clear all right up to the Ten Million Mark, but there are queer little disturbances around the Age of Problems."

"Oh!" The memory of Jelfel flashed into my mind. "What sort of disturbances?"

"Well, there's some queer behaviour on the part of the atoms composing the time-line. Looks as though they've been pushed to one side, or something. Have a look, sir—I can't quite fathom it myself."

I crossed over to the Vibrator, similar in every respect to the instrument used by the testing department at Headquarters, and looked at the recording needle keenly.

Upon a long sheet of parchment the path the liner would take through time was scale-drawn, with the various Ages marked at the correct points. The Vibrator, in effect, was something like a "stationary" time-machine. That is to say, it sent forth a beam of pure energy, allied to positive electricity, along the time-line. This energy beam had a fading point set at infinity, so that it lost nothing by radiation during its travels. Some wit had called the instrument "The time-machine's Ghost!" for the simple reason that whilst the Vibrator projector itself was firmly embedded in 2000—or any other age, if desired—the beam itself went onwards to futurity or back into prehistory, as the case might demand. In this case it was the former, of course.

The energy of the beam, therefore, if it struck anything unusual in its course along the time-line, was repulsed slightly, and the effect instantly recorded upon the chart. This repulsion caused powerful springs to move backwards in the projector, which in turn deflected the delicate tracery needle on the chart. Naturally, the result looked something like an old-time seismograph record, only that the line was usually perfectly straight. I saw now, however, that noticeable zig-zag deviation occurring exactly at the spot 22,000, designated as the Age of Problems.

"From the look of that line," I said, turning to the watching Aldbury, "I should say that a beam or something is being projected from the Age of Problems, or from its area. The energy of our projector beam is positive electricity—that beam from 22,000 is perhaps also positive electricity. Positive always repels positive, and if sufficiently powerful it could blow this time-liner completely to one side—blow it to pieces! I don't like the looks of it, Aldbury."

"Neither do I, sir. What are we to do? Not make the journey?"

"We can't stop now," I answered. "Keep on until we approach more closely to the disturbance; then I'll give orders as to what is to be done. I have an idea that one of the passengers can explain this."

Aldbury looked at me in astonishment. "One of the passengers, sir?"

"Yes. There is a man aboard who is the Master of the Age of Problems; I have an idea he might be able to explain this."

"But, sir—" Aldbury stopped in mid-sentence as the warning gong sounded on the wall. Without another word he turned away to his post with that incontinent obedience to duty that is a byword with a time-liner employee. I took one last mystified look at the Vibrator, then, mentally resolving to see Jelfel at a later date, I too turned to my controls, issuing instructions through the radio-phone.

"Close the outer doors! Stand by there with the repellers! Throw on the lead shields!"

This latter order, by the way, concerned the movable lead sheathing with which all time-liners were equipped, in exactly the same manner as all buildings. In the time-line of course cosmic rays are exceptionally prevalent and the lead sheathing was our safeguard.

I watched the exterior workers through the televisor, and presently Chief Engineer Caldon raised his hand in readiness.

"O.K.!" I said sharply, and threw over the master-switch of the repulsion generators. Again I must digress for explanation's sake; I am inclined to forget you know nothing of operating a time-liner.

The gas Carrenium was drawn through powerful suction engines into sealed tanks and remained there under "movable" pressure. This gas pressure was transmitted to pistons at either the front or the rear of the liner (as our way of travel demanded). At the extremities of these mighty pistons were affixed objects that I can only assimilate to immense plungers—great round discs of a rubbery consistency and yet enormous toughness, which had the power of pushing upon the gas stream itself and so moving the vessel forward, much the same as oars move a rowing boat. Our fuel, therefore, cost us nothing, as we merely used the contents of the time-stream itself. The greatest cost to the Corporation lay in the upkeep of the sealing-tanks and repellers.

At my order of "O.K." the exterior repellers got to work. The time-liner had been lying on a cradle of metal plates. Actually, these plates were energized, containing enough electric current to hold the time-liner to their surfaces until the contact was broken. I have mentioned that the liners were made of an alloy much lighter than the time-gas: this alloy, even when sheathed in lead, still floated with the same perfect simplicity. The only thing to anchor the vessel was, therefore, magnetism, of a quality capable of holding the alloy immovable.

The repellers, therefore, once the current was broken, permitted the vessel to move upwards and diagonally. The outcome of this was to drop the vessel into the time-line, and also allow it to float in the air, and thus save a possible materialization under an ocean or inside a solid body at some point in the future. Not that this was likely to happen, for the future was perfectly mapped out—but caution was never overlooked… Another detail too was the terrestrial gravitator, by which, as the passage through time went on, the liner kept constantly in the same position in relation to the earth as the planet moved on in its orbit—otherwise we very probably would have been left in the void.

I waited intently at my controls until I felt the slight jolt that announced the impingement of the liner with the timeline. Looking through the observation window I saw the crowds on the departure platform waving and cheering vociferously as we moved away from them; then suddenly they commenced to fade, and for an instant I had the familiar vision of seeing them merge peculiarly into a square transparency; they seemed oddly bisected by cubes and oblongs, as for a moment I caught a glimpse of them subtended into the fourth dimension.

The view, from then on, was one with which I was well acquainted, but I can well imagine that to a stranger it must have been inordinately fascinating. From the window one saw the panoramic confusion of changing time—an astounding view indeed as seen from the vastly accelerated speed of the time-line, comparable in a way to a movie film enormously speeded up.

One saw the cascading confusions of melting and rising cities, superimposed upon mirages of oceans and landscapes that rose and fell with the phantasmal incredibility of a nightmare. The sun resolved itself into a golden streak embedded in a purple sky, and the moon as an intermittent silver streak—the inter-mittence being caused by her phases as she changed from new to full.

The average speed of a time-liner was about six years in one minute. When a long distance journey was made, such as the final stop of Ten Million, we used to reckon it would take two ordinary years t get there. Such journeys were rare, and only done by relays of pilots when attempted. For a reason that only Carreno knew it was quite impossible to exceed six years a minute. To do so meant dissolution. Only his lost accelerator could make it possible to enormously increase our speed without danger.

Our journey this time was due to end at the year 40,000. The destination of Elna was, of course, 20,000, and her Age would be our first stopping place—about forty-eight hours' trip. I make all this clear, you understand, so that you may follow how our system worked.

It was a remarkable sensation, even to a hardened pilot like myself, to watch the incredible weavings of time as we moved silently onwards through it. Since our departure had been from New York, we naturally would come to rest in New York some twenty thousand years later. Be it understood that the time-liner itself never moved in relation to stationary objects, except for the diagonal movement into the fourth-dimensional timeline. All we saw was the movement of Ages speeded up, which normally would have to be evolved through.

I stood for a while watching the intermittences of summer and winter on the changing face of the city, watching the mad chaos of clouds moving at desperate rates, and the swinging of the sun from solstice to solstice. I looked upwards in the brief flashes of night and beheld the shifting orbits of the planets, the phantasmal appearance of a comet about 2034, and so on. Somehow, I never lost my absorption at the almost uncanny wonder of it all.

"Everything's O.K., sir." Sub-Engineer Aldbury's voice aroused me from my preoccupation.

I nodded. "All right. I'm going on deck for a while. If anything's wanted, let me know. I'll be back shortly."

"Yes, sir." He saluted and took over the controls. There is little to do in controlling a time-liner. It is understanding it which counts.

# CHAPTER III

## *Resolved into Atoms*

I went up along the enclosed lead-sheathed deck, with its specially-constructed glass outlook windows. It was, as usual, filled with passengers, either promenading or reclining, the majority looking at the amazing view through the windows. The solar generators provided the liner with a comfortable degree of heat and light, for the exterior lighting during these trips was of bluish green, and utterly impossible to properly read or see by.

I saluted those whom I knew as regular travellers and continued on my way, stopping at last at Elna's suite. Lightly I tapped upon the door, but, somewhat to my surprise, there was no response. I gently tested the door and found it locked. Puzzled, I looked through the window, and beheld Elna seated in the armchair, engrossed in a novel. Evidently I had not knocked hard enough, so I tried again, and still I got no answer. A second look proved that she still was reading. A panicky thought seized me that something had happened to her. Being in control of the ship, I had duplicate keys of every room and cabin. In less than a minute I had secured the one for her suite, and flung the door open wide.

"Elna, what's the matter?" I exclaimed in alarm, striding forward.

Still no movement from her. She remained in the same position, head slightly bent to shield her features, her hands gripping the novel with its slightly lurid cover. She did not seem to have heard my entrance. Mystified, I went closer to her and seized her arm. At least that was what I intended to do, but can you imagine my astounded feelings when I went right through her! I fell heavily on the armchair, right through her body—yet when I staggered upright again she was still there, absorbed in that book. I looked underneath at her face, but it vanished in an impenetrable shadow.

"What on earth's happened?" I panted, looking about me. The first thing I beheld was the inter-connecting door to the next suite. Rapidly I searched out the necessary key, twisted it in the lock, and entered the next apartment. A familiar figure moved from the table in the centre of the room and stood standing watching me with a little smile of amusement puckering his thin, harsh lips.

"Elnek Jelfel!" I said, drawing a deep breath.

"A rather sudden entry, Commander, but perhaps the captain of the ship has certain rights of which I am not aware," he said coolly. "To what am I indebted for this visit?"

"There is something peculiar connected with Elna Folson, in this next suite," I said, striding towards him. "As Commander of this ship I must ask you to explain. You are the only man aboard likely to know anything about it."

He stood silent for a moment, and my eyes wandered to a group of queer devices upon the table. Then he shrugged his shoulders, closed the connecting door, and smiled again.

"I have said before, Commander, that there are a lot of things we know in the Age of Problems, that have never been even heard of elsewhere. Perhaps, after all, you are entitled to an explanation. There is, as perhaps you know, a certain scientific theoretical reasoning that it is possible for me to put into practical use."

"What reasoning is that?" I snapped.

"The endowment of a two-dimensional image with the necessary third-dimension to make it a three-dimensional solid."

"This is all by-talk!" I said hotly, but he interrupted me with raised hand.

"Far from it, Commander; far from it. The endowment of a two-dimensional image with a three-dimensional solidity is but an elementary effort of the Age of Problems. In fact, this three-dimensional effect produces a perfect solid, so life-like that you mistook a photograph of Elna Folson for the real thing!"

"Good heavens! You mean I spoke to an *image* of Elna?"

He nodded and smiled sardonically; then I seized his shoulder in a clutch of iron.

"You swine!" I breathed. "I never liked you anyway, and this about finishes it! Where is Elna herself?"

"Would you really like to know?" he asked pleasantly, shaking my hand free.

"Of course—and hurry up about it!"

"Very well, then…"

He led the way to the armchair and motioned me to be seated. His green eyes surveyed me thoughtfully for a moment, and I returned the gaze with as much coldness as I could muster.

"Commander Lee, I think you are a man of average intelligence," he said at last.

"Thanks," I returned laconically.

"No offence, Commander, I assure you. I say that, merely because what I am about to expound to you might tax your credulity a trifle—but, if on the other hand you are scientifically inclined, it will leave you with an unbounded appreciation of the Age of Problems."

"You can cut out all this grandiloquence," I said curtly. "Get on with it. My time is valuable, and unless you can very satisfactorily account for the disappearance of Elna Folson, I shall be forced to put you in charge."

Jelfel chuckled oddly at that remark. "At the present moment Elna Folson is imprisoned in my Age, quite unaware of how she came to be imprisoned, and will stay there until I see fit to release her."

I caught my breath sharply. "But that's impossible!"

"Not altogether, Commander. Observe!" He moved to the instruments upon the table and finally set to work with one that reminded me very much of an old-time cine projector. It evidently was something of the kind, for presently upon the cream enamel of the opposite wall there appeared Elna, once again, seated apparently in mid-air, reading. I stared at it in amazement, so utterly life-like was it; then with a grin that had something devilish in its quality, Jelfel switched the instrument off.

"That, of course, was Elna," he said sardonically. "On the trip up last time I took a photograph of her on the promenade deck. She was reading a novel—the one you have seen. Careful treatment on my part enabled me to remove everything from the negative except her own form. I even eradicated the chair in which she sat. The finished effect is that she appears to be lounging in mid-air. Naturally, I reversed the negative to positive by including thiocarbamide in the developing solution. All that is necessary to resolve this positive photograph into a three-dimensional solid of the original, is to use this three-dimensional ray." He switched on another of his small instruments, and the resultant beam seemed to pass right through the wall.

"You see, this ray contains the power of having infinite wavelength; it passes through anything. Now, what is done is this: the original film or slide of Elna is put in the projector gate in the ordinary way, and shown—but the illuminant is not a carbon arc, but this ray. I had better add that the ray can be shortened or lengthened as desired, so as to resolve the image at any desired distance; nor, by a secret process of my own, does the image ever get beyond life-size, no matter how distant it might be. Hence, this photographed image is projected wherever necessary, and the screen on which it appears is merely created by the motes o: dust in the air itself. The finished result is a projected photograph so natural and solid that only careful inspection can prove the difference. I had merely to project Elna's image into the next suite about the position of the armchair—observe if I had it correctly arranged by the simple expedient of the keyhole—and there you are. Nothing can block the ray, of course, not even this solid wall."

"I admit the cleverness of the idea, but what use is it?" I demanded. "Why do you want to project this picture of Elna, anyhow?"

"So that anybody would swear, if necessary, that Elna Folson was sitting reading in her suite at such and such a time. Just a little safeguard, though it will probably never be needed… There is another thing. I usually take a moving picture instead of a still, and also a voice record. This of course is merely an advanced system of this childish slide idea. I knew I should need that photo of Elna Folson when I took it—and I knew also that you would come and ask me all about it."

"How?" I asked.

"Time has many things to tell," he answered quietly, looking at me with those big green eyes of his. "Of course, I have not all the energy contained in these little boxes. The real source of energy connected up with these machines is in the Age of Problems, which perhaps I will have the pleasure of making clear to you at a later date…"

He paused and came slowly towards me, contemplatively.

"There is one thing about the Age of Problems I must make clear to you, Commander."

"Indeed?"

"You know nothing about it, do you?"

"No man does—it is apparently impenetrable."

"Quite so; but you know what Age comes immediately before it?"

"Certainly. The Age of Security—the two-thousand-year span to which Elna Folson belongs."

"Just that. And what comes immediately after the Age of Problems?"

"Why, the Age of the Second Birth, when the earth apparently starts anew with the rudiments of a shattered civilization—rises from a world of blackness and ashes."

He nodded silently. "You are a good pilot, Commander—you know your job! The Age of Problems, let me explain, represents the peak of intelligence, the climax of the Second Intellectual Cycle. It happened in the past. The last civilization ended in the Era of the Egyptian Intelligences, when they reared those mighty pyramids and Sphinx from the very atoms of the sand, and were then wiped out in a cosmic disaster, from which the later races sprang. My Age represents our own peak of intelligence—the Second Cycle. It starts again on the Third Cycle immediately after my age, and ends once more with the period known as the Age of Intelligence, after which the earth can no longer safely hold life. There are three cycles of intellectual growth in earthly history. The Egyptians came first; my age constitutes the peak of the Second; and the Age of Intelligence constitutes the peak of the Third. Rather incorrectly the Age immediately after mine is called Age of Second Birth. It should be Third Birth, but we will waive that matter. My Age is, without egotism, the supreme Age. Never before or since has anything equalled it; I have seen that for myself. About my Age I have girt powers which no ordinary intelligence can understand or penetrate—hence it is known as the Age of Problems, and I, Elnek Jelfel, am its Master."

Somehow I had lost some of my distaste for the man as he went on talking. He had a gripping quality about him.

"Your explanations are very interesting," I said, "but it doesn't explain the reason for kidnapping Elna Folson, when you've finished!"

"Patience, Commander, I beg of you. It is impossible for me of the Age of Problems to advance further than a few months from the present—and by 'present' I mean my own time, 22,000. The reason for this I cannot quite understand. To try and force myself forward beyond a few months causes dissolution, disintegration of my bodily atoms and molecules. It has been said that my Age has been seen towards its close as a blackened wilderness, devoid of life. That I cannot understand, either. But, however, I am digressing again. Elna Folson, as you will know, is the daughter of the President of the Time-Liner Corporation in the year 20,000, which naturally is in conjunction with the Corporation of 2000."

I nodded.

"As you will also know, the President of 2000 and the President of 20,000 have the original formula of Carreno's for the making of time-machines. For a reason not altogether clear those time records are not to be found in my Age; possibly they were lost in an intervening period. I desire that formula, Commander, to make time-machines of my own. Carreno was the only man in all earth's history who had the power to solve that supreme mystery; I admit him as my superior in knowledge. But I must have time-machines of my own."

"Why?" I asked, giving him a keen look.

"For the simple reason that my Age is thickly over-populated. I must have extension; I propose spreading my people back into past Ages, despite the fact that no record is ever shown of anyone accomplishing the fact."

"You can't cheat Time," I said quietly. "What is writ, will occur!"

"The record of the incident might have been obliterated in past time," Jelfel returned calmly. "Anyhow, I desire that formula, and I mean to get it. Until Folson, the President of 20,000, gives up the formula, and agrees to withdraw and destroy all time-machines from the service, Elna Folson shall stay in my Age. Her liberty is the price. No rescue can possibly be effected. By the same token I plan to put you in such a position that your death shall be forfeit, if your own Corporation in 2000 does not accede also to the same demands. I must have the formula from both Presidents, and a guarantee of stoppage of all time-machine communication. I require past ages for my own uses, and will have no interference."

"You mean you would dare to imprison me? "I demanded harshly.

"Without the least hesitation, Commander."

"You forget. That formula is recorded upon machines, besides being in the minds of the two Presidents."

Jelfel smiled coldly. "You may rest assured, Commander, that when that formula is given to me, all other traces of it will completely vanish. I will be the only one to know the secret."

"You would kill?" I said hoarsely.

"If necessity demands it—yes."

"You devil! And you dare to tell me—the Commander of the ship—all about it!"

"Why not, my dear sir? I may as well be frank."

I breathed hard. "So it's you who's wrecking all our time-liners! I thought so when I saw the Vibrator report a little while ago. I was going to tackle you about it. I have been assigned to finding the cause of this fiendish destruction!"

"Quite an interesting vocation, I'm sure. The other time-liners have been flung into infinity by a beam of pure negative electricity, which resolves the time-liners into atoms. No soul ever knew what happened. The same fate awaits this ship!"

I sprang to my feet. "Not if I know it!" I grated. "I'll have the ship stopped!"

"I think not, Commander," Jelfel said softly, now holding in his hand something like a cigar made of aluminium. "Keep patient, please, or I may find it necessary to resolve you into atoms also—before your time! Don't move!" His face set in ruthless lines for a moment; then again he was all smiles. "If you will step over here. Commander, I will show you how Elna Folson was transferred to my Age."

I obeyed perforce and watched whilst he indicated certain instruments.

"All matter, as you know, is composed of atoms and molecules?" he said, looking at me interrogatively. I nodded assent.

"Have you ever heard of the transportation of matter?"

"Only in theory," I answered, though I guessed what was coming.

"I have perfected a ray, entirely invisible, which has the quality of resolving any form of matter into its constituent atoms and molecules, afterwards reassembling them in the original form without any harm to the object concerned. In this wise anything can be moved from place to place in atomic form, within the beam itself, and reassembled wherever desired. In the case of Elna Folson, I focused the beam upon her suite from this little instrument here"—he pointed to a machine resembling a small searchlight—"and having ascertained beforehand her exact position in the room, I set to work with the detector. That is this dial here. The needle always points in a direct line with the object to be dematerialized, by what is called 'sympathy with the aural frequencies'—the aura being the electrical emanation of the body. The beam has then only to be set in parallel with the detector needle. Thus, Elna was resolved into atoms and molecules and projected down the fourth-dimensional timeline at a speed approaching that of light—186,000 miles a second. Elna, being in atomic form, could not disintegrate at that speed, as would a solid mass of matter, such as this time-liner.

"Upon her atoms reaching my own age, my chief engineer would project the atoms to the prison, and reassemble them. Elna Folson would wake up in prison, her only memory being one of being in her own suite one moment, and, after a transient feeling of faintness, waking up in her prison the next. Of course, these instruments are also remote-controlled, the real source of power being in my own Age. This same system materialized me aboard a time-liner. There was no other way."

"Why did you travel to past Ages in any case?" I demanded.

"For two reasons. One to find Elna Folson and imprison her to further my plan; and the other to determine the possibilities for my people when I move them."

I shook my head slowly. "Your tale sounds thin to me, Jelfel. You have some other motive behind all this—something different from merely securing a time-machine formula and finding an outlet for your surplus populace."

"I have told you the truth," he replied in a hurt voice; but still I did not credit his words. If I judged the man aright he had far mightier plans behind it all, but what they were was an entire mystery at that time. Unable to make further advances on that subject, I returned to the one on hand.

"I don't see how the atoms of any particular form of matter can be detected," I said. "How does your engineer know?"

"Entirely by his instruments. How does one identify a radio wave? It can't be done; the receiving apparatus does it for you. It is merely a system of vibration, by which the invisible is rendered visible. I will show it to you when we reach my Age."

"You are very confident, Jelfel," I said grimly.

"I have every reason to be, Commander. You may as well realize that you are quite in my power. It is my intention to project you also into incarceration in my Age. You are the 2000 Corporation's best man. They will do much to save you."

"Don't be too sure," I replied grimly. "And in any case, if you can do all this dematerializing process, why do you need time-machines, anyhow? Can't you project your surplus people into past Ages?"

"No; I must have a medium. That medium is a time-machine. In any case, I have not sufficient power to project a surplus two million people down the time-line, even if it were possible to do it without the medium of a time-machine—which it is not. The only way is to use time-machines themselves."

"If that be so, why wreck the entire fleet of time-liners? They would be very useful to you, I should think."

He smiled grimly at that. "You evidently forget, Commander, that to take the ships would mean taking the people. I do not want them; they might even prove very dangerous. No, I must build my own ships. I give forth my ultimatum to the two presidents merely to avoid using too much power to destroy the machines if they don't agree. Simplicity first, action afterwards…"

The more he went on the more I doubted his story. I wished I knew what his real scheme was, wished I could penetrate this feeble plot he had outlined. But no—I could not advance any further at that moment. Through the window on the wall I saw the speeding ages of time slipping by with confusing rapidity. I was in a tight corner, and I knew it. That gleaming weapon of his—I fancied it was a ray-gun—was no weapon to be trifled with.

Presently he spoke again. "Sit down!" he said in a grim voice.

I obeyed, and watched with an intense gaze as he swung round his Dissembler so that the gleaming lens faced me.

"There is no other course, Commander," he said coldly. "You will go, and I will follow. In time this liner will be destroyed—but that won't worry either you or me. Please prepare yourself."

"Stop, you infernal devil!" I shouted hoarsely, and unable to restrain myself any longer I leapt for the alarm on the wall. I was too late, however. The ruthless lens followed me, and from it there suddenly stabbed a ray, a ray that could not be seen, but could be felt. I took one last look at all those portable instruments on the table, no larger than ordinary luggage. Then I became aware of a sensation of hurtling through the air. I seemed to fall over, and pitched helplessly into an abyss that seemed nought but a tumbling emptiness dotted with the glowing of innumerable stars.

# CHAPTER IV

## *The Movable City*

I have not, of course, any means of discovering the period of time taken during my transition from the time-liner into Jelfel's Age of 22,000. The darkness, and my plunge into a seemingly electronic world seemed to last a short time; then I felt a distinct tug at my invisible form. I presumed this was caused by the atoms and molecules of my body being deflected from their path into pre-arranged channels in the Age of Problems. Followed a moment, transient and fleeting, of almost unbearable pain… I found myself standing upright in a room of moderate proportions, lined with walls of metal, possessing only a small ventilator in the roof, and one metal door with a small grille.

I blinked, rubbed my eyes, and then felt myself. I was as normal as I had ever been. I fell to pondering for a space upon this scientific miracle of reassembly; then, my mind clearing from the fog of transition, I began a tour of inspection.

My discoveries were not comforting. The metal of my prison was composed of some curious substance that seemed to be a cross between iron and glass. I later learned it was called iralium, and possessed the curious quality of being transparent to all vibrations and rays, from the highest to the lowest—and yet it was of almost inconceivable toughness. Its melting point, it appeared, was somewhere in the region of 6,000 degrees Centigrade! Considering the melting point of tungsten, the hardest metal discovered up to the year 2000—its melting point being about 3,450 degrees Centigrade—I came to the pretty obvious conclusion that any attempt to melt iralium with the ray-gun I had in my uniform, would be pretty futile! All this about iralium, as I have said, I learned later. At the time I was busy seeking a way out of the prison.

The lock of the cell door was the most curious thing I ever saw—remarkably fragile, the ward being no thicker than a lead pencil, and fitting into a similarly thin clasp. The actuating force of the lock seemed to lie in a little box about four inches square, riveted to the door itself. Yet, although I tried to break that ridiculously thin bar, although I tried my ray-gun upon it, I failed to make the least impression. I was contemplating what to do next when a voice, quite familiar, spoke to me. I looked round, but saw nobody; above there was only the ventilator and little yellow lamp.

"Commander, I shouldn't waste time trying to break that lock if I were you," said the voice of Elnek Jelfel. "The lock is controlled by thought-waves, and the metal is known as iralium." He then proceeded to tell me what I have already related concerning it, continuing: "My voice is of course coming to you over the radio beam, which I told you could be connected to my three-dimensional projector if necessary. It is my desire to have a talk with you. In a moment the door latch will be open by thought impulses. You will walk down the corridor and turn to the first door on the left…"

"You seem mighty confident of it," I said into the air, and evidently he was tuned in to my voice with his marvellous instruments, for he answered:

"From the moment the latch opens, until you are with me, you will be controlled by what is known as radio-hypnotism. You remember the remote-control wireless control of the old days? Radio-hypnotism is a ramification of that art. It is a system of impulse, so tuned that it is in perfect alignment with the frequencies emanating from your brain. Now get ready!" The voice ceased, and I watched the door tensely.

Sure enough the ward slid back, and, suspecting his radio-hypnotism to be something of a bluff, I jumped forward, intending to make a dash for escape. To my horror, the effort was completely useless. A sound echoed through my head, very much the same as that in a loud-speaker, when a valve in the wireless set is struck. In that moment I became bereft of all thought and reason; I saw nothing before me but a long corridor of iralium, curiously superimposed upon by a vision of cogs, meters, flickering needles and electric spark-gaps. I can only presume this latter effect was occasioned by viewing, semi-hypnotically, the instrument which was the cause of my mental enslavement.

My next really conscious realization was of being before Jelfel in a remarkably large, brilliantly lit hall, flooded with the glare of colossal arc lamps. This effulgence glinted upon machines and instruments of which I had no knowledge, and threw back their brilliant rays from droning engines and generators of immense power and voltage.

Against a great black wall of switches, dials, and controls I found Jelfel, attired in a close-fitting black costume. The material of this costume, as tough as canvas and yet as elastic as silk, clung rather tightly to his form, and revealed every line of his almost more than perfect figure.

His brooding green eyes were upon me, half in amazement.

"Greetings, Commander," he said a trifle dryly.

I moved towards him. Somewhere behind me a door slid silently into place and locked itself. I had been prepared for remarkable science in the year 22,000, but never had I expected such a veritable multitude of scientific apparatus, as that which now closed me in. I did not hesitate to admit to myself that I was beginning to feel a trifle afraid.

"One hour ago, Commander, you were aboard Liner 48," Jelfel remarked, pulling forth a chair and inviting me to be seated. "In exactly ten seconds"—he looked at a queer clock upon the wall—' 'your liner will pass across the beam of negative electricity I am projecting at the time-line. The reason for the alteration in time, by the way, is caused by the advancement in time in relation to yourself. You may, or may not, understand that. Time is full of paradoxes. Days pass in seconds in Time. However, Liner 48 will be hurled into infinity, and it is my wish you view the proceedings."

I half-rose to my feet in anger, but his compelling eyes forced me back. "Don't attempt any moves, Commander. Tampering with millions of volts of electricity won't do you any good. And besides," he added, with a most unholy smile, "I don't want my apparatus to be short-circuited!"

For a moment there came a silence between us: silence that is, save for the drone of generators and dynamos. Then Jelfel turned to me again, his hand upon a massive, four-pole switch. He nodded his black head toward a three-foot screen of what seemed to be ground glass. "I'm going to show you the actual destruction of your beloved time-liner," he explained grimly. "The machine I am controlling now is a Light-Wave Trap. That is to say, it imprisons the light waves within a narrow beam and reproduces them upon the ground-glass screen there. The beam is now tuned directly upon the spot which Liner 48 will cross. You will see everything for yourself. Just watch."

He pushed up his four-pole switch and a stream of blue fire flared from point to point, and jumped across a gap between, two pencils of copper like a writhing snake of turquoise. A resistance-coupler, low down by the floor, hummed transiently as a powerful voltage passed through it to some hidden earthing system. In awe I watched, and wondered, if this was only a Light-Wave Trap, what on earth must his beam of positive electricity be like! I was shortly to discover!

I looked at the ground-glass screen and failed to observe anything beyond blackness for a space; then very gradually I beheld the vision of my own beloved ship, as yet unharmed, appearing in view. Mentally, I pictured Aldbury, the engineer, at the controls, wondering what had become of me—and Elna Folson. Unless Jelfel had left his shadow image of her to disguise suspicion. I did not know… Very slowly the vessel came into full view. I could imagine Aldbury's misgivings at approaching that mystery disturbance, but evidently, having received no other orders, he was going on.

Then, suddenly, there came a soundless coruscation of astoundingly brilliant light. I was compelled to shut my eyes for a moment. When I looked again I beheld just—blank nothing! The ship had been completely disrupted, hurled into the enormities of endless space and time.

I had hardly absorbed the horror of this fact when two one-hundred-foot tall pillars of copper at the far end of the vast room turned green. The energy emanating from them hurled itself upon the resistances lined against the wall, and streamed with devilish, terrifying power into colossal earthing contacts. Tubes—colossal six-foot tubes of tremendous thickness of glass—flared through all the colours of the spectrum, emitting beams of pure ultra-violet that stung the eyes and blistered the skin. A bass humming shook the iralium floor, and from somewhere came the twanging of enormous percussion springs. Then abruptly all was as it had ever been.

I turned back to the grimly smiling Jelfel.

"What caused that?" I demanded.

"Merely the throwback from the beam impinging upon the time-liner," he said in a matter-of-fact voice, then turning aside he switched off his numerous instruments, presently looking round again and surveying me thoughtfully.

"I have sent a message on beam radio to the Presidents of 2000 and 20,000, concerning my ultimatum," he said slowly. "I expect the answer any time."

I looked at him stonily. "And you're fool enough to think they'll agree?"

"It would be to their advantage to do so," he answered "If they do, I will return you and Elna Folson to your respective Ages without molestation. If they do *not* agree, I shall wreck every city in the time-line from 2000, to 20,000, and obliterate, by the same token, the fools who control them. Then I will transport my people as I planned, by securing the information from the dead brains of the respective Presidents."

Again I felt he was disguising his real motives, but for the life of me I couldn't fathom him.

"If you can get the information from the Presidents, even if dead, why do you have to wreck all the cities?" I demanded.

"Because, my dear Commander, I do not require time-liners to operate any longer. Even the death of the Presidents, if I am forced to it, will not stop the running of time-liners. Complete obliteration is the only course. You see, I am trying to be amicable and pleasant by making an ultimatum."

"If flinging thousands of innocent lives to doom is your idea of being pleasant, I don't want to see you when you're really annoyed," I grated.

He revealed his teeth in an irritating smile. "To be *certain,* is always my way," he answered calmly. Then, easing himself from his indolent position amongst the instruments he said: "Perhaps you would like to see some of my machines, so that, should you at any time conceive the utterly absurd idea of opposing me, you may realize what you are up against!"

He motioned me to follow him, and leaving the hall of complexity we entered another one of even vaster proportions. I cannot describe it to you; it was a riot of engineering genius and scientific apparatus raised to the *nth* degree…

It possessed a glass roof, through which the morning sun was streaming. I noticed that the sunlight had an odd coppery tinge, the reason for which I did not discover until later.

Jelfel pointed to a barrage of wires and enigmatic boxes and dials.

"With that," he said, with merciless decision, "I shall destroy every city in the time-line between 2000 and 20,000 if the reply to my ultimatum is not satisfactory! It emanates a vibration of such force and depth that it excites the atoms of any given body so violently as to cause the collapse of that body. Not disintegration—not dissolution—just collapse, you understand. For instance, it would raze a building to the ground by perpetual vibration and tremor. It causes, in effect, a perpetual earthquake, so persistent that everything must finally crumble before it. It is sent through Time by a process of deflection. First on to the time-line itself, tuned to any given Age, then deflected once more from the line into the Age, forming, if you can mentally picture it, a figure like a square U, the base of the U being the time-line."

I listened in aghast silence and wonder to his cold-blooded exposition.

"This is the Atom Reassembler, of which I told you. This dial here registers the position in space of any given number of atoms, 'one' counting as 'one million' on account of an atom's smallness. This other dial shows approximately what the atom will resolve into when reassembled. The instrument is attached to a propulsor, which propels the atoms to any desired place."

He walked on casually as he explained, like a guide in a museum.

"This instrument here is pretty similar to the one I explained—only more complicated. It is the automatic Atom-and-Time-Dissembler. It also embodies a Reassembler, timed to work at the limit of projection. That is to say, the Ages are indicated here on this chart. If you wanted to visit, say, 1600 A.D., you would set the pointer to that point and throw in this switch. That switch would dissolve you—or any amount of people at once up to six—and would project you to that pre-decided Age—1600. Upon your arrival there the reassembler switch would operate and you would materialize—all automatic. I've made many a trip with that. I have a bigger one that needs an operator, but this is a perfect self-functioning machine. You will notice I have a wide range of Ages—anything from prehistory to Ten Million…

"Now this instrument here is rather clever. It is an Emanation Detector, and beside it we have a chart of computed emanations. Every form of matter, organic or inorganic, has a certain quality of emanation, has it not?"

"I suppose so," I answered.

"Of course it has! For instance, light emanation to start with—and many other forms of vibration besides. Light emanation or vibration was the basis of this instrument, which I discovered for myself. A white object has naturally a higher order of light emanation than a dark object; whilst a medium white object has an emanation between the two. You understand?"

I nodded.

"Well, my further investigations revealed that all matter has also another emanation, besides that of light. This emanation is created by the protons and electrons themselves, but is inconceivably minute, requiring a power amplifier to bring it into proper focus. Now, in inanimate bodies, such as soil, metal, and so forth, the emanations are very low, due, I imagine, to the stationary condition of the object. But in the moving objects, such as human beings, animals, etc., the emanations are very high, due to the *constant movement* of the object concerned.

"Now again, like fingerprints, no object has exactly the same emanation as its neighbour, and, as there are upwards of fifty thousand important forms of matter in everyday knowledge, it took me some little time to tabulate the approximate frequencies of matter—but it was very interesting! I did at last succeed in fixing what I call degrees of emanation—from one to fifty thousand. There you see the numbers on the dial, and the big pointer ready for moving.

"When that pointer is set at, we will say, a stone of about four inches circumference five miles away, we have to find the approximate frequency of that stone and calculate the distance and the area." He made astounding calculations on a sheet of paper. "The frequency of that stone, in accordance with the five mile distance, is about 480. We will turn the pointer of the Emanator to that number."

He suited the action to the word, and there appeared on a metal screen before us a dim vision of some object lying upon the ground, presumably five miles distant. What system of magnification and telescopic device he used, I could hardly guess at—or how he overcame the bend of the earth's surface. Elnek Jelfel to me, at that time, was a man of complete mystery. From his hints I gathered his telescopic work was done by a reflected-image system at the horizon limit. The system was a trifle too complicated to make clear in ordinary language.

"There we are," he said, adjusting a knob, and I looked in the screen to see such a stone lying upon the ground in the sun light. "A trifle more than I expected," he said; "492, to be exact. You see, with this instrument, I can usually find anything at any time, providing it is within a five-mile radius. Later I shall solve how to increase the radius indefinitely."

My interest in this particular product of a genius was more than normal. A vague idea was forming in the back of my mind that I might find it quite useful to me in making an effort to escape; indeed, not so much use to me as to finding Elna's whereabouts. This idea in mind, I stepped closer to the machine and looked at the tabulator. I noted that Jelfel's green eyes shone with genuine pleasure at my interest; manifestly he was a man who lived and died for machinery and achievement.

"Suppose—suppose one wanted to find a human being?" I asked him, trusting to luck he would not suspect my motive for asking. Evidently he did not, for he went to great lengths to fully explain to me. The gist of it was that all human beings have a different emanation, according to age, colouring, state of health, sex, and so forth. I gathered enough to know that a blonde has a higher emanation than a brunette, that a woman has a higher emanation than a man, and that the emanation of a girl like Elna would lie in the region of Emanation Number 1016. If this was not correct I knew enough to perform those gymnastic mathematics that would prove, to a fraction almost, where she was. I held that number, 1016, firmly in my mind.

"Another masterpiece," Jelfel said fondly, becoming so absorbed in his scientific achievements that he seemed to be forgetting I was a prisoner and not a visitor. He indicated a tall stand akin to a tripod, with an affair on the top like a reflex camera. On the floor, in line with this "camera," was a metal plating.

"The Growth Determinator," he explained. "This instrument contains yet another of my special rays, and anything within its focus is either reduced or enlarged from normal size by altering the vibration of the atoms and electrons in the body."

"At that rate, Jelfel, you could visit an atom," I said.

"I don't think so," he answered. "To visit an atom would mean crossing a gulf of void at some period, in order to alight on the minute planet. It could be done with a ship of some sort, not otherwise. Hmm, I must ponder that problem. Thanks, Commander." He dabbled about with the controls, increased his size by double to prove it to me, and then, normal again, continued the tour.

The amazing trip came to an end at last, and I was, I must admit, aware of great admiration for his genius and inventive powers. A pity, I reflected, that his real aims should be so ruthless and warped.

Then it seemed he suddenly remembered I was his captive. He became once more suave and sardonic.

"Have you any idea, Commander, what the world looks like in this Age?" he asked.

"The New York of 22,000!" And as I shook my head he continued: "Come to the top of the observation tower. I feel sure you will be interested."

"Look here," I said grimly, taking his arm, "don't you think this business has gone far enough, Jelfel? You are only showing me these marvels of yours to entertain yourself, and instil within me a fear and respect for your undoubtedly brilliant achievements. But I'd rather you did something definite! I would rather you put your cards on the table, and let us fight it out. Where, to start with, is Elna Folson?"

He shrugged. "Really, Commander, this is a sudden divergence, is it not? I might even say a breach of etiquette. Here am I, endeavouring to entertain you as your host, until I have the replies from the Presidents, and instead of reciprocating my generosity you ask difficult and entirely needless questions."

"My host!" I echoed bitterly. "That's amusing, anyhow!"

"I'm glad you find it so," he returned dryly. "Until I hear from Messrs. Templeton and Folson it is my duty to entertain you and protect you, and so long as you do not attempt to do anything foolish I will do that. As far as Elna Folson is concerned, she is quite safe, and will be. Unless…" And the compression of his hard mouth into a thin slit left no doubt in my mind of the merciless cruelty to which he could descend if necessary.

For the moment, it appeared, it would be policy to comply with his wishes, much though it went against the grain of the compiler…

Turning, he opened the door at the end of the great hall, and indicating an iralium staircase, motioned me to go up. I found the staircase twisted in spirals upwards for quite five hundred feet. I confess I didn't relish that climb, but I went upwards steadily, glancing at the blank iralium walls as I progressed, and remarking the neat bulbs of white light placed in them at intervals.

We came at last to the broad, flat platform of the summit, five hundred or more feet above the city level. It was, of course, sunny, and once again, as I glanced up, I noticed the odd coppery tinge of the sky, and even more coppery sun at the zenith. I was studying the phenomenon when Jelfel came to my side.

"The coppery sun?" he asked, interpreting my thoughts.

"Yes. What is it? Cosmic dust?"

"No; etheric vibration, with which this entire Age is sheathed. It is absolutely impossible for anything solid to get through those vibrations. So you see"—he smiled that strange smile—"I am quite isolated. The vibrations emanate from those towers you see over there." He pointed toward a spot about a mile away, and, taking my first look at this city of 22,000, I gave an involuntary start.

The place was a machine-mad riot!

The only thing that allied it to an ordinary city was the layout of the streets, arranged with an orderly and geometrical precision. The buildings themselves, however, whilst they did not any of them attain sky-scraper proportions, were all circular, and built upon what were evidently enormous wheels. To each building there was fitted something resembling a gleaming cylinder. For all the world, the city looked like a vast mass of inverted metal basins, with the mystic cylinders and wheels attached thereto.

I turned and looked at Jelfel.

"You have a curious city," I remarked.

He nodded. "In that respect, I think the Age of Problems is unique, Commander. All the buildings are built upon wheels. The cylinders you see are atomic force motors, which, if necessary, can propel the buildings from place to place. I have already told you of our excessive overcrowding. That is why I gave orders for all buildings to be made movable, so that, as the race multiplies, they can spread farther and farther afield."

"Surely you can stop this constant increase?" I asked.

"Yes; but why should I? The Age of Problems constitutes perhaps the most intelligent race ever evolved. Why should I stop knowledge? Better to wipe out the lesser intelligence and let my own spread—than stop mine and let the others stay."

His ruthless viewpoint was obvious. I turned to the rail and looked over the side. More movable buildings—everywhere the same—from horizon to horizon. I turned back and found that Jelfel, deep in thought, was eyeing the horizon broodingly from the other side of the platform. For a moment his vigilance was relaxed; his extraordinary mind was groping with deeper problems than my own precise whereabouts…

My eyes moved from his slim back to the square trapdoor opening in the floor that led to the lower regions. I did not know at that time whether my next action was foolhardy or not, but seeing an opportunity I put my innermost plans into action. Springing forward with one bound I seized Jelfel round the neck with one bent arm, and dragged him down to the platform floor. He fought furiously, but having precipitated matters I resolved to see the thing through. I may not have been his match mentally, but when it came to physical power, I was easily the master. For only a short time we rolled about the floor, then at last I managed to secure his feet and hands with the belt from my uniform.

As I struggled to my feet he glared up at me.

"You fool! Do you think this is going to do you any good?"

"If I didn't think so I shouldn't have done it," I answered curtly. "You can stay there for a while, Elnek Jelfel, away from your beloved instruments, whilst I get busy on my own account." My words seemed to goad him utterly, for he struggled with might and main to tear himself free from the tough leather that held him.

I took little heed of his threats and curses. I knew I had stranded him in about the best place of all—at the top of the observation tower. I plunged forward to the spiral stairway, slammed down the trapdoor behind me (I could find no means of locking it), and commenced to climb downwards as rapidly as I could go. So far I had succeeded by pure simplicity; everything else depended upon my speed.

Gaining the enormous instrument hall I ran across to the Emana-tor, searching the shelves of my memory for the number Jelfel had said would coincide with a girl of Elna's build and formation.

"1016," I breathed, swinging round the heavy pointer to the hair-degreed number in question. "One—0—one—six!" I was biting my lower lip with the intensity of my effort, one ear cocked for the first signs of danger. Securing the number at last I threw in the switch and stared intently at the metal screen facing me.

Something merged out of the vagueness, something amorphous and extremely blurred. Something that moved to and fro like a nebulous smudge on a velvet blackness. I looked about me and found the focus-sing knob. Gently turning it I was rewarded to find the blur decrease a trifle; then at last it came into perfect distinctness.

It was Elna herself, pacing to and fro in an iralium prison, similar to the one in which I had found myself. I looked very closely and dimly beheld the number "9" on the cell door.

"Elna!" I breathed, forgetting that she couldn't possibly hear me. "Now I know where you are. Cell 9, wherever that is." I pondered for a moment, then made up my mind.

Hastily switching off the Emanator I leapt across the great room to the Growth Determinator. Switching on the power, as I had seen Jelfel do it, I put myself in the full intensity of that beam, enlarging my size gradually until I stood quite fourteen feet tall. I reflected this would be useful in case of danger… I became aware that I was enormously heavy. Though not a brilliant scientist, I knew enough to realize that the ray had in some way altered the normal vibration of the atoms and electrons in my body, and hence had increased the energy in my body. Naturally, the result was that my weight had increased in proportion to my size. There were no scales handy on which to weigh myself; and in any case I had not the time.

Reaching forward with a mighty hand I switched off the ray, and stalked with Brobdingnagian strides down the hall. The various instru-ments seemed to be much smaller to me now, of course. Everything in size is relative. I felt curiously unafraid of anything and everything. I only paused once, and that was to pick up a massive girder-wrench from the floor. I doubt if I could have even raised it normally. As it was now, it was comfortably heavy in my grasp.

Gaining the outer door of the second instrument room I found myself in the iralium passage-way. No sounds came to my listening ears, so I advanced, looking about me keenly in the light from the yellow ceiling bulbs. I wondered why no sunlight was admitted to this prison building; perhaps it would tend to make the hapless inmates too cheerful!

So I went on down the long passage, until at length I came to the first cells. These were different from my own, mainly by reason of being smaller, and because they had ordinary key locks, and not thought-impulse. I came at last to Number 9, which I had seen in the Emanator so dimly, and looked inside.

"Elna!" I said softly, and that something stirred within and she herself came to the bars, looking out on my colossal form in something akin to awe.

"Why, Sandy—Oh, thank heaven! But what on earth has happened to you?" she went on rapidly. "Have I shrunk, or have you grown? I—"

She stopped suddenly and my hand tightened on the girder-wrench as suddenly, from round the nearby corner, there appeared a guard. At the sight of me he stopped in dumbfounded amazement, then he bravely tugged out his disrupter and levelled it. In one gigantic stride I was upon him, had flung the ray-gun from his hand, and lifted him on a level with my eyes by a slight effort of one massive arm.

"I have no wish to hurt you," I said, "but if you are sensible you will do as I order. Have you the key for Cell 9?—this one here?"

"Yes, but—I dare not betray Jelfel. I dare not defy orders. It means death!"

"You will do as I say, or it will not be left for Jelfel to kill you," I answered grimly. "Open that door!"

He had no alternative. I lowered him to the floor again and he opened the door with a rattle of keys. Instantly Elna tripped out into the passage way, and with one shove I sent the guard sprawling into the cell, in her stead. I snatched away his keys, locked the cell door upon him, and then flung the keys away down the passage.

"Quickly," I said to Elna, and gathering her up under my arm as though she were only a china doll, I sped back towards the instrument room as fast as my enormously long legs would carry me.

I lowered Elna to the floor when at length I arrived there, and stepped across to the Growth Determinator. It was but the work of a moment to reduce my size back to the normal five foot ten again.

"What's all this about?" Elna demanded tensely. "Have you beaten Jelfel at his own game?"

"For the time being, yes," I answered her, and as quickly as possible explained what had transpired since seeing her last. "So the thing to do is get back as quick as possible," I concluded. "The only way to do it is by the Atom Dissembler—the same thing that materialized Jelfel on the time-liner. We've got to beat him to it. He means business. Come quickly."

I strode towards the instrument in question, seizing Elna by the arm—then I paused as a sudden steady ticking upon the great ebonite wall arrested my attention. I looked closely at the maze of instruments, and at last traced the cause. A mechanical device of some sort was rattling out printed characters upon a thin sheet of white metal. Intently, Elna and I surveyed the message as it came through, and it did not take long to apprehend that it was the answer from Templeton and Folson.

"OFFER REFUSED. ULTIMATUM WILL NOT BE CONSIDERED TEMPLETON."

"OFFER ENTIRELY BEYOND THE BOUNDS OF POSSIBILITY. FOLSON."

"They refuse!" Elna breathed. "My own father refuses! They would rather we went to our deaths than give in to Jelfel! It's monstrous! I'll tell Father something when I see him!"

"Duty comes before flesh and blood," I replied quickly, turning away. "I'm glad that has come through, for we know now what to do. We've got to get back to 2000 and warn Templeton of what's coming. He can tell your father. Jelfel will stop at nothing now. Come on!"

I clutched her again and almost dragged her to the Dissembler.

"But look here," she said, as I set the controls of the instrument to 2000; "if this Age is sheathed in etheric vibration we can't get through it!"

"The vibrations stop all solid matter, but not atoms," I answered, preparing the switches. "There is nothing to fear. We will merely be projected into 2000, and upon reaching there the automatic control here will work and resolve us back into our original form. Jelfel told me all about it."

"I have a cheery thought," she said, with that infectious little smile of hers. "I wonder what it would be like to *never* materialize…"

"Good heavens, Elna, don't say such things! Now, are you ready?"

I stopped and looked across at the open doorway leading to the observation tower. There stood Jelfel himself, dishevelled and furious! So he had managed to get free after all—probably with his ray-gun. He stood still for just a moment, then he positively hurled himself across the room, was even touching the controls of the Dissembler as I flung in the master switch…

The next instant Elna and I were hurled into that strange, seething fluctuation of an electronic world. For my own part I seemed to hang thus for eternities, like a lost soul between worlds; then, after a duration of such length that I began to fear something had gone wrong, there came again that transient pain and I materialized, to find Elna, a trifle pale but otherwise unharmed, by my side.

"Done it!" I breathed triumphantly, looking at her; then I turned to lead the way up the small hill upon which we found ourselves. I thought it queer that we had moved so much in space in the interval as to land upon a hill; at the least we ought surely to have materialized somewhere in New York or its Environs…?

As I toiled to the summit of this mound of curiously mushy soil I began to notice that the air was abnormally warm and stuffy. There was a steaming dankness over the land, a vast moisture, and overhead a mist and cloud-beridden sky. An inner consternation began to grip me. Elna came up to my side, and on her bright, intelligent face I noticed the same expression of incipient alarm.

We topped the little hill at last, and then stopped dead at the astounding, unbelievable sight that met our eyes.

Ahead of us there was no New York—no sign of man's handiworks at all!

Purely a vast extent of marshy-looking land, bordered about two miles beyond with a jungle of colossal, titanic proportions. To the left there was a range of mountains, and to the right a great swamp and more jungle. Once I fancied I detected something fuming, incredibly huge, rise and fall in those oozing waters.

"Good God!" I said at last, my mind reeling before the frightful realization that swept into my mind. "Elna, this is the work of that devil Jelfel!"

"But—what?" she asked, utterly perplexed.

"Jelfel! You remember he was dabbling with the switches even as we dissolved? Well, we're not in 2000; we're right away back in the age of monsters and saurians! Back in the beginning of the world!"

## CHAPTER V

### *Primordial Terrors*

"The beginning of the world!" Elna whispered, her grey eyes staring out over the steaming wilderness. "We—Then, we're trapped, Sandy! Marooned—just like the old castaways we used to read about!" A faint, brave smile twitched her lips, as she turned to look at me.

"No castaway ever got in a jam like this," I replied. "Here, sit down. We must think this out."

I took off my heavy tunic coat, grateful to be only in my cool shirt, and laid it on the mushy ground, Elna, too, removed the coat she was wearing and did likewise, attired now in strong, serviceable skirt and thin, sleeveless, grey blouse. And so we squatted there, baffled and perplexed, and gazed away for a space, in utter hopelessness, across that awful morass to the primordial jungle beyond.

Undoubtedly we were in the dawn of the world, perhaps so far back as to be before the coming of Man. Later I found this was indeed so, though what exact Age it was I never discovered.

"Sandy," Elna said at length, "we're in a most difficult position—I might even say awkward. We're marooned in a past age, and have no means of getting out of it. We have no food, no water, and no shelter..." She sank her fair head into her hands and ruminated deeply. She did not cry; she did not become hysterical even. Elna Folson was a product of the year 20,000 A.D., trained through years of evolution to meet a crisis not with panic and tears, but with intelligence and resource. I felt proud to have her as my companion on this new startling episode.

Presently she looked up with a start, and then down at herself.

"Look," she said, and pointed to steadily spreading patches of moisture upon her blouse. I looked at my shirt and found it likewise. So wet and humid was the atmosphere it was steadily saturating us!

This was a contingency we hadn't reckoned with. Scrambling to our feet we decided we might as well get wet walking as sitting still, so we set off, purely at random, in the direction of the distant jungle. I had an idea in the back of my mind that it might be possible to light a fire or something with the little ray-gun I always carried with me, though I frankly doubted ever igniting anything in this sodden immensity.

Coats slung over our arms we commenced to walk, skirting the edge of the morass. Its waters were entirely devoid of any growths whatever; no water plants of any description seemed to be visible. It was just a sheet, extending heavens knew how far, and from it arose, in occasional sickening waves, the most overpowering stench. I could only presume that stagnation was the cause of it.

The ground itself was excessively mushy. We found ourselves sinking over our ankles at each step, and the alarm that at first assailed us that we had stepped into quicksand was presently allayed as we found solidity seemed to exist at a depth of about four inches. It was slow, filthy progress, that slopping about in the mud and ooze of a prehistoric shore.

The more I saw, the more convinced I became that we had arrived in a very early Age indeed. The dense mists overhead, the excessive warmth and humidity, the great inland lake—all this pointed to extreme youth on the planet's part. The lakes were of course condensed steam, and the heat occasioned by the fierce internal fires of the earth, still extremely active from disruption from the sun...

"Look!" breathed Elna suddenly, stopping and clutching my arm. "What on earth is *that*?"

I followed the line of her indicating finger, and beheld something towering out of the distant centre of the lake, something that made me gaze fixedly and with a growing sensation of horror. I could see a mighty head, immense bone-rimmed eyes, and triple rows of backwardly slanting teeth, but the rest of the body was submerged. The awful creature wallowed for a while, about as gracefully as an elephant in a public bath; then it plunged below the surface and vanished, sending wavelets splashing up upon the shore.

"What—what was it?" Elna breathed.

I shook my head. "Don't ask me! It doesn't come into the classification of anything I ever heard of before. I thought it might be a stegosauras, at first, but now I'm quite sure I've never seen it reproduced anywhere, either as a skeleton or in illustration. We're in a nightmare Age, Elna; let's push on."

I took her arm and we squelched off towards the now slightly nearer jungle. I kept one eye on the lake in the meantime, but saw nothing else appear. I racked my mind as I progressed to try and classify that hideous specimen, but without success. Evidently its bones had never been found in a latter period...

By the time we reached the jungle we were thoroughly exhausted. The intense enervation of the air seemed to double the amount of energy expenditure. We were two very strange figures. I dare say, could some superhuman onlooker have seen us—two lonely beings on the edge of a mighty lake, with an even mightier forest beside us. Two hopeless, weary creatures, drenched with humidity and perspiration, heads aching, and feet caked almost ludicrously in sloppy, dripping mud.

The forest itself was the most astounding thing I ever saw. The tropical forests of 2000 Central Africa have nothing to compare with it. The trees of this place shot up quite three hundred or more feet, and the boles at the base were of tremendous girth, I am sure that some of the larger ones must have measured quite twenty feet across.... And everywhere within was nought but a riot of foliage, a mad profusion of great vines and astounding tough ivy. Everything was a poisonous-looking green; and nowhere could I behold a single flower to relieve the monotony.

It was the Age of the Big. The little things were yet to come. Somewhere in all this slime and filth must lie the chemical qualities—the protoplasmic slime—which eventually would evolve into man. But not before many cycles had passed...

As we gained the edge of the forest, I noticed it was becoming suddenly dark. I remembered then that, being so far back in time, the earth was spinning far faster than in my age. The complete rotation could not be more than five or seven hours. It all depended upon the exact period we were in.

A strange, primitive fear of the darkness assailed me. God knows, the Age was terrifying enough by daylight, without the awful abyss of night surrounding us… But there it was. Beyond all doubt night was falling, and once it began, it slipped into complete darkness without any suggestion of twilight.

Everywhere it became oddly silent, save for the faint rustling of great leaves in the scorching, thirst-torturing wind.

"Sandy, what are we to do?" Elna whispered.

"How can I say, Elna? I've only a ray-gun with me—that's the only weapon. We need shelter and food—and water. I wonder if—if that lake water is drinkable? My throat is like a lime-kiln."

"But the water is putrid!" she protested.

"Mebbe," I assented grimly, "but if you ask me anything we'll be glad of even putrid water before long. Don't you realize what has happened to us? That we're completely trapped? We have no way out… "

"We have—death," she answered quietly. "Oh, I'm not afraid of dying, Sandy. I know my limits. If there is no way out, there is only death for it."

I seized her hand in a tight grip. "Spoken like a true native of twenty thousand," I murmured. "Good girl! But we won't do it yet; we'll look around first. We have always the disrupter if all else fails. Now I'm going to try that water."

I turned to move to the lake edge, when Elna suddenly gave a startled cry and pointed skywards. Almost immediately I saw what had astounded her, and I admit I stood in sheer awe at the sudden majesty of a celestial spectacle.

For a moment the dense mists had drifted apart, and there, just clear of the horizon, hung a colossal moon—not a perfect globe, but apparently a gigantic pear, visibly slowly turning, with the passing moments. Not an argent-faced, dead moon, but a grey mystery, a cloud-enshrouded world.

"Is that the moon?" Elna asked, a trifle doubtfully, all her fears and troubles forgotten for the moment in the contemplation of the astounding spectacle.

"Yes. And it proves, Elna, that we are amazingly far back in time. The moon has only just started its journey which will finally bring it to a stop 240,000 miles from the earth. The pear-shaped swelling is caused by the portion still slightly protruding where it was torn from the earth. As it continues to revolve it will gradually assume globular form, and at length become a dead world. Being a much smaller body than earth it will cool more rapidly and hold life a far less time. When it has reached that cooling period, Man on earth will be just beginning his upward climb."

My words floated towards the forest and died into silence amidst faint echoes. A very brilliant speech to make upon a primordial shore, forsooth!

The moon covered again by the ever-encroaching cloud and mist, I went down to the lake edge, and, lying on my face in the mud, tested the water's qualities. It was fresh water, certainly, but the flavour—! Thirsty though I was I could not bring myself to drink that foul liquid. I turned and beheld Elna watching me from a little distance, in the diffused light of the hidden moon. How unutterably lonely that shore looked! It was enough to strike terror into the heart of the strongest man, let alone two beings accustomed to the refinements and polish of unguessable ages of evolution and experience. Left alone there amidst the wilderness of the unknown, it came to me more clearly than ever before that education is an error in many ways. It had bereft both Elna and me of all knowledge of fighting instinct, of how to meet brute with brute.

I was soliloquizing thus, and returning to Elna, when I suddenly heard the dry beating of leathery wings above me. I looked up and simultaneously yelled out a warning. A vast shape, not unlike a monstrous bat, was outlined against the silvery mist. I caught a glimpse of a vile, wickedly hooked beak, and distended jaws. As fast as light the awful thing swooped from the direction of the jungle tree-tops, straight towards the now desperately running Elna!

"Quick! Quick!" I bawled hoarsely, tugging at the ray-gun in my trouser pocket. "Lie flat!"

The mud hampered her movements, however, and mightily though I struggled through the ooze to reach her, I was like a crawling snail compared to the bullet-swiftness of the pterodactyl, for such I took this flying lizard to be. Since the pterodactyl was the product of the Jurassic and Cretaceous Periods, I am inclined to think this creature was some kind of pterodactyl prototype, or else unknown altogether to science in later ages.

To my horror, I saw it sweep down in a graceful curve, seize Elna by the shoulder of her silk blouse—and flesh as well for all I knew!—and lift her, struggling and fighting, into the air.

"Great God!" I breathed, and felt cold sweat pour down my face in the passing frightful terror of that moment. I have often lived it over again in my dreams since.

That infernal ray-gun of mine came free at last from its special pocket in my trouser leg, but now I dared not to focus it upon the rapidly receding pterodactyl, for trembling as I was, I might disintegrate Elna at the same time... Then, with a curiously musty odour, the flying horror veered off over the jungle.

I stared dumbfounded after it, then my gaze became fixed—for, just as it was about to vanish from sight over the tree-tops I distinctly saw the dangling figure of Elna drop from its jaws and disappear in the foliage of the topmost branches! For a space the monster circled with an angry beating of wings about the impregnable foliage, through which it was too big to penetrate; then, evidently sighting me with its astoundingly keen eyes, it made a sudden swoop in my direction.

I acted half mechanically in the succeeding moments of terror. Even as I saw the glint of terrible teeth in the distended jaws I sighted my disrupter full upon its hurtling form. Calling into being all the steadiness I possessed, I focused and fired.

Instantly a blinding ray of light stabbed through the moonlit gloom towards that flying five-foot of armour-plated toughness. Came a sudden loud explosion that echoed resoundingly in the rather dense air—then I looked for the thing again. It had vanished! With the explosion, it had disintegrated into atoms...

I took a deep breath, thrust the ray-gun back in my pocket, and squelched off as rapidly as possible to the forest to find Elna, if indeed she still lived.

Fortunately, I had made a mental note of the tree in which she had fallen—a towering monster with two upper branches reaching out like titanic arms to the swirling grey scum of sky. Without a moment's hesitation I began to climb the tree, tearing my clothes and flesh on three-inch thorns in the doing.

Up and up I went, hand over hand, calling her name as I did so, and finding my heart sink as there came no reply. I tore away leaves with an intense fury that they should dare to block my path, barked my knees and elbows in my scrambles, until at last I commenced to reach the thinner regions of the topmost heights. Once, an affair like a foot-long centipede scuttled across my vision, and was gone. What it was I never dis covered.

At last I found Elna. She was lying inert in the crotch of two immense branches, their natural, pronged shape gripping her about the waist, but leaving beneath her feet a sheer drop of thirty feet into a leafy abyss below. One of her hands was clutching a branch above, the other was dangling limply behind her. From her general attitude, and the closeness of her head to the main tree-trunk, I imagined she had made a desperate effort to save herself falling, had succeeded in fact, but had stunned herself in the doing.

Edging forward carefully, and bracing myself in the branches for the effort, I managed at length to haul her free. My balancing act was dangerous work; one slight miscalculation could easily have hurled us both into the foliage beneath. But by dint of clutching her under one arm with one hand, and hanging on to the tree with the other, I at last succeeded in bringing her to the comparative safety of the main crotch of the tree.

Her shoulder was bleeding freely, and the silk blouse was practically torn to shreds. I thanked the fates that had prompted her to wear that flimsy garment, for beyond all doubt she owed her escape to its parting under her weight. Carefully I set to work to bandage up the wound, and as I did so she began to recover consciousness. At the sight of me she murmured a low expression of thanks.

"What happened, Sandy? I—Lord! My shoulder!" She winced and bit her lip to stifle an exclamation of pain. Then with another grunt of discomfiture she rubbed the back of her head tenderly. "Always in the wars!" she said, with an effort at a smile. "Oh yes, I remember now what happened. My blouse ripped and I fell down here, leaving our charming visitor with a mouthful of silk and, from the feel of my shoulder, several inches of first-quality female flesh. I clutched at the branches as I fell, but toppled backwards and hit myself such a whack… H'm—I don't know what happened after that."

Briefly I explained to her how the tree branches had saved her from disaster by gripping her waist. She smiled faintly and held the torn shreds of shirt I was using for a bandage more closely to her bleeding shoulder.

"Well, all in a day's march!" she said sombrely. "But Lord, how my shoulder hurts. It's more than a mere bite. Sandy; it stings as though my arm were being pulled off."

I looked at the wound closely in the moonlight. It was unpleasantly inflamed. I hesitated to tell her my innermost thoughts.

"Well, what's the matter?" she asked almost curtly. "You needn't try and hide anything, Sandy. I'm not a kid. What is the matter with my shoulder?"

"The venom in the pterodactyl's jaws," I said worriedly. "It seems that it has poisoned your flesh. Heaven alone knows what sort of filth those creatures feed on; naturally the bite has affected you."

"Better get down and bathe it," she said steadily, with another revelation of that calm, unshakable courage that made her so fine a companion. "No sense in sitting up here like tin gods." She spoke with effort; I think that shoulder was causing her far more pain than she would ever admit. She turned, wincing, to commence the descent, when I halted her with an exclamation.

My eyes, quite by chance, had become fixed upon something on the farther shores of the lake, something distinctly visible from the elevated view of this horror-ridden land.

"Elna, am I seeing things?" I asked at last. "Over there—on the lake edge—moving points of phosphorescence."

She looked in silence for a space, then nodded. "You're right, Sandy. There are six spots of luminosity over there, and they're coming towards us. There seems also to be like a thin streamer of luminosity extending from them to the distant mountain range behind."

"But what can they be?" I asked, rather absurdly.

"I'm not a magician, Sandy. Let's get down."

I went first in the descent and assisted Elna from branch to branch. It was hard going for her in her unfortunate condition, and the fear was obsessing me that, if I didn't find something remedial before long, the venom would poison and kill her whilst I helplessly looked on.

At the base of the tree she sank down on the ground, exhausted by her experience and the ever-increasing stiffness and pain of her shoulder. We both sat still, oblivious to the dampness of the ground, watching those six luminosities approach. From our vantage point the lights seemed to be moving slowly, but when I came mentally to compute the immense breadth of the lake, I began to realize that the strange objects were moving at something like thirty-five miles an hour. It was perhaps odd, the manner in which we sat and watched the things approaching, but to tell the truth we were so glad of the rest after our harrowing experiences, and so convinced that nothing could be more terrible than our present position that we made no effort to escape.

The Luminosities came close at last, and quite distinctly we could see a thin streamer of light appended to them and reaching to the furthermost edges of the lake's other side, wherever that might be. It seemed that in some undefinable way these bodies were connected to some mysterious source or other...

The first premonitions of some danger knocked at the portals of my reason. The amazing glow from the Things was of a curiously restful quality; very soothing to our overwrought bodies There were six, as I have said, moving now around the bend towards us, at a slightly-slackened speed, moving like five-foot transparent candles of flame towards us.

Silently I got to my feet, and Elna did likewise. I put a protecting arm about her shoulders. As the Things came closer and closer I at least felt a sudden mad urge to turn and fly blindly into the unknown forest behind, but something, even then, held me back.

"Are they alive?" Elna said in a low voice, her eyes chained to them, every little detail of her face lit up by their effulgence. "If not that, they are at least intelligently propelled," I answered her. "They seem—"

Abruptly I ceased speaking. The entire six had come to a halt on the shore about eight feet from us. To gaze upon them was a most unusual sensation. Suspended there in the air, having no definite, definable form, seeming nought but some beautiful form of gas, it was an experience as singular as any I ever came across.

"They're watching us!" Elna said in amazement. "Sandy, I think I'm dreaming!"

She had hardly ceased to speak when we both fancied we heard a voice answer:

"No, you are not dreaming. Those upon which you gaze live, move, and have their being. Strange phenomena to you, but actually sentient entities. Life of the fourth planet come to end its civilization upon the third."

"Did—did you hear that?" Elna stammered; and I clutched her hand reassuringly.

"Elna, it may seem incredible, but I'm beginning to get the idea. These glorified Roman Candles are living beings. They spoke to us by thought; naturally their thoughts form into the words we understand. The fourth planet is Mars. They're Martians!"

"Now I *know* I'm dreaming!" Elna said. "Space-travel is impossible. Science has proved it."

"Impossible!" derided the mental voice of the tallest pillar of light. "Nothing is impossible! It is the will of the Highest that you come with us and explain the mystery surrounding you—the mystery of how two Earthlings of another Age come to be in the pre-protoplasmic era."

I began to wonder myself if I was suffering from delusions. I knew life might evolve in strange forms upon other planets, but pillars of light were a trifle beyond even my scale of imagination. And again, what on earth had these intelligences in common with a young and terrible world? I remembered the last mental remark that the beings were "ending their civilization upon the earth." But why?

"That which baffles you will be explained by the Highest," came the thought-words. "Prepare for transition to our abode—you and your female counterpart."

At that Elna aroused herself from her pain to look transiently indignant. "Female counterpart!" she expostulated. "What do you think I am? An animal?"

"I have spoken," came the thought response. "Prepare."

Elna and I just stood there, not knowing what was going to happen, when suddenly a dense column of light streamed from the uncanny creatures and enveloped us. For my own part I felt a sensation of comfort beyond all earthly parallel, and seemed to be buoyed upwards in a canopy of soothing light.

# CHAPTER VI

## *The Luminous Intelligence*

I have reason to think that by some process of great intricacy—which later was explained—the Luminosities transferred Elna and me simultaneously across the primitive lake to a spot somewhere in the mountain range we had seen. However, the next thing we knew with any degree of certainty was that we were lying on our backs in something that felt like the softest down. All about us hung an iridescence of white rays, emanating from a source unknown.

I raised myself on one elbow and looked about me; then a voice in my mind said:

"Before you, you will find food. Eat—you and your female counterpart. After that, sleep. I have willed it,"

Elna sitting beside me, we found the food as promised on the ground before us, reposing in a bowl of curious bluish metal and resting in the downy stuff in which we ourselves were enmeshed. Only too thankful to comply with the orders of the uncanny being—whose actual whereabouts we could not for the life of us discover—we ate the stuff. It was beautifully sweet and palatable, having the curious quality of both satisfyinf hunger and slaking thirst simultaneously.

When we had concluded, the voice in our minds spoke again.

"Man, your female counterpart is suffering acutely from a wound in the shoulder. By degrees that wound would get worse until your female counterpart died of poisoning. So be thankful to the intelligence of another world that you were both discovered by the detonation of your interesting toy, the atom disrupter. I command that your female counterpart no Ionger suffer—that she shall no longer call her admirable courage into being to shield from your blind eyes the tortures of the monster's venom. I command that the wound cease to be. Begone!"

With the ceasing of the peculiarly worded communication I turned to look at the astounded Elna, and before my eyes, in the odd light, I distinctly saw a thin streamer of light writhe forth from the all-surrounding radiance and touch her flesh. In an instant that ugly, bleeding gash on her shoulder had gone; was as if it had never been. Instantly the drawn lines of suffering vanished from her mouth and round her eyes. She turned to look at me in dumbfounded amazement and lifted an investigatory hand to the now smooth skin. The light streamer faded and vanished.

"I—I felt it go!" she whispered, not unnaturally overcome by the almost uncanny power of the baffling intelligence.

"Sleep!" said the mental voice; and almost instantly we dropped into deep and singularly dreamless slumber.

\* \* \* \*

I awoke again slowly, to the dim grey light of that early and incredible Age. Above me was the leaden, mist-smothered sky, but upon every side—slightly less luminous now, was that brilliant light that lacked a source.

Lifting myself on my elbow I found Elna just awakening a few feet away from me. We were both lying upon a mass of substance that looked like transparent feathers—a glorious filigree of gleaming, spider-web strands.

"Eat!" said one word in our minds, and once more we consumed a meal of that delightful stuff. This done we rose to our feet, and more from force of habit than aught else, straightened out our filthy, torn, and muddy clothes.

"You are wondering," said the voice, when we had finished, "who I am—who we are—and what we are doing in the age of the earth's dawn."

"It seems like a dream," I said, and evidently the spoken word carried sufficient mental impulse behind it to become intelligible to the all-embracing light.

"In your terms, I and my counterparts are of the planet Mars, I see you understand, it is a planet many thousands of years older than the earth. It has been the lot of Mars, for many ages, to support life of our type by exuding from the dampness of its atmosphere a chemical quality upon which our gaseous forms thrive. Some time ago, however, that humid quality began to evaporate. The thing to do was to remove what remained of our race to this young world, and, whilst it continues in this humid state, continue our lives. When that humidity has gone—for it does not last long—we will either take the long journey into the infinite, or else move to yet another young planet… We know it will not be long before this planet becomes capable of supporting the grosser forms of life. That will be our signal to depart.

"You and your female counterpart are products of a later Age, which, although quite advanced in scientific accomplishment, is but slight compared to the massed force of the intelligence of our planet. You, or at least your counterparts, understand the mysteries of time and space, otherwise you would not be here, millions of years back in the past. Mayhap, as time advances, your people too will merge into one—but being solid matter, by reason of the planetary conditions, that is not likely. Be it understood that we of Mars can either become independent units or one massed whole at will. Through the circumstances of our planetary conditions we have evolved into beings of transparent gas, containing none the less intelligent and far-reaching powers. Mars, even at this stage, is an empty world—but the coming of ordinary man upon that planet is due to begin. That is, solid man.

"Ah! You wonder at our merging into one body? Let not that puzzle you, man. Gas can merge where solid matter cannot. The words that come to you, are the concentrated force of four million individual units of intelligence, merged into a common whole, which to you appears nought but a wall of light. Were it necessary, the four million could split up into individual units, even as six did last night—but even so they would still be held by a gas line to the greater body.

"I have told you that your atom disrupter, or ray-gun, was heard. We had no intimation of your coming; so it was that we came to you and transported you to our little domain here in the valley of the hills, through the medium of paralleled interstices."

"Paralleled interstices?" I repeated.

"A process of which I fear you know nothing. It involves a complicated law connected with the varying forms of light waves, by which light waves are transformed into vibration by inclining them at an angle to the rotation of the earth. Ii brief, the interstices of one place are made, by vibration of light to change places with another. Hence, you were moved in space by what might be termed an invisible rod, the centre of the rod having its location in hyper-space. The two points metaphorically swung round and instantly moved you from one end of the rod to the other—or rather from one place to the other. A fourth-dimensional pivot… "

"Oh!" I said, comprehending very feebly. Then: "My companion and I are marooned in this Age; we have no means of getting back into our own time. Do you understand Time well enough to send us back to our home?"

The luminous intelligence seemed to consider. "That could not be done," came the reply, at length, and I felt my heart sink. "You being solid matter, and ourselves gas, we are not trained to the transportation of matter through time. It would be impossible for us to so alter the time regulation as to transport you. From the standpoint of our mathematics, it would result in you and your female counterpart being dissolved. But, however, you need not fear. At some point in future time a man named Ino Carreno will discover how to conquer time… "

"He did!" I exclaimed excitedly. "In the year 1980."

"From your standpoint he is past; from ours, he is to come," the mental voice said, and the oddity of the paradox impressed me. "However, that man will send forth a time-machine into the past, fully equipped, as a test machine. The point in the past, to which he will send it, corresponds exactly with this Age and with this day. I have just computed the necessary mathematics that prove it. That machine will appear here for a moment, on the hillside there, which marks the spot where eventually Carreno will build his laboratory after thousands of years. We will attend to it that you safely board that time-machine in the instant of time that it merges into this dimension. Be thankful that some force through the ages prompted the man Carreno—or *will* prompt the man Carreno—to send his machine back to this spot."

"Elna, it's a miracle!" I said in delight, turning to her.

"Not a miracle," she responded, in that practical tone of hers. "Just mathematical coincidence, and very fortunate."

"It is not our will to retain you in this Age," said the voice again. "We seek nothing but our own intellectual pursuits whilst the earth can support us. When Man begins to appear we will depart, for we have no wish to encroach on the rightful preserves of the real inhabitants. Man, perhaps, will carry our memory down through the ages, and so will spring up legends and tales of past beings, that in future time will seem to have no foundation."

"Great heavens!" I breathed, a sudden thought striking me. "Elna, we're gazing upon the source of Greek mythology, folklore, witchcraft, and a hundred and one other unexplained cults and sciences… "

"You speak truly," assented the voice. "It is written in the Ages that we shall be spoken of; that men shall die for daring to utter legends of our having been here."

"Even in our time there are legends of beings who came with the clouds about their heads and whose bodies were made of light," I said thoughtfully. "Who can say but what the first men, glimpsing your wondrous forms, handed down the story from father to son, until in the printed world of civilized beings such stories are looked upon as legends? Privileged we are indeed to see you and know you for what you are. But tell me, All Highest, why do you call this—er—lady companion of mine, my female counterpart?"

"Because that, in all truth, is exactly what she is," came the answer. "We ourselves long ago evolved into the condition where the existence of two separate sexes was found to be unnecessary. We are a hermaphrodite race—we combine the two sexes in one, and multiply upon ourselves where necessary. That necessity is rare."

"Will such a thing ever come to pass upon the earth?" I asked eagerly.

"No. I can never foresee solid matter merging both sexes in one, unless the ordered processes of time ultimately bring it about, even as in your age some plants are of the hermaphrodite species... But the time grows short, man. You and your female counterpart must go to the time-machine, before the exact moment is lost to you for ever."

"One thing, before we go!" I exclaimed. "In my own Age of time I am fighting a man with thousands of years greater knowledge than my own. I fear for my people. Can you tell me what to do to overthrow him?"

"No. It is not our way to give counsel to men of another world; it too often leads astray. I can only see one thing in the future—a future so incredibly distant that even my massed intellect reels at the computation of it—and that is a vision of a galaxy unknown; the movements of a planet as yet unborn and your own visage visible upon that planet. There you will meet a power that will dwarf anything you have ever known, an intelligence that will make our greatest efforts seem but the feeble efforts of an insect. More I cannot tell you... One thing we will do for you. We will speed up the vibration of the time-line so that your journey to your own Age will be rapidly accomplished. Without that you would take years to return, and die in the meantime. And now begone!"

And almost simultaneously as it seemed, due no doubt to that marvellous system of paralleled interstices, Elna and I found ourselves upon the hillside. Below, covering the entire valley floor, stretched a billowing mass of gently undulating luminescence, glowing beneath the grey and troubled sky. Intelligent life! Life in gas! I wondered again if I was dreaming after all—then a writhing appendage to the gas about the forms of Elna and myself convinced me once and for all that it was truth.

"The time is nearly due," said the voice again. "High up on this hill corresponds with the height from the floor of Carreno's laboratory when he will project his machine, into time. Do nothing. I will set the controls to 2000 A.D. Farewell... "

Elna and I stood perfectly still. Then abruptly I felt a sudden whirling, as though I were being pitched bodily through the air. I cried out, struck something hard, and then fell back in total darkness. Something moved beneath me...

Came a streaking band of light from some point in space, then through the thick glass window I beheld the mad chaos of the Ages, enormously speeded up, against which the passage of my own beloved

Liner 48 would have seemed the veriest crawl. I found that I was lying on Elna. With a profuse apology I helped her to her feet.

"This is the machine that has the accelerator," I said. "The one that was lost, and which, by some strange mathematical coincidence, we have found... Maybe that's it," I said, and pointed to an unusual equipment allied to the controls.

"Don't touch anything!" Elna counselled, holding my arm. "The Martians said we were to rely on them."

I dropped my hand. "True enough. Thanks for reminding me."

I looked around in the yellow light of the hurtling sun, and then glanced at the dials and recording instruments.

"The Highest has kept his word," I said quietly. "He has turned the machine back in time and we are hurtling towards 2000 at a speed beyond compute...."

# CHAPTER VII

## *The Shattering of New York*

We returned to the year 2000 A.D. in Ino Carreno's original laboratory, turned, as I have explained elsewhere in my narrative, into a museum for those curious and interested enough to observe the actual environment of perhaps the world's greatest scientific genius.

Since the test time-machine had not moved in space at all, and since it was fitted with a terrestrial gravitator to hold it always to the earth in her passage round the sun—and also because the original site of Carreno's laboratory had not been moved at all—we merged into the mundane again through the medium of falling out of the time-line to the floor. I had been unprepared for the arrival. I could not bring myself to believe that the intelligence of the gaseous Martians could so faultlessly have set the switch to 2000. However, they *had* done so, and, being such a fool as to disbelieve, I succeeded in causing both Elna and myself a pretty rough landing.

Fortunately, we were none the worse, save for minor bruises, and opening the rubber sheathed airlock we stepped out upon the wooden floor. The museum was all in darkness; all about us, tabulated in orderly fashion, only just visible in the reflected light from New York's city lights, were the instruments with which the great Carreno had once worked.

"All safe," I whispered, taking Elna's arm. "We're back, thank God! The job now is to find the way out of this place. Come on."

On tiptoe we went to the door. As I had expected, it was locked. Turning, we made for the window. This proved an easy matter, and within a few moments we were out on the fire-escape, with the panorama of New York's glittering lights and beacon-towers before us—the same spot where the valley of gas intelligence had existed thousands of years before! Never before had I realized quite so vividly how much a man relies on beings akin to himself to keep him alive.

At the bottom of the fire-escape, which led into a little deserted alley, we held a brief consultation.

"No use doing anything tonight," I said. "Besides, we don't know what day it is, or how long we've been away. I'll go first thing in the morning and see Templeton, and warn him of the danger. You'd better come with me for verification. I'll pick you up at your apartment at eight sharp tomorrow. How's that?"

She nodded. "That'll do splendidly. I'll have to take the quietest route home—certainly not along the pedestrian ways or I'll be arrested for indecency or something. Look at the mess I'm in. I look like having a job getting my apartment back again. I'm supposed to have returned to my own Age in 20,000, you know. Ah, well, all in a day's march. See you tomorrow."

"Right. Sleep well!

"Who couldn't after what we've done?" was her parting shot, and with a merry laugh she turned and vanished in the night.

Here, in case any of you in the past might think my manners crude, I had better explain that in the Age 2000, men and women were treated as equals. Whilst woman was still considered the weaker sex physically, she was admitted to be every whit as clever mentally as any man—and sometimes more so. All the old-time curriculum of hat raising, bowing, kissing, taxi-calling, and so forth was buried underfoot by the march of progress. Whether wisely or not is not for me to state here.

I found my flat exactly as it had always been. At my entrance, which by the way I made by the fire-escape, my servant, Hilton, came into the drawing room, stopped in horror, and then rushed forward.

"Good heavens, sir, whatever has happened?" he asked blankly, pulling forth a chair and quite needlessly helping me into it. "Pardon me, sir, but have you been involved in an accident?"

I filled myself a glass of ekrimar, a beverage of the time, and drank it down in one clean gulp. Hilton watched me with something like awe in his pale, solicitous face. It was not often I used so forceful a refreshment.

"Hilton," I said grimly, "I've spent half a day and all one night in an age before the coming of man!"

"You astound me, sir. I really do not know what things are coming to."

"I do, Hilton. There's trouble coming—hellish trouble—unless I can stop it. We are going to be shattered to pieces. The cause of all the trouble lies in the Age of Problems, and the Master of that Age is a bright specimen called Elnek Jelfel. He tried to be rid of Miss Folson and me by hurling us into prehistory. Thanks to a test time-machine made by Carreno we got back," and so I told him of our various experiences. When I had finished he stroked his smooth chin. Hilton was more to me than a mere servant. Frequently, I had found him a very intelligent adviser.

"It was this man Jelfel then that destroyed the time-liners, sir?"

"It was. Templeton shall know everything in the morning."

Hilton shrugged. "I shouldn't place altogether too much assurance on the President, sir. Corporations are not gifted with imagination."

"They'll have to believe me!" I answered grimly, fingering my empty glass.

"Yes, sir. As you say, sir. The news came through on the radiovisor last night about Jelfel's ultimatum. The President seemed to imagine the whole thing was a hoax."

"He would!" I snorted, rising to my feet. "Damn it all, you'd think after all this time that Government and Corporations would try and be sensible—but no! Always the same doubting suspicion; always the same difficulty in making oneself heard and understood! They make me sick, Hilton!"

"Yes, sir. Would you care for a meal, sir?"

"Yes—I'll have a bath and a change whilst you prepare it. Oh, by the way, what day is it?"

"Thursday, sir.

"Ah! Then, including my time on the liner, I've been away about four days, and one day since Jelfel's ultimatum. Hmm, I may yet be in time… All right, Hilton, just talking to myself."

"Yes, sir, so I gathered."

* * * *

Eight-thirty the following morning saw Elna and me, both neat and spruce again, being ushered into the Debating Chamber of the Time-Liner Corporation. To be sure of a full audience for my most important narrative, I had made the appointment the night before over the teleadviser. The earliness of the hour meant nothing.

Sure enough the entire complement of directors was present at the horse-shoe table, with Templeton, as usual, in the centre I saluted smartly and Templeton bowed very slightly, as was his wont. I remarked, however, a curious stiffness in his manner and a cold glance in the ice-blue eyes.

His opening words were not reassuring.

"Well, Commander Lee, what have you to say?"

I didn't know whether to construe that sentence as a question or an invitation, so I plunged straight away into my story.

"I have called you together, gentlemen, to warn you of an attempt being made by the Master of the Age of Problems to secure complete control of all the ages from this one up to his own—22,000. He it is who is responsible for the constant loss and wrecking of our time-liners; he also it is who sent that ultimatum to you and President Folson. We have got to fight him, gentlemen. If not, the ruination of our cities, our Age, and our people, will be the result."

The craggy lines around Templeton's mouth did not budge at my remarks. Instead, he leaned slightly forward across the table and gazed at me long and steadily with those boring, implacable, eyes. I read in them a growing hate and ruthlessness, and vaguely wondered why.

"Perhaps, Commander Lee, you will be so good as to tell us why you deserted your ship in the time of need? Why you were nowhere to be found when danger threatened?"

I started violently and gazed at him blankly. I spread my hands. "But, sir, I was positively kidnapped from the ship. Both Miss Folson and myself were powerless in the hands of Jelfel. He was a super-man of science."

Templeton's thin lip curled slightly. "We had the radio-vibrator on your ship all the time, Commander, and we distinctly saw you enter the suite of this young woman here—Miss Folson. But you *did not come out!* What you went in for, you know best yourself. The next thing we heard over the radio-vibrator was the cry of Aldbury, your sub-engineer, for assistance. He called for you—you were the only man to give orders on the liner; the only man capable of stopping the ship when that mysterious force was found to be close upon it. But was there a sign of you? No! You had gone in Miss Folson's room, and that was all! As you know, the radio-vibrator covers the whole area of the decks and engine-rooms. We cannot see into cabins and suites. What were you doing. Commander Lee?"

"Good God, President, you don't mean you're accusing me of—of desertion?" I stopped, my brain whirling at the ruthless construction that had been placed on my quite innocent actions. "I went from Miss Poison's cabin via a connecting door to the suite of Elnek Jelfel, next door. He had kidnapped Miss Folson, and I meant to find the reason for it. I never left his suite in person. He projected my atoms into his own Age—22,000."

"Yes, and my atoms as well!" Elna put in hotly. "You have no right to dare to suggest anything else, President Templeton!"

"I speak the mind of the Directors at large," Templeton answered coldly. "It matters not to this organization, Miss Folson, whether you be the daughter of President Folson or not. Duty is merciless—but just!"

"Just!" Elna echoed in derision. "Hand me the ekrimar, somebody! Every word that Commander Lee has spoken is absolute truth."

"We rely on machines, on radio-vibrators, that cannot lie," Templeton said, his lips closing like a vice. "You will now explain, Commander Lee, where you were all day yesterday, and how you managed to get off the time-liner before it was flung into sub-atomic space."

"I have told you, sir!" I said, almost despairingly. "Miss Folson and I were projected into the Age of Problems. Then, in our efforts to escape we were outwitted by Jelfel and flung into pre-history, amongst the age of monsters."

"Indeed. And how did you get back?

"By the test time-machine Carreno sent into the past many years ago. You can see it now in the museum. The time Miss Folson and I landed in, happened to coincide with the time of Carreno's machine."

"Granting the truth of that statement, it would take you years to get back. You did it in a day! Explain that, Commander Lee."

"We encountered great intelligences. They helped us…" I felt the net drawing round me inextricably.

"Great intelligence in a prehistoric age?

"They were from Mars, President! For God's sake, you've got to believe me! The very safety of an age—of all future ages—depends upon it!" My voice rose to the great roof on rising note and died away into silence.

Just silence. I realized how hopelessly awry everything had gone. Mule-headed disbelief! Damnable, infernal machines that misconstrued everything! Hilton had been right in his assumption, after all. I could have cursed aloud. Poor Elna was nearly on the point of hurling herself on the cold, inscrutable President, so violent was her inward rage.

"Commander Lee—Elna Folson—it has been proven that you are lying. You, Commander Lee, in particular. You we missing from your ship when you were most needed; you knew when that ship would be blown to atoms, so vanished in a safety machine with Miss Folson before the event occurred. In some Age—whether the Age of Problems or otherwise I am not prepared to say—you sent forth those ultimatums, mainly because you knew they would never be acceded to, and also because it would seem that you and Miss Folson were beibg held as involuntary hostages. After that, knowing the plan had failed, you returned—which would only be a day's journey—to this Age, with this unutterable tissue of falsehoods! Commander Lee, you will be relieved of your commission forthwith! Come here!"

"But, President, I swear to you by heaven above that I am telling the truth! You have *got* to listen! We escaped from that Age. We have come to warn you—to have the necessary facilities to carry war into the enemy's camp!"

"Commander Lee, you will please be silent!" Templeton ordered stonily, then as I mechanically reached his table he extended his arm and swiftly wrenched the badges of authority and power from my uniform. They tinkled on the metal floor. I stood looking down at them dumbly, bereft of all power to think for the moment. The glaring, fiendish injustice of it all engulfed me.

"You fools! You insane fools!" Elna shouted, striding forward and glaring into the unmoved President's face. "My own father would have had more sense—he would have listened! But you... Bah! You're nothing more than bunglers—muddle-headed, stone-brained idiots!"

"Your own father, Miss Folson, would do exactly as duty merited," Templeton replied calmly. "Whether you be related or not you are one of the community, and you must suffer if you outrage the laws of the community! You have assisted *Mr.* Lee in his nefarious work, and no mercy will be shown. You hear, *Mr.* Lee?"

The "Mr." stung me to the quick. I looked up and glared sullenly.

Templeton paused for a space and considered the matter, assisted by the mutters of his fellow-directors. Elna and I stood looking at them, stupefied. Then presently Templeton spoke again.

"Sandford Lee, you are found guilty of the highest treason—the wrecking of time-liners by some form of electrical energy from some inaccessible spot in the time-line. You are also found guilty of desertion and endeavouring to wrest control from the Corporation by false representations. The penalty is death—tomorrow morning."

I staggered as though I had been forcibly struck. "What!" I gasped dazedly.

His monotonous voice went on. "You Elna Folson, are found guilty of abetting Mr. Lee in his work, but are not guilty of treason. You will be sent to the Machine Factories at Polar City for a period of seventeen years. That is all."

"But—but—" I began hopelessly, the faces before me seeming to dance in a mist. "You're signing your own death warrants! It means—"

"Be silent!" Templeton ordered curtly. "Guards—your duty!"

The two guards by the door strode forward and seized Elna and me in an iron clutch. We were both of us too utterly dunbfounded to comprehend matters fully. Death for me! Seventeen years in the terrible Arctic workshops for Elna! Why, the thing was absurd—insane! There must be a mistake! My mibd whirled in giddy orbits of irresolution as we were both piloted down various regions of the great edifice. I remember seeing a grilled door open and shut, heard a metallic clang, and then realized I was in a cell.

Stupefied, I sat down on the hard bench and felt at the place where my medals ought to have been. Death! Death! Death by the dematerializer—to be dissolved into atoms for trying save an Age! Good God! Was this, then, the outcome of education and machinery?—that it should condemn two innocent beings without a hearing? One to death, and the other to a small lifetime of perpetual toil! I groaned deeply and sank my aching head in my hands.

I do not know how long I sat trying to think things out before I heard Elna's voice from the next cell. I rose to my feet: crossed over to the door. For the moment the corridor outside was free from guards.

"Sandy, have you thought of anything?" she asked. For all the good we've done, we might just as well have stop behind and provided a diplodocus with a good dinner. It would have been useful, anyhow!"

I swore violently.

"Oh, what's the good?" I snarled. "Ruthless law, ruthless decisions! No chance at all! The blistering, damnable—"

"Turn off the gas," she said tersely. "That won't do any good. The thing to do is to think of a way out. How I wish I were a Martian!"

I stilled the string of invectives I had marshalled into perfect order, regretting that I could not blast forth for once in my life.

"There isn't a way," I told her. "The prison is guarded from floor to roof, and these doors can't be shifted. We're absolutely cooked, Elna. Done for! By God, how I'd like to tear the heart out of that devil, Jelfel! He's responsible for all this. One can'r altogether blame the views of Templeton."

"Oh, can't one!" Elna objected truculently. "I blame him for one! He relies too much on machines! My own father would not have—" She stopped. Then: "Did you feel that?"

"Yes," I said, and stood still for a moment. I had distinctly noticed a peculiar trembling of the floor, as though an engine were at work somewhere underground, and its vibrations were making themselves manifest. It stopped for a moment, then it began again with increased force, becoming gradually stronger, until it felt for all the world as though a colossal dynamo were at work underneath the building.

"What on earth is it?" Elna asked at last.

"Hanged if I—" I began; then suddenly it dawned upon me. An extraordinary feeling that was both relief and anxiety swept over me. I gripped the bars of the door. "Elna!" I panted. "Elna! It's Jelfel's vibrator machine! You remember—he told us it would raze every building in the Ages to the ground by vibration. He told me, anyhow, and I told it back to you. He's started the war he promised... "

"You're right!" she breathed. "Then that means—collapse!"

"Let it collapse!" I snapped. "It'll perhaps teach them a lesson. Whoa! He's putting the power on, isn't he?"

At that moment the vibration had increased to a positive shaking. I could feel my body and the wall and door of the cell trembling at top speed as the vibratory force increased. Feet were echoing down the passage now, feet running in alarm, and from the various cells came shouts and exclamations.

"What is it?"

An earthquake!"

"Let us out of here! The building will come down!"

I pressed my face closer to the bars. "Elna," I said, "I do believe that Jeifel is going unconsciously to do us a good turn. If this trembling keeps up at this rate it won't be long before these walls and doors warp and crack under the strain. If that happens, stand by and I'll get you. I've got an idea, and it's a thousand to one it will work. Don't get out of touch whatever happens!"

"All right. Count on me."

The shaking increased until it reached a certain frequency, but of such an order that presently to my delighted eyes there appeared a gradual thin crack down the farther wall of my cell. I watched it with a burning stare. It widened by imperceptible degrees. My whole body was trembling as though with ague from the constant dithering of the floor.

Almost as things apart I heard the clanging of cell doors, hoarse voices, stamping feet—a vast miscellany of noises with the lower undercurrent of the vibration running across the whole unintelligible din.

There was a sudden lurch and I found myself hurled against the door. A roar and crash from somewhere outside. Pressing my face against the grille I saw a massive piece of the corridor ceiling come crashing down in a cloud of dust, sending a nerve-cracking clangor, like a titanic hammer striking an empty boiler, echoing down the prison's dreary reaches.

I tried mentally to picture what was happening outside. The prison, I knew, was only one portion of the great Time-Liner Building, and situated, luckily, on the ground floor. This being so, the prison would naturally be the first to suffer. If other buildings were being affected in the same way, New York must be on the verge of ruin...

I did not have long to think, for presently that which I had hoped for took place! The door, unable to stand that constant and unremitting tremor snapped at the lock and swung outwards, presently even trembling from the broken hinges. I could hardly keep my feet. Outside in the passage, as I stumbled into it, I beheld guards and prisoners alike scrambling to their feet on the vibrating floor, only to be hurled over again.

Clinging to the trembling metal-work, I edged along to Elna's cell, next to mine, of course, and found her clutching the door-bars tenaciously. Furiously, I kicked at the lock, and at last, my foot aching from my efforts, I was rewarded. My repeated blows, and the force of constant vibration had been sufficient to break the metal clamp, and Elna came staggering out into my arms, hardly able to stand on her feet.

I hooked one arm around her waist, and with my free hand I hung on to what metal projections I could find.

"Keep together," I said in her ear. "I've got an idea."

We went away from the struggling, cursing figures on the floor towards the big arched doorways that led to the street levels. This necessitated negotiating three passages, but, so busy was everybody with their own safety, we were paid no attention to.

The entire edifice was filled with the most uproarious din, upon which was imprinted the frightful row of splitting and disintegrating metal, and the deep roar of Jelfel's hellish vibratiom system. Evidently, I thought, he had tuned his machinery s as to be at the exact periodicity necessary to cause the collapse of the particular metal of which practically all New York was composed. Evidently, during his trip to 2000, Jelfel had been very observant.

We gained the street without molestation, and there found the most indescribable confusion and disorder. Crowds of people were straggling desperately to keep their feet, the great majority failing. Remote-controlled cars were skidding and twisting sideways, hurling themselves into the midst of the shouting, terror-stricken mobs. Occasionally, great blocks of metal and stone from the towering edifices came crashing down in the street amidst clouds of dust and debris, crushing and maiming the unfortunates who happened to be beneath...

"Confusion!" I whispered. "This is what we want! Elna., are you game to take a chance? Game to come into time with me and meet Jelfel on his own terms?"

Her face became filled with an eager anticipation, like the grand old warrior she was!

"Of course!" she answered promptly, pushing the hair back from her face as a rising wind, caused by the perturbation of atmospheric currents, blew it into her eyes. "I'm game enough, Sandy, but what do you propose to do? Everything is collapsing. Even if we dared to steal a time-liner to travel in, it's doubtful if the metal hangar housing it is still standing. Everything is just dropping to pieces."

"Everything of *metal*!" I said quickly. "Carreno's time-machine is the thing for us! Don't you realize that his laboratory—the museum—is preserved just as it used to be? It's made of wood and brick. It should have escaped the destruction of metal buildings for that very reason, unless such buildings have fallen upon it. Come on, let's make for it. We haven't a moment to lose."

We turned about, and bracing ourselves against the violent tremors and lashing wind, made our way down the congested, confused main street. I have little conception of how we successfully battled our way through the yelling figures, or how we managed to dodge the uncontrollable motor-cars and crashing masses of masonry that fell ever and again. I only know that we did at last arrive bruised and exhausted in the little alley-way where the Carreno Museum was situated.

At this point of the city, it being the oldest part and mostly composed of brick and timber, after the old style, the vibration-force had done little harm, the reason being, of course, that the periodicity was not tuned to that particular form of matter. Jelfel, even as he had intimated, was concerned mainly with the formation of New York's bulk of buildings.

Without hesitation we climbed the fire-escape, which was dangerously loose in its supports, and smashed the window of the ground floor—the first floor up. The Museum was empty. Even the caretaker was missing, evidently driven out by the strange things happening within the city. To my intense relief, the time-machine was still there, in exactly the same position in which it had been left the previous night. For a moment I wondered what the caretaker must have thought when he had found it during the morning. There was no time for useless conjecture, however.

"In you get!" I said to Elna, and pushed her through the still open manhole door. She stepped inside the machine with a calm courage, and I swung the ordinary propeller-motor (to raise us to the time-line). After a few efforts the synthetic-fuel compressor worked and projected its contents into the firing cylinders. Instantly the engine burst into life amidst a cloud of blue exhaust... And here may I add a point? The only way of keeping this time-machine on the ground was by the gravitator-anchor, a rudimentary version of the idea that led eventually to those great magnetic plates capable of holding a time-liner. But for this anchor the vessel would always have floated in the time-line. The anchor being used it necessitated an engine of some kind to raise this old-fashioned machine to the timeline itself…

To get inside, close the manhole door, and move to the control board was but the work of a moment. Setting the dial to the Age of Problems I threw in the various, archaic switches. Followed a jerk, a flashing glimpse of the four-dimensional landscape, then we were in the time-line and moving forward at our normal rate of six years to one minute.

I looked through the window, and to my mind there drifted another paradox. The view outside showed New York as *perfeet*, and quite *unshattered* after we had left behind us in that moment of chaos… I pondered upon that matter, feeling very small and unintellectual when faced with so profound mystery.

## CHAPTER VIII

### *Hurled into Futurity!*

Elna aroused me from a profound preoccupation by a typical remark.

"Sandy, I suppose you know we've no food or water aboard?"

I turned to her. "I know it—but what could we do? The was no time for it, anyway,"

"Then what do you propose to do? Exist on air?"

"The journey won't be so long in any case. We'll have to last out. My proposition is to go to the Age of Problems first and see if we can find a way through that etheric vibration. If we can't I'll stop the machine at your Age and we'll have a rest and nourishment; then we'll go on to the Age of Intelligence and ask their advice on the matter. Jelfel seems mighty sure that his Age is the only one worth calling intelligent, but I prefer to find that out for myself."

"But Sandy, if you go forward past his Age it will mean you're crossing that barrier of electricity he's hurling at the timeline. We'll be blown to atoms."

"I don't think he'll be using his electricity for that purpose now," I answered thoughtfully. "So far as he knows there are no time-machines coming along the time-line now. He's quite convinced that he's stopped all that. And so he has—for the fact that we happen to be here is just an exception. Anyhow, I'm taking a chance. If I know anything of Jelfel, he has better uses for electricity than to waste it. Are you game to take that chance, or shall I drop you back into the comparative safety of the Middle Ages?"

She looked at me coldly and put her hands on her hips. "What do you take me for, Sandy? A mummy? Of course I'm coming with you… " She relaxed and looked wistful for a moment. "I would have liked to have seen my father," she said sombrely.

"You know that can't be done," I answered quietly. "Every Age in precedence to Jelfel's—as far back as 2000—is being destroyed by his vibrator. We cannot enter those Ages without destruction."

She fell to pondering at that. Rarely did her quick mind accept the obvious; she was born of the spirit that penetrates beyond and solves.

"But," she said presently, slowly and thoughtfully, "if every Age is being destroyed simultaneously, how is it that in between we view Ages where the buildings are as solid and impregnable as ever? If indeed every Age from 2000 to 22,000 is being destroyed simultaneously, it would mean a shattered world for something like twenty-two thousand years!"

"Time is, and ever will be, something always just beyond the grasp of mortal mind," I said solemnly. "I've spent years navigating Time, and long ago I ceased to try and solve its intricacies. Explained geometrically, it is rather puzzling. Thus: Synchronism prevails only if a radius vector of one object is always parallel with the corresponding radius of another. Explained in more ordinary language, it is like this: Jelfel, by vibrating his machine into all the Ages from 2000 to 22,000 is, in truth, veering away from that essential parallel of one radius corresponding with another. By doing that he has made a great mistake. During his activities, every Age is made to link with one present period of time—the period of time he is using—but the instant he stops to exert his powers, time resumes its normal course, and the Ages are as they ever were, because they come *after* the moment when he linked past with future. It is mathematically impossible to link past and present together for an indefinite length of time, and expect time past to take on the aspect of the future. It cannot bridge the intervening gap of what is called 'blank' time. Generally, there are two elements of time as we see it with our physical eyes, excluding all logic and natural reasoning. Those two elements are conscious and subconscious time. The one—the former—is that which is before our eyes and true; the other is the less understood state wherein time and the activities of Nature continue to take place, dissociated from our state of perception."

Elna placed a hand on her brow and whistled. "You don't think I'm Einstein or Kant, do you?"

"It's not difficult!" I insisted. "Imagine a smooth-flowing brook, carrying upon its surface a piece of wood. Now, take the banks of the brook as the different Ages. For convenience, we will say that trees are placed at equal distances along the brook banks—those we'll call Ages. Now, imagine your brook dammed at some point, yet with just enough outlet in the dam to keep the water at a constant level without overflowing. What happens to your piece of wood? It stops opposite a tree, or, to show the analogy, time, to you, is made to stand still for a given period. From your standpoint on the piece of wood time *is* standing still, but all the same the course of time is going on—that is proved by the outlet in the dam which keep the water at a constant level. The instant the dam is removed you on the piece of wood, will move on. But, whilst you were standing still, anything could happen in that Age. Cities could rise and fall without there being any appreciable movement of the time-line—or brook. Yet, all the same, time has been going on. That is what Elnek Jelfel is doing. By his methods he is making time stand still, but he forgets that once his influence is removed time will be as it has ever been. The whole thing lies in our state of perceiving it, which, from a human standpoint, is pretty feeble. Now do you see?"

"Well, I'll take your word for it," she smiled. "It must take brain of hypertrophied dimensions to understand that clearly."

"It is not understood clearly by anybody," I assured her. "It is known what use time can be put to, but to understand it, is, it seems, the Almighty's prerogative."

She shrugged at that, but I was inclined to think that far more went into that keen brain of hers than was apparent on the surface. She said nothing further, however.

Crossing to the window, she stood for a space looking out on the kaleidoscopic upheaval of passing years, I, for my part, turned my attention to the instruments. Then presently Elna spoke to me again. I found that she had moved from the window, and was standing close to the controls, poring over a queer, circular cylinder, with two pencils of metal, presumably copper, projecting from the top.

"What is it?" she asked, indicating it; and I recognized it as probably the lost accelerator for the controls. I went to her side and looked at it; looked also into an open box by its side which contained perhaps twenty-five of the copper pencils, for what purpose I did not then even guess.

I looked at it thoughtfully for a time, lying there on a small bench between the control board and automatic solar energy heaters. The cylinder was a trifle complicated, even to my expert eye, seeming nought but knobs and push-pull switches. Finally, determined to discover the thing's possibilities, and satisfy myself that it *was* the accelerator, I pushed in a large, bulbous-looking knob in the centre of the thing.

Almost instantly a blinding blue-green flash leapt from the copper pencils on top of the thing, a flash of such brilliant intensity that Elna and I both fell back dazzled, covering our eyes with up-flung arms. Simultaneously, almost, we were flung to the floor of the time-machine by a sudden terrific forward surge. Try as we would, we could not raise ourselves from the terrific acceleration for quite a space. We just lay there, helplessly panting, feeling as though bands of iron were slowly crushing in our chests.... Then at last the frightful pressure began to relax, and I got shakily to my feet, practically dragging Elna to hers.

"What—what happened?" she asked, her eyes on the now dully glowing copper pencils.

"It is the accelerator!" I panted. "Lord, yes! Look!" I pointed out of the window to the cascading mysteries of hurtling Ages, and to the jerking, shooting sun. We were moving at a speed far and away greater than anything ever attained in my knowledge.

"Naturally, the sudden terrific acceleration threw us over," I went on. "So long as the acceleration kept on mounting we could not get up, but when at length we attained a constant velocity, such as it is now, we became normal again... "

I went across and scanned the recording dials. I stared hard at what I saw and looked back at Elna again. "We're past the Age of Problems already! Heading into the future at top speed! This is a bit too much of a good thing!"

Feeling rather worried, I crossed over to the switches of the accelerator again, but to my growing horror found that no means I could devise would stop the infernal thing! I am inclined to believe, in the light of later happenings, that the extra propulsion was created by some form of atomic disintegration—the two copper pencils being used for the disintegration, and their energy transmitted into the interior mechanism. The whole system of both disintegration and atomic energy conversion, therefore, lay in the interior of the cylinder. Later I proved the truth of this. I was struck at the moment with a chilling fear that, if indeed these pencils of copper were used for disintegration, the accelerator would continue to operate until the last scrap of atomic energy had been exhausted! And heaven alone knew how long that would take!

"Can't you stop it?" Elna asked, a catch in her voice.

I pulled and tugged at the queer switches, kicked at the ebonite facing, did everything in my power—but no! We still hurtled through Time at a steady, terrific pace. I noticed that Elna was biting her lower lip agitatedly, nor did I blame her for feeling afraid. I was little better myself. I jumped across to the normal control-board and pulled at the levers and braking switches with the ferocity of a madman—but by some peculiar electrical linking the accelerator was mated to the control board, for it was impossible to use the switches without first stopping the accelerator.

I felt little beads of perspiration gather on my brow as I stared dazedly out of the window. We had passed the barrier line of the Ten Million mark, and were still hurtling into futurity at an undiminished, constant velocity.

Elna came to my side presently and joined me in dumb gazing. Already the vision of the landscape had changed. We caught glimpses of eternal wastes of sand, of a black, inimical sky, and occasional strange things that fluttered in a ghastly twilight.

Through the thousands of years we were hurtling, watching—dumb, helpless beings—the earth slowly come to the end of its life. And still we watched, fascinated...

Through the thousands of years we passed into the millions. Fifteen Million, Twenty Million, Thirty Million, and... Forty Million! Through the early facets of the earth's eventide we beheld little change beyond a strange cosmic spectacle—the vision of the moon increasing in size and sweeping ever closer through the awful gulfs of time and space towards the earth. Its transient eerie light threw a pale radiance upon unthinkable desolations. Craggy hills rose evanescently against the changing almost black skyline, hills that were monstrous ridges of inkiness.

Once, something like a flying shark shot across our vision and was gone. Very slowly the earth was becoming older, until at last we were occupying a steady position on one point of the earth—or rather above one point of the earth. We saw that the sun had come to rest near the horizon, a glowing red ball bisected by the horizon. A ball sullen and friendless, almost burned out. The work of solar, tidal drag was done. The earth had stopped revolving and was still, one face always to the sun, the other always to eternal night...

The moon, which during this period had been approaching ever closer, had vanished from view, but there was much in the sky—a sky of inky black—that led me to think that the satellite had broken up into the form of innumerable small particles, and had formed itself into an asteroidal belt, girt about the earth, like the rings of Saturn.

And still we went on, despite an occasional wrench at the instruments, and a dull feeling of growing despair. If Time was endless, where were we to end our astounding journey? How far would the disintegrating atomic force carry us before it expended itself? I glanced at the copper pencils—as yet only a quarter of their length had vanished.

A new aspect of the problem was commencing to worry me now. If this speed kept up we would ultimately come to a point where we would be adrift in space, with the earth no longer beneath us. Our only chance lay in the fact that Carreno's gaseous fourth-dimensional time-line extended through space itself. I saw no reason to doubt it if Time be endless. If, by some chance, it did *not*—if it was confined only to the earth—we would ultimately be flung into the void as a free body, to what end could not be computed. If the time band passed onwards into the void we would carry on until the gravitators anchored us to some other solid body converging with the timeline; or else… I didn't dare to think further. Quietly I made my conclusions clear to Elna.

"Perhaps a quick death in the void would be preferable to starving to death," she said quietly. "For starve we shall if this atomic force goes on for a long time."

"Everything depends on the atomic energy," I assented sombrely. "Fool that I was to ever tamper with it!" And in savage fury I kicked the base of the control-board.

Presently, unable to control myself any longer, I made another attempt to stop that infernal accelerator. I studied with cold precision, I made calculations upon the possible time it would take to expend the atomic energy in a pencil of copper, a quarter of an inch thick and four inches long; I considered the velocity of the current used to disintegrate the copper, but here I was stumped, for I did not know the nature of the current. I pulled switches and pushed buttons, but never once hit on the correct combination. My efforts were as successful as those of a half-wit trying to stop a power-house. At last I desisted and admitted myself beaten.

Disconsolate, I went to the window again and put an arm around Elna's shoulders. We stood looking out once again upon that astounding vision.

"To think Jelfel has again escaped us!" I muttered direfully. "It's adding insult to injury!"

"There are more things to worry about than Elnek Jelfel," Elna answered quietly. "He can be attended to later—if we ever get the chance."

"True enough," I said in a low voice, and silence fell between us.

As the time-machine travelled onwards a slow darkness began to envelop us, the cause being the gradual diminishing in the amount of light from the sun. There was much that led me tc believe that during the middle of that journey we travelled at a most prodigious velocity, covering, I am certain, thousands of years to the minute.

All sparks of life had vanished from the earth at this unthinkable point in the future. Everywhere there lay as nought but a craggy, solidified hardness—and, very presently, we beheld a solidity appearing on the earth's surface, a solidity that reached upwards and all about us.

"Great Scott!" I exclaimed. "The atmosphere is freezing!"

I spoke the truth indeed. For quite a time afterwards we were enveloped in a dense white solidity that hid all vision, but of course, being separated from that dimension by the time-line, we did not experience any discomfort. The solar heaters in the time-machineparadoxically enough using up the energy of a sun disappearing before our very eyes!—were functioning perfectly…

Then very gradually all this whiteness began to disappear, and we glimpsed the earth again, lying now a white-bound, ice-sheathed landscape, devoid of air, life and warmth. The faint light from the blood-red sun was rapidly waning, as we hurtled with incomputable speed through centuries upon centuries.

One thing now was obvious. Outside was the perfect vacuum of interstellar space, a temperature of minus two hundred and seventy-three point one degrees centigrade. The earth was a dead world—and yet the time-machine was still going on! Proof enough that the gaseous fourth-dimensional time-line was independent of earthly conditions…

And still we went on, on surely the maddest, most incredible adventure ever meted out to two human beings! Still on, and ever on through the endless immensities of time. My mind reeled at the contemplation of the Eternal; the efforts of Man seem incredibly inadequate when placed in line with the Almighty's perspective.

## CHAPTER IX

### *The Planet Brain*

I have no means of computing how much time we spent on our journey into incalculable futurity. It must have been quite a long spell, for we suffered all the pangs of hunger and thirst before the copper pencils began to reveal that they were slowly coming to the end of their existence. Even so, our speed was still tremendous. Weary and aching, we dragged ourselves to the window and looked out again. During an interval—which had ended with our view of the airless earth and dying sun—we had slept. How long neither of us knew, but the sight that met our eyes when we came to look out again left us dumbfounded.

For earth and sun had gone! Everywhere about us lay the intense, indescribable blackness of the void—above, below, on every side. Smudging this horizonless enormity was something misty, a nebulous swirling, only dimly visible to the unaided eye, and by far outshone by the brilliant, dazzling pin-points of stars, and the lesser luminosity of strange, unknown planets. The time-machine had become a space ship!

"What does it mean?" Elna asked, in a hushed, awe-stricken voice.

"Only one thing, Elna. We have gone so far into the future that the earth has dissolved into atoms; the sun has cooled, died, and done likewise—unless it has become a dark star which we can't see. Anyhow, the earth has crumbled into cosmic dust to form one day, who knows, the nucleus of another solar system. The inevitable law, Elna—birth, maturity, and decay. We are in the void, heaven knows at what period of time, amidst the stars and planets of a time beyond comprehension. See, over there we have the birth of a solar system—that flaming nebula, with the brilliant nucleus and rotating, less brilliant edges. And all about us, empty space. True indeed it is that Time is eternal…"

"Does this mean we can never get back?" she asked quietly.

"Of course we can get back, granting we stop this journey at a spot where there is solid matter. But if we don't use the accelerator to take us back, we will be dead before we even move a quarter of the journey. We'll be old!"

"What Age are we really in?" she asked me, and I turned to the dials and surveyed them closely in the starlight.

"Impossible to say, old girl," I replied, turning. "They have reached maximum and broken. The last reading was three hundred and twenty billion years."

"That's a long time," she said, with a trace of her old spirit, and forced a laugh.

I turned my eyes to the distant nebula and watched the slow movement of the unknown constellations as they changed their positions in the infinite, controlled by a power which, although science may claim to understand it, could not be reproduced by all the scientific genius ever evolved. The power of the Creator. I assure you that it was a solemn outlook.

The only consolation was that we were slowing down very, very gradually. The energy of those copper pencils was expending itself. After it had done so, if nothing solid merged beneath us, it would be a case of going on at the normal crawl until something did! I hardly felt inclined to dance with joy at that contemplation.

So our life went on for what must have been several days of normal time. We could only sleep, but, as time passed, even sleep became impossible, so torturing was our hunger and thirst. We were weak, cross-tempered, unutterably weary—almost at the point of wishing the damned time-machine would blow itself up and drop us into the death-dealing void that enclosed us…

And all this time the nebula we had sighted at the beginning was going through the inevitable cycles of cosmic progress, until there came a time, as our copper pencils were nearly at vanishing-point, when a solar system was born! This amazing spectacle we did manage to observe, and of all the astounding celestial things I ever saw, It was the most amazing.

Conceive it if you can! I realize the inadequacy of my pen. That spiralling nebula, now grown quite distinct in the firmament—the tremendous speed of its gyration. Then suddenly came the hurling forth of blazing, blinding fragments of light into the infinite! Seething fluctuations of eye-searing luminosity that travelled outwards like the sparks from a child's Catherine wheel. At our rate through time we watched the process speeded up, of course, and saw the invisible drag of the central nebula, as its gravity held the disrupted, flaming pieces, and very gradually drew them into orbits, until at last four boiling planets were moving at varying distances in ellipses around the parent sun. How long that process took I don't know. I only recall that we viewed the greater part of it at one sitting, and it will linger forever in my memory…

After the birth of this solar system had taken place we again relapsed into a state bordering on semi-stupor, both of us incapable of speaking or moving, so utterly exhausted had we become.

We were unconscious of anything that happened for a long time afterwards, but at last I did manage to crawl about a little, and noticed that our speed had considerably diminished. The accelerator was no longer at work, but we were still being carried forward far beyond a normal rate by the tremendous momentum.

On hands and knees I dragged myself to the window and looked out; a choked cry escaped my broken and blistered lips.

"Elna! Elna!" I croaked huskily. "A world! Arid we are materializing upon it! A planet from that solar system we saw being born. A world of steam and vapours—a young world, as what the earth once was. The orbit of the planet must have brought it so that our time-machine gravitator has anchored us to it during its travels around the sun… "

With what little assistance I could muster, Elna managed to drag herself to the window and gazed out upon the landscape of seething mists and steam through which we were passing. Our view was perforce limited to this kind of vision for a long space, but as we passed age upon age we saw the gradual cooling off of this process, saw the formation of lakes and seas, saw titanic upheavals, as the expanding heat within the planet's core hurled up mighty mountain ranges and belched forth masses of volcanic matter. I am inclined to think the process was more rapid than upon the earth, this planet being of somewhat smaller dimensions, and naturally the smaller a body the less time it will take to cool.

You may imagine our astonishment, when this planet cooled down enough to support life, at beholding no form of life whatever—not active life, anyhow. We beheld merely a bluish-white sun and sea-green sky. And below a land of deep blue lakes and vivid green moss-like grass. A pleasant land indeed; but no sign of life.

I was too weak to make any remarks when we reached this stage. One thing was obvious, the time-machine was now controllable again, since the accelerator had finished its dastardly work. Therefore I reached out my hand, pushed in the switch of the gravitator anchor, and tried to start the motor engine. Naturally, after the journey through space, it refused to respond. The result was that we fell out of the time-line into the mystery world with a resounding crash. Like a fool I had put on the full power of the gravitator-anchor.

I fell backwards against the wall, banging my head, but not severely enough to stun me. Poor Elna was unconscious in any case; the strain and complete exhaustion had proved too much for her at last. She was slumped at an odd angle in the corner, her arms sprawling wide apart, her body curled up—just as though she were dead.

Fumblingly, I felt around the screws of the man-hole sheath. I knew only too well that the atmosphere outside might be poisonous to our type of life, but even if it was, death was preferable to this everlasting moving onwards through time. It was literally a case of life or death at that moment.

Then the air came whistling into the time-machine. Just for an instant it caught my lungs and made me cough, but adapting myself to it was not a tremendous task. It was indeed very similar to earthly atmosphere, save perhaps that it had slightly more oxygen content.

Outside, lay a view of a small lake, and about it was clustered a bright green forest. The sunlight seemed tempting, and except for its heat and curiously dazzling light, it was not particularly unusual, being about the same distance—some ninety-three million miles—as our sun is from the earth. Feeling slightly revived by the fresher air I turned to Elna and shook her gently. She stirred slightly and turned a worn face upwards.

"What?" she muttered, between blistered lips.

"We've stopped, Elna. Stopped on the unknown world. There is water at hand. Come along."

She tried to get to her feet, but her legs crumpled beneath her. I doubt very much if, had she been on the earth in that condition, she could have raised herself at all. This planet, due to its smaller size, had of course a lesser gravity, which, whilst imparting a pleasant lightness, did not make walking difficult.

"Come on, Elna," I murmured encouragingly, slipping my hands under her arms and raising her to her feet. "Water... You'll feel better... "

With my support she managed to stagger along the soft, springy-textured moss towards the lake. Then I laid her on her face before it, threw myself down beside her, and tested its qualities.

"Fresh!" I breathed, smacking my lips. "Drink your fill."

She plunged her face into the shining coolness. The long draught we took revived us enormously. We were able to sit, able to stand, and contemplate our surroundings. And the sunlight, too, was pleasantly warming: almost too much so; it made us both feel unaccountably sleepy. This I attributed at first to hunger.

"Wonder if the forest holds anything edible?" I said, pointing to it. "Let's go."

I took her arm and we moved towards it, but at each step that tremendous lethargy increased. It was more than tiredness; it was pure hypnosis! It dulled our brains, dulled our faculties, bereft us of the power to reason. I have only one last memory—that of falling flat to the ground, and losing all conception of everything material!

\* \* \* \*

My return to consciousness was slow, but it was with a feeling that I was very comfortable in mind and body. I had entirely recovered from my former incapacitation; I no longer felt hungry or weary. Indeed, I felt amazingly strong, as though some unknown power had doubled the power of my muscles.

Opening my eyes, I became aware of lying on my back under the shade of an overhanging rock. All about me were towering mountains, reaching green-sheathed slopes to pale green skies. I found Elna also just returning to consciousness beside me, and she too remarked upon the astounding strength that had come to her during the period of unconsciousness. Together we looked out over the unfamiliar landscape. It was certainly not the same place where we had fallen to the ground—indeed somewhere very far removed from it.

"Where's the time-machine?" Elna asked suddenly.

That was a discomforting thought. The time-machine was nowhere to be seen. With a mute accord we rose to our feet and looked about us.

"A planet of mystery indeed," I murmured. "Who moved us to this spot? How comes it that we see no signs of life? And again, how is it that we feel so well in health when before we were half dead?"

"Perhaps something to do with the sun," Elna said, glancing up at it under her hand.

"It's certainly conceivable that certain emanations from it might help our health a great deal, but even that couldn't explain our moving," I said, puzzled; then I suddenly staggered backwards as a profoundly deep bass voice spoke through the air, a voice such as I had never heard before. It came literally from the very bowels of the planet, of a depth so profound and vibrant that I could never have thought so bass a pitch existed in the realm of harmonics. One felt, rather than heard it.

"Stand still!" it commanded. "Be not afraid at what shall take place before you. Be patient!"

I looked at Elna's astounded face; the thing was real enough, then.

"That sepulchre voice," she muttered. "Did it really… "

I nodded dumbly, then I almost jumped out of my skin at what took place on the stretch of level ground before us. A building had appeared as though by magic—a magnificent, many-windowed edifice of white stone, and of considerable size. It appeared to be anchored to the ground by fine tendrils. Nor was this all, for a very earthly-looking man came out of it, fine tendrils were draped to his form and attached to the ground. He came towards us like one in a trance, and stopped about six feet away.

"This is impossible!" I breathed, dumbfounded.

At that, the tremendous voice spoke again.

"It is not impossible! You will follow this man to the white house, and be seated in the room he will direct to you. Do not touch anything unless instructed to do so; you are not mentally alert enough to understand the cosmic forces and areas of refracted space, that makes this seeming miracle possible. To tamper with it might destroy you, and I have no wish to be inimical. These manifestations are attached to the parent body—so watch, and hold your counsel. Now, follow the man."

In a complete daze, Elna and I did as we were bidden. The "man" turned about and walked with a steady tread, and I noticed that it seemed as though the tendrils attached to him passed through the solid ground and vanished as he walked! The Voice's words, "attached to the parent body," obsessed my imagination. Little by little, the amazing truth was commencing to seep into my mind. The voice—the magical manifestations of the building and human being… Great heaven above! The planet itself was a living thing! Had an intelligence, of such indescribable power that we could not hope to glimpse the meaning of even its most childish efforts! Even as I thought of this startling possibility, the words of the gaseous Martian in pre-history returned to me: "… a vision of a galaxy unknown; the movements of a planet as yet unborn, and your own visage visible upon that planet. There you will meet a power that will dwarf anything you have ever known, that will make our greatest efforts seem but the strugglings of an insect."

I remarked these thoughts to Elna, and an expression of profound wonderment came to her face. In silence we mounted the broad steps of the building—it was composed of a stone that had no earthly parallel—and were ushered by the mysterious individual into a broad, cool room equipped, curiously enough, with very comfortable easy-chairs, and all the appointments of a modern flat of 2000.

I noticed that the manifested human always kept about six feet away from us, and never spoke. He was perfectly formed, dark-haired and brown-eyed; indeed, in some odd way he was *too* perfect in formation.

I began to suspect, and correctly as events proved, that he was only a manifested thought-image, created by the astounding intelligence that had us in its grip.

We seated ourselves, and waited for something to happen. With startling abruptness, the man vanished. One moment he was there; the next he had snapped into extinction. The room was empty. We felt a sense of vast, intellectual forces and presences grouping about us, preparing for communication with our little, uncomprehending minds...

Presently the great Voice spoke again.

"My friends, I have studied you carefully in these past few moments, and have taken unto myself a complete knowledge of all you possess, both mentally and physically. You are both extremely low in the scale of knowledge and perception, but by the same token are highly developed creatures of your own particular sphere. It would, however, be quite impossible for you to conceive any of the problems I would like to place before you, for the simple reason that you have not the faculties for understanding. You understand space and time, which is useful, yet you seem to have no conception of what is meant by Eternity, or what is meant by the term Universal Mind-Force. I am one unit in an inconceivably vast universe of colossal mind forces—forces of vibration, radiation, emission, hypnotism, and the entire area of the subconscious, which latter it appears you do not fully comprehend."

For a moment the Voice paused again, and then went on to mutter incomprehensible remarks about "fissure of Sylvius," "parietal lobe," "medulla," and so forth, all parts connected with a human brain, I realized. When, however, comments such as "trimagnetic rotating impulse," "outward force of space particles," and "constitution of emission cells," were uttered, I was hopelessly at sea.

"You must understand, my friends," the Voice went on again, "that you are now dealing with a mind force beyond the powers of anything you have so far experienced. Yet, I am not the quintessence of mentality by a long way. There are intelligences in the vast cosmic universe of such awe-inspiring force, that even I cannot grasp their smallest meanings! Mind—thought vibration—call it what you will, is an infinite power. It perpetually increases, until it reaches some ultimate force that no thing can understand. This ultimate force may be what is termed the Almighty!

I am not in a position to say. What you must realize at this moment is that this entire planet is a brain... A brain!"

# CHAPTER X

## *The Return*

"I thought so!" I said, half aloud, leaning slightly forward ii rapt attention.

"In this exact position in space there once stood the earth, the planet from which you have come. To your own perceptions that planet has ceased to be—yet you know in the innermost recesses of your mind that that world still flourishes. Why? Because you have merely gone such a distance along the time-line as to lose all concept *of* that planet. This world you are on now is child of the parent nebula, which you saw in space during your time transition. That nebula was nothing but *pure mind force*—not solid, unintelligent matter as was your earth. My reasoning leads me to believe that, at some unthinkable era in the past, a scientist set to work to make a brain. He was successful, but that brain became hypertrophied, lived and multiplied upon itself, reasoning higher each time, until it developed such intelligence that it wiped out its creator. From then on, age by age, it increased atom by atom, until at last it formed itself about the entire planet. Came the time when that planet, by Nature's law,, collapsed into cosmic dust. Followed a period wherein it floated in space—a period corresponding to the time when your earth came into its brief life spell. After the death of the earth that cosmic dust, which had been a smudge in your own terrestrial heavens, condensed into a nebula—a flaming nebula of intelligence. That nebula was the one you saw during your time travelling. And so it came to pass that the intelligent sun gave birth to its intelligent children—this planet, and three others. So you perceive the coming of a planet-intellect, of immense and far-reaching power. Apparently just an ordinary world with water, hills, and landscape, but intelligent none the less. Hence a power to which the concept of time and space, the practical application of every dimension, the knowledge of every atom and molecule, is but a child's problem..."

I felt strangely wedged between gigantic forces. Elna, I imagined, from her expression, felt the same way. She was sitting quite still, listening in utter silence to every word. Long since had we ceased to conjecture where that bass voice came from.

"You have yet to learn that the need for sustenance in the form of food and water is unnecessary," the Voice continued steadily. "When you reached this planet you immediately partook of water. You felt better.

Why? Because you *thought* you felt better! Had you fully believed you would have felt worse, you would have got the physical result of that belief. The physical, my friends, always reflects the mental. I threw you both into a state of hypnotism, and whilst in that condition brought you back to a normal condition merely by altering your thought perception. In the same manner you were transported, in a 'blank trance,' to a more convenient spot for communication, but as your minds are adapted to material things I willed this house and the human being to appear, so that you might be more comfortable."

"We are indeed grateful," I said, feeling something was called for.

"It is nothing, my friend. I also perceive that you came to this time through no apparent fault of your own. Your real desire was—and is—to overthrow one war-like specimen in an earthly time known as the Age of Problems." The Voice became cynical. "Age of Problems! I can see every mystery solved in that Age even now!... I notice also that your motives are for the right thing—to perpetuate good on the earth. Right is the only correct reasoning; if you would succeed, my friends, I am minded to help you..."

"In what way?" I ventured.

"I have made an examination of your respective brains, and, whilst they are small, and singularly incapable, I can nevertheless convert them into such high-powered organisms that very few problems of your planet will baffle you. The mysteries of Elnek Jelfel's Age of Problems will no longer trouble you... You will be able to save the earth—for there is every need of it, believe me. Elnek Jelfel is not what you think he is!"

"Why, what is he?" I asked quickly.

"That you will find for yourself in time, my friend. Believe it true that the earth is in dire need of your assistance, and I shall make you capable of giving that assistance... The brains of yourself and of this young woman are merely a mass of multitudinous nerve cells and fibres—in embryonic formation compared to mine. Each of those cells responds through chemical changes to some form of external energy. To descend very low in analogy, you must imagine that the impulses are akin to the conduction of electricity in a wire—only in your case mental impulse is a great deal slower than electricity. When this impulse reaches a nerve cell of your brain that cell liberates energy, and this energy is transmitted to other cells. The cells which are needed, be they muscular or nervous system, immediately respond to life. In the former case, the impulse will of course be transmitted to the contractile cells, and in the latter to the neurones. You understand that?"

"In a way," I said.

"Since the greatest brain activity takes place around the region of the cerebrum, and since the speed of impulse to that nerve cells is so slow, it is my intention to so alter the cerebrum in your brains that your powers of perception and retention will be greatly increased, and also I shall remove from the cells a great deal of needless material, which will mean, to you, greatly increased intellect. In time the effect will fade, and you will become normal, due to the fresh clogging of the cells. But my reasoning tells me that your clarity of thought will last long enough for you to outwit your enemy."

For some reason, sudden fear clutched at my heart. Elna gripped my arm and looked at me in alarm.

"But surely we will do as we are?" I panted, horrified at the plans of this all-powerful intellect.

"You have nothing to fear," the Voice responded. "The operation will take place immediately."

We both jumped to our feet, but before we could make a move three white-garbed men emerged from the air and walked steadily towards us, those queer fibres extending down into the marble floor as they walked.

"Obey!" the Voice commanded.

We had no alternative. That hypnotic mind had us in its grip again. We made a last desperate stand against it, fought with every vestige of our puny will-power, and failed. I dimly remember being lifted into the air by some invisible process and floating down the long hall, Elna by my side in a like position, and the three silent conceptions of a super-mind following with a steady tread in the rear…

* * * *

My sensations during what I correctly presumed was the operation— performed by the three automata surgeons under the mighty mind's con- trol—were amazing in the extreme. There was no pain or discomfort; I seemed just to be comfortably asleep, and yet, in some unaccountable way, awake. I could see everything with my eyes shut! Could see the white-garbed surgeons working under a brilliant light, which had, I fan- cy, some radium content in it, and glimpsed the occasional glitter from electric knives and marvellous surgical implements that put anything I had ever seen before, completely in the shade. I think Elna was some- where near me; I could not be sure.

As the process went on I felt queer little impulses in my head—im- pulses that I can only liken to little hammers beating in my skull. And for each beat, it seemed, my sense of imagination and sensation increased. I found that I could still not only see with my eyes shut, but I could even see through the walls of the room; and through the floor and ceiling!

Just like glass—the green heavens above, and the utter blackness of void beneath. For an instant a terrifying dizziness and nausea seized me, and passed. I felt for a space as though I were floating like a disembodied spirit between the real and the extramundane... Then I awoke!

I became conscious of a strong arm about my shoulders, and of an expressionless face looking into mine. I felt very strong, astoundingly strong—the exact antithesis of the close of an earthly operation. Also unlike the sequence of an earthly operation, I got off the operating-table of my own accord and gained my feet, flexing my arms, and feeling a sudden desire to hurl things right and left... Then the mood of transient savagery passed. I turned about and saw Elna being helped to the floor by the third surgeon.

Little by little, as I stood there, I began to feel the effects of the operation, so marvellously and painlessly performed. At the first my sensations were normal, then I began to sense matters take on a change. At will I could, in a sense, become as though possessed with X-ray eyesight. By a slight effort of concentration I could change my normal vision and see right through any object, in the same manner as I had done whilst on the operating-table. I looked at the surgeon before me and felt a passing phase of amazement at seeing the skeleton formation of his body through his clothes and flesh. Then I ceased to concentrate, and, to my vision, he became a solid man again.

As I was pondering upon what next to do, the surgeons vanished. The tables also melted, and the instruments. The entire operating-theatre was empty, save for Elna and me. I went across to her and laid an arm about her shoulders.

"How do you feel?" I breathed, and learned that her sensations were very similar to mine, only in a slightly lesser degree, probably because of her smaller proportions.

"The operation is ended," said the Voice. "In time, as I have already told you, the effect will pass, due to fresh clogging of the cells; but now you are equipped with the power to fight for the good of your planet. Make notes whilst in this high stage of mentality, so that problems which baffle you may still be solved when you return to normal."

"Will our state of perception increase as time goes on until the zenith is reached, or will it decrease from this standpoint?" I asked.

"It will increase for quite a time yet. As new problems rise up you will exert your mentality to overcome them. Exercise of anything is the only key to its practical use. Stagnation is anathema to a brain, as it is to anything else. You will reach a certain peak of mental perfection, then gradually you will drop back. There will be times when your brain will think faster than your body will move. You will do and say unpremeditated things. But do not worry; a brain always works for the good of the body. You will never regret these impulses… And now, before I bid you farewell, is there anything more you wish to know?"

"Yes," I said. "Is there any way we can speed up our time-machine in order to return in reasonable time to our own Age and world?"

It seemed that the brain planet laughed.

"I did not arrange for your brain to be operated upon for nothing. That problem will not baffle you when you see your time-machine again. I will transport you to it, and that must end our communication. If ever you come far enough along the time-line again to seek my counsel, I shall always be ready to give it. Goodbye."

The Voice ceased to speak; came a sudden wave of giddiness. I seemed to reel helplessly, then I was standing not ten yards from the silent, motionless time-machine with Elna at my side, as usual.

She looked about her, and remarked: "We're back again where we first landed."

I nodded. "Now evidently comes the time when we must exert these 'speeded-up' brains of ours and see what we can do. Let's get inside the machine and think it over."

We walked slowly towards the one link with our Age and planet, and as we did so I turned the matter over in my mind. I had hardly started to think the problem out when like a flash of light the solution came to me. I stood astonished, amazed to think that I could ever have been so dense as to not see it before. I felt like a child who has been unable to open a door by pushing it, and had suddenly found it opened inwards instead. I laughed with the sheer joy of mental accomplishment.

"Yes, it's easy enough," Elna nodded, as I turned my delighted face towards her. "I can see the solution as well. What dunderheads we've been! All that is needed is to use those 'refill' copper pencils in the accelerator cylinder, set the electric disrupter at work, and the rest is automatic. Let's look."

Eagerly we went inside the machine, and amazingly enough, without the least effort, found how to open that cylinder which had formerly defied all our efforts. Inside were the controls for the disintegration of the copper pencils, and the neat little apparatus for converting that tremendous energy into propulsion. Silently, comprehending everything as we looked, we surveyed the neat, gleaming pistons of the propulsor shafts, and saw, too, the complicated connections that mated the whole thing to the master control-board.

I looked again at the box at the side holding the twenty-five copper pencil refills, and placed two in the sockets on the top of the cylinder.

"And of course," I said, looking the thing over again, "this switch here starts the motor, but you can't stop it without throwing in this break-contact plunger. We failed to understand that the only way to stop the constant disintegration was by using this plunger, which, coming into contact with this magnetized plate, throws out a radius of pure energy of exactly the right frequency necessary to stop further atomic disintegration. We pushed the wrong knobs. It never occurred to us that this thing was on the plunger principle. Beats me how we were fooled by it!"

Elna smiled faintly. "What is past is done with, Sandy. We're going back home as geniuses, and we're going to wipe Jelfel off the map before we've done… " She stopped and frowned in sudden annoyance. "No food or water during the return journey!" she snapped. "What fools we've been to overlook it. I don't want to go all through that misery again—" Here she stopped dead and stared at something on the floor. So intent was her gaze I looked too, and can you imagine my feelings at beholding a hamper standing there, lidless, and filled to the brim with the choicest viands of earthly Ages. We went closer and found upon the handle a very earthly-looking label with words printed by some marvellously flawless machine:

"A PARTING REMEMBRANCE TO THE EARTHLINGS."

"The Voice has given us food," Elna said needlessly, looking at me in rather an awe-stricken manner. "What a mind—what conception… Oh, look here! A chicken, perfectly cooked—and champagne—and ekrimar! Truly nothing is impossible to a mind that understands what to us *is* impossible." She paused and smiled dryly. "Looks to me, Sandy, as though we'd better get lost in Time again!"

While Elna attended to the accelerator, I set to work upon the controls—after the airlock had been securely fastened, and that precious hamper removed to a safe corner. I got the machine rising on a long slope into the air (it appeared that the motor was working perfectly again after its travels through the void, either through the warmth of the sun, or else further work of that astounding planet brain), and presently we impinged upon the time-line with a slight jar, seeing once again that familiar four-dimensioned view. Then once more we were firmly embedded in the time-line, hurtling backwards along that endless stream to our own position in space and time.

For the time being there was nothing more to do, so we set to work on perhaps the most delicious meal I have ever known. Chicken and ekrimar! I live again those moments of palate paradise.

Certainly there was no discomfort on the return journey. We saw, of course, that amazing planet brain in the reverse order of time. We saw it return to the parent nebula, and recede until it again became that dim smudge from which it had evolved. Once more we passed through the incomprehensible gulfs of infinite space, until at last the earth began to reform below us.

Backwards we went, and still farther backwards, through the countless centuries. Through the age of frozen air, the age of ice, the earth's last days, and still back, and ever back. The journey took, I noticed, practically the same time as before—but without its attendant discomforts.

Came the time at last when the sun resumed its golden tint, when it again swung with terrific velocity; when at last the moon swept through all her phases in a violet sky. At this point Elna threw in the plunger of the accelerator, and instantly the copper pencils ceased to liberate their disintegrating energy. Our speed began to slow down. The Age of Safety, the Age of Danger, the Age of Security—all moved before our vision in running, turbulent panoramas of four-dimensioned incredibility…

And so at last the Age of Problems once again!

Here we halted the time-machine almost to stopping-point, and considered the best course to adopt. The Age was, of course, shielded by etheric vibration, through which nothing solid could pass. To attempt it would mean immediate repulsion. The only thing to do was to consider the matter very carefully. We now had superior brain force; here was the chance to test its powers.

By mutual assent we sat down and thought it out, and very amazing it was how fast our ideas flowed.

"It's simple!" I exclaimed at last, and once more experienced that amazement at being so little-minded before. "This atomic disintegrator, which we use for the accelerator, can now be dispensed with. We will increase the field of disruptive force and turn it *on Jelfel's vibration screen!* That will disrupt the atoms of the vibration screen and allow a clear passage for the time-machine. Easy!"

"How do you propose increasing the field of disruptive force?" Elna asked.

"Not difficult. The heaters work from solar energy—stored solar energy. The pressure-gauges show we've an enormous amount of surplus solar energy still in store. Dismantle the heaters and convert the energy into the energy already in existence in the disintegrator. Release all our surplus energy at one go—and whoof! Bang goes Jelfel's precious obstacle! Some of it at least—enough for us."

We set to work right away. First we dismantled the accelerator and set it up in the nose of the time-machine. The next task was to connect the flexible leads of the disrupter to the exact centre of the ship's metal nose, and so allow the current to pass into the exterior of the ship. The task of riveting the cables and fusing them through the metal itself we accomplished with that very useful heater. By stepping it up in power and choosing one particular degree of heat, we managed to obtain enough brief incandescence to fuse the cable into the metal... Next we set to work to remove all the surplus ebonite casings we could find, and put them on one side to be used for encasing the motor when finished, and so stop, as much as possible, the spread of dangerous electric discharges...

The arrangement of the heater was not particularly difficult to our amazingly clear minds. Between us, we found it fairly simple to attach the solar energy converter to the one in the accelerator, and arrange the cables to stand the load of considerable extra voltage from the stored solar energy. True, we equipped the motor with resistances to avoid the chance of burning it out by overload.

The rest of the work was simple. Without any trepidation, so confident were we of the correctness of our plans, we switched on the storage batteries of solar energy—taking care first, of course, that the whole apparatus was shut in with ebonite so far as we could manage.

What took place was exactly as we had calculated. The stream of disintegrating force was transmitted into the air outside. That field of disruption struck the shield about the Age of Problems almost immediately, and there was a sudden blue-white flare that nearly blinded us with its terrific effulgence.

"Quick!" Elna breathed tensely. "Forward! We're blasting the way through!"

I flung in the control switch, set my teeth, and drove the time-machine through the white hot gap. I made the jump with terrific velocity in order to avoid the melting of the ship itself, so terrific was the heat. Then, at my order, Elna cut off the disintegrator's power, for already it was cutting a hole in the ground itself!

The time-machine staggered slightly as I swung it sideways out of the time-line, lurched, and then started to fall downwards. In a moment I had the normal engines going and arrested our fall. I felt my heart beating with delight and excitement as I beheld below the familiar round, wheeled buildings of Jelfel's Age, glittering and gleaming in the dying sunset.

Lower we dropped, and lower, until at last with a thud we came to rest a trifle to the left of the city.

# CHAPTER XI

## *Outwitted!*

As we descended from the time-machine, the lights of the city suddenly sprang into being, as though in salutation of our arrival, I reflected. Instantly the machine city became a wilderness of gleaming, bellying edifices, the lights within them shining through the windows, and turning them into square eyes.

Elna came to me, and together we looked up in silence at the Emanation Towers of the etheric barrier. A cold smile touched her lips.

"That didn't prove so much good!" she said dryly.

"Nor is that anything to what is going to happen," I supplemented; then before I could say anything further a quartet of men padded silently up in the arc-light. I turned with a little start, my eyes dropping to their levelled ray-guns.

"What are you doing here?" one of them asked, evidently the leader, judging by the array of badges adorning his chest.

Somehow, my extra fast mentality flung the next words into my mouth.

"We seek Elnek Jelfel, the Master."

He looked at us suspiciously for a moment, then cocked his eye on the time-machine.

"That's a time-machine, isn't it?"

"Yes. What of it?"

"Just this. How did you get through that vibration screen?"

I smiled a trifle grimly. "I don't consider myself answerable to a guard," I replied. "Take me to the Master at once."

For an instant the guard looked at me with more than a hint of fury; then he relaxed and shrugged his broad shoulders. "All right. Follow me."

He turned about and we followed him between the wheeled edifices. His walk brought him, as Elna and I had expected, to the door at the base of the observation tower. We were led in, the door closed, and there followed a march across the familiar, smooth expanse of floor. At the footsteps, a slight figure at the far end of the room turned and looked up from surveying his banks of instruments and dials.

It was Jelfel, of course. Nor could he conceal the astonishment in his features as he gazed at Elna and me. With a curt nod he dismissed the guard, and came towards us with a face that slowly became impassive once more.

"This is a surprise, Commander Lee—Miss Folson." I looked at him, and felt, for the first time in my experience, capable of overshadowing him in intellectual force. Even his many complicated instruments no longer baffled me.

"I thought you'd find our visit a trifle unexpected," I responded coldly. "You see, Jelfel, neither your efforts to maroon us in prehistory, or the powers of your vibration screen served to keep Miss Folson and me out of your plans."

"You interest me. Tell me, Commander, how did you ever get through that vibration screen? There must be a fault in it somewhere."

"No there isn't, Jelfel. We literally burned our way through it. We disrupted your screen. It's composed of vibration forces set up in the nitrogen atoms, isn't it?"

"True enough. But—"

"The disintegrator we used has a radium content. We merely shattered your nitrogen atoms—and incidentally your screen—with alpha particles of radium, allied to solar energy."

Jelfel stroked his chin. "Then of course the atoms were transformed into hydrogen atoms?"

"Yes, but that was of no consequence to us. We broke your screen and got through, anyhow. I claim no credit for the idea. Nitrogen atoms were exploded by radium particles thousands of years ago. This was merely an improved version, aided by stored solar energy."

"A feat like that, Commander, must have taken a power of reasoning I hardly suspected you possessed," Jelfel remarked dryly.

"That is but a trifle compared to what I am going to do later," I returned grimly. "You may as well realize right away that both Miss Folson and myself are here to exterminate both you and your machines—and all the machines you may devise to block our path will avail you nothing!"

He raised one eyebrow half amusedly. "Really, Commander? Well, I'm sure that is very interesting. You are delightfully frank—the one really interesting trait in your otherwise diverse character... Of course, though, what you say is so much absurdity, for the simple reason that I have you covered at this very moment with magnetic poles which can produce instantaneous paralysis. Just try and move," he suggested coaxingly. I did try, and cursed myself inwardly for a precipitate fool. I could not shift an eighth of an inch from where I was standing on the metal floor. Neither could Elna move.

"Very rash, Commander—very rash," Jelfel murmured pleasantly. "However, it may be of interest to you to know that my plans are working splendidly. All the cities of the Ages from 2000 to this Age are in ruins. Every time-liner has been blown clean to hell, and the Presidents Templeton and Folson are both quite dead! My machines fully recorded all I needed to know from the still retentive brains of the dead men; then they were rayed out of existence. Time-machines are now being rapidly built. This Age, as I have told you before, is overcrowded. Daily it becomes worse."

"Yes, so you've said before," I returned tartly. "I don't believe that stuff. You've got bigger schemes up your sleeve, and I mean to find out what they are!"

"You mean that you have killed my father?" Elna put in, in a low, tense voice.

Jelfel smiled twistedly as he looked at her. "You know, Miss Folson, there is a very old saying—'All is fair in love and war.' This, of course, is war!" he added, with entirely needless emphasis.

I looked at him steadily.

"So you succeeded in wrecking every civilized city with that infernal vibrator of yours?"

"Exactly, Commander. It was an interesting sight, viewed in my Wave Trap, to see the poor fools scuttling like rats for shelter as the buildings fell about them." Jelfel brooded for a moment and clenched a thin hand ruthlessly.

I stared at him in bleak hate for an instant; then suddenly I summoned every vestige of my abnormal will-power in an effort to break the magnetic bonds that held me. He was too goading; more than flesh and blood could stand... The strain was terrific, and the first time it failed. But the second time I succeeded!

So sudden was the breakage of magnetism, I toppled forward clean on top of the thoroughly astounded Jelfel. I think it was not so much the mental effort I made as the physical one. That titanic strength that had come to me aided me enormously. I closed my hand about Jelfel's throat in a grip of iron. He struggled feebly, rage contorting his features. I forced him to his knees.

"Now!" I breathed exultantly. "I've got you where I've wanted you for many a long day! You are going to give immediate orders for the stopping of all time-machine building; then you are going to tell me your real motive behind all this. I'll decide later what plans to make. You smashed all those cities in the time-line, for instance, and you're going to rebuild them. Understand?"

"And the alternative?" he choked, clawing at my hand.

"This," I said in a low voice, and crushed my fingers with almost frightening power into the soft flesh of his neck. At that he fought frantically, and I eased off a trifle. "Well?" I asked. "You have ten seconds."

He seemed to think swiftly. Then, gurglingly: "I agree."

I let him up, covering him with the ray-gun I snatched from his belt.

"First of all, release Elna," I ordered.

He reached out with his foot, moved a control on the floor, and Elna came forward to my side.

"The communicator to your workshops is over in the corner," I said, not stopping to comprehend how I knew all this. "Give those orders for stoppage immediately."

Jelfel looked at me strangely, as though uncertain as to how much I knew, then with a curious little smile he walked over to the instrument in question and made a few adjustments to the mechanism. I watched him narrowly.

"No tricks," I advised him. "I happen to know far more than you realize, Jelfel. My mind is quicker than yours. This is war of wits and speed—not of blood."

"True," he assented, with a little shrug; then with astounding swiftness he suddenly flung out his right arm and knocked the ray-gun clean out of my hand. Another swift movement, which I recognized as a ramification of the ancient art of ju-jitsu, and I found myself lying on my back on the floor with all the wind temporarily knocked out of me. Automatically I kicked out my foot and struck him full in the stomach. Rather to my surprise he was not winded in the least. He merely staggered, and I noticed that my foot had brought forth from his middle a curious metallic sound. I had no time then to conjecture on this curious occurrence, but later I had great reason to remember it.

I scrambled to my feet as he staggered, retracting my arm for a punch that would certainly have cracked his jaw had it ever landed. It never did so, however.

"Stand still—both of you!"

Both Elna and I stopped dead in a forward movement. The cold-faced guard who had escorted us from the outside was now standing in a farther doorway, ray-gun levelled. He advanced with a glint in his eye.

I dropped my arm and waited grimly for the next. Jelfel recovered his balance and stood in silence by the bench for a moment, his green eyes upon me.

"So!" he panted at last. "You thought, by primitive methods, to outwit me, Lee? You consummate fool! Your brain greater than mine! Bah! You have not the brain of an ape to descend to that sort of foolery. Barbarism died out in the atomic war of 2468; after that it became pure mind-war if there was any at all. But you're going to pay for that lapse.

You hear me? You are going to—pay!" He spat out the word with vicious satisfaction, and came closer to me. "Death is too pleasant and swift a passing for so worthy an enemy. It must be something lasting; something to carry in the memory… "

He began to pace up and down, chin sunk on his chest, hands clasped behind him. I followed his every movement with burning eyes, wondering in my innermost mind what conceivable notion had ever prompted me to be so utterly ridiculous in my behaviour. Naturally, I might have known I could never hope to overcome a man like Jelfel by mere barbaric methods. Still, I had obeyed a mental impulse and felt vaguely satisfied.

Presently he ceased his pacing and came towards Elna and me with a slightly sardonic smile on his cold face.

"I have a wonderful idea," he said softly. "An idea worthy of a genius—and also an idea that will give you ample scope to exert your—er—super-brain. Correct me, Commander, if I have designated your intelligence erroneously."

"You infernal—" I began, then I stopped hopelessly. He went on monotonously.

"Undoubtedly, the best place for you and Miss Folson is in the Machine Department. There, despite a certain amount of rigorous confinement, you will have ample scope for exerting all the intellect you desire. You will be able to help in the actual making of my time-machines! You will be able to help with the assembling of them. In brief, you will be able to help in the construction of the machines, the secret of which I obtained from the brains of two dead men. One your father, Miss Folson!" He turned to her, his icy smile broadening into an unholy grin.

I said nothing; neither did Elna. What could we say? I assure you it was only a remarkable effort of will power that prevented me hurling myself again on this scoundrel of the Age of Problems.

"Naturally," he went on calmly, "the time will come when the constant toil, the privations, and the iron rule I enforce, will break you. You are a strong man, Commander Lee, and Miss Folson is anything but lacking in physical endurance. But even so, the strongest body and mind break under perpetual hardships. That is what happens in the Machine Department, my friends. The workers there are really criminals—prisoners—but naturally it is my desire that they perform useful service whilst being punished at the same time. They die in the end, so what matters it?"

Again came that involuntary action that made me utter words entirely apart from anything preconceived.

"If you only knew it, Jelfel, you are signing your own death warrant by sending us to the Machine Department you speak of. Elna and I returned to wipe you out—and nothing you can do or say will ever alter our purpose. It is written in Time that it shall come to pass."

Jelfel shrugged.

"I have an intense appreciation of the melodramatic, Commander, but I usually like it in the proper place, where the general perspective lends itself to the atmosphere of the drama. You, to use a vulgarism, are merely drivelling." He stopped and looked at me with his burning eyes for a moment, then turning to the instrument board behind him he pushed in the switches of the Light-Wave Trap. Instantly the attached ground-glass screen flared into life, and there came a vision of the arc-lit world outside. Swiftly, as Jelfel operated the controls, the view changed, until at last Elna and I beheld our time-machine clearly in view in the picture.

"That, of course, is the time-machine in which you came? Jelfel said, without turning his head.

"What about it?" I snapped.

"Sorry though I am to state it, Commander, it will have to be destroyed forthwith."

"Destroyed!" I breathed thickly. "You're marooning us again, eh?"

"It is really necessary, Commander. You remember when I destroyed Liner 48? Well, this machine will go in the same way. The only difference will be that I shall use a Disintegrator, instead of the beam of force, such as I used before. They are both similar in ultimate results."

He moved to his Disintegrator, threw in the switches amidst a flaring of electricity, and then stared at the screen… Came one brilliant flash and the time-machine had completely vanished. There remained only a smoking patch upon the dry ground.

Dully, I heard the contact being broken on the devilish machine, and looked round again to behold Jelfel complacently smiling.

"Just—dust!" he said pleasantly, switching off the Light-Wave Trap with a slender, skilful hand.

I felt unable to speak in the intensity of the moment. I only comprehended in a dazed kind of fashion that the link with my own time—with Elna's time also—had been ruthlessly destroyed. The only other way was with Jelfel's own time-machines, and as for getting a chance with one of those! The farcical side of the idea almost prompted me to a bitter laugh.

"And now, my friends," Jelfel went on, "I will personally conduct you to the Machine Department. I feel sure you will feel honoured," he added, with that cutting sarcasm that was the grim shield of his cruel, merciless nature. "Pray come with me."

He turned about, and I watched his slender form for a moment; then, at a jab in the back from the guard's ray-gun, I proceeded to follow him,

Elna walking at my side with footsteps that were noticeably weary, not so much from physical exhaustion as mental hopelessness. True enough, the position at that moment did not seem to warrant any overflow of joy. For some reason, then incomprehensible, I had walked right into a trap, and had dragged Elna down as well. Silently I felt the pangs of remorse, and above all a seething fury against myself.

# CHAPTER XII

## *The Devil's Workshops*

I need not explain at length the journey to the Machine Department. It was reached by a devious system of stairways and winding passages, all flooded with the glare of arc-lights. Jelfel kept constantly in the forefront, walking at a steady pace, and behind was the guard, with levelled ray-gun.

Then presently we emerged from the silences that grouped about Jelfel's domain, into a region of steadily increasing sound and warmth. Sickly warmth that clung to the shining iralium walls, warmth that literally stunk with chemicals, and had within it all the qualities of the revolting and obnoxious... The noise increased steadily, merging from the steady, deeply pulsating thuds of distance into more clearly defined hammerings and roars that brought before my mentality visions of immense pile-drivers and electric saws of colossal dimensions.

The nature of our surroundings changed. The passages became bleaker in aspect and less luxurious. The iralium walls seemed to shine inimically, and had lost their former cleanness and brightness. For some obscure reason I was reminded of a visit I had once made from the dirty working quarters of New York to the sea-coast. The change in appearance here, reversed in order, was very analogous.

At last Jelfel passed before a grilled gate, possessing bars of three-inch thickness. Beyond, Elna and I had a vision of a repellent, uninviting enclosed square, lined on either side by doors, from behind which emanated this constant and almost distracting din.

"I am afraid you will find your future abode a trifle noisy," Jelfel said dryly, turning. "However, it is a fact that the eardrum can become attuned in time to almost any vibration periodically. You will have ample time and scope for proving the authenticity of that statement."

"Don't you think you've done enough torturing without adding more?" I asked him bitterly. "If ever I get my hands on you again, Jelfel—"

"You won't!" he assured me coldly, fingering his throat tenderly. "I have an intense dislike of having my throat interered with." He stopped at that and looked back into the square as an armed guard approached, moved the switch that operated the electric lock on the prison gate, and we saw the entire thing move slowly to one side.

"It took you long enough!" Jelfel snapped, glaring at the guard.

"My regrets, Master," the sentry answered humbly; and I felt within me a sickening disgust at the fawning manner of this sycophant. No wonder, if all the slaves of the Age of Problems were like this, that Jelfel was the undisputed ruler and dictator.

We were then conducted across the square to one of the many doors. Once again came the operation of the electric locks, then we were inside the place, on the threshold of the workshops of this machine-crazy Age.

I will not say my brain reeled at what I saw, for in my clearer state of mentality I comprehended much of what lay before me; but I do say that, had I seen it a few weeks previously, I should have stood before it all like a child. The infinite complexity of it all! The labyrinth of astounding and unexpected things!

And the heat—and the light! The heat struck me like a physical blow, a mighty upper-surge of super-charged warmth, having with it the obnoxious odour of molten alloy and strange chemicals. It blanketed Elna and me instantly, setting us gasping for breath for a moment. High up in the lofty ceiling were arc-lights of terrific power that drenched the seething flow of activity and metal beneath. Everywhere was metal, and strange, unaccountable instruments. Dials that glittered strangely on the metal walls, flickering lights that leapt perpetually across blank emptiness, men that moved in orderly formation upon towering platforms of metal, with tortuous staircases rising upwards to the lofty metal roof. Here and there an electric welder flared into blinding life, and I caught a vision of a crouching figure in grey overalls with a shield of purple glass before his eyes…

And din! It deafened conception, it robbed me of the ability to even think for a space. Roaring, beating, hammering—a modern Babel!

"Interesting, is it not, Commander?" asked Jelfel's voice, close to my ear.

I spun round on him, so suddenly that he took a step back.

"Don't worry; I can't do anything to you!" I shouted harshly, speaking with all my power to make myself heard. "But, by heaven, Jelfel, you're going to pay an account to me one of these days—not only as retribution for these poor devils here, but for the murders you have committed, and for the supposed fate to which you have condemned Elna and me."

"Did you say 'supposed'?" he asked, with that sardonic grin of his.

"I know you'll never succeed," I answered grimly, and I dare say it sounded at that time a very absurd remark; yet I felt I had grounds for uttering it.

Jelfel shrugged indifferently and turned back to the scene before us. Presently he raised his hand and motioned to a distant guard. He came up the long flight of steps from the hall floor at a run, and saluted.

"You will take these two and set them to work with the others," Jelfel ordered. "You will treat them exactly as the others. The only exception is that they must be watched more closely."

"Master, it shall be done."

Jelfel turned back to Elna and me once again. "I am afraid that this is where we must part—at least for the time being," he said, with a plainly mock bow to us both. "Maybe we'll see each other at some future date— if you live that long," he added thoughtfully; then he turned to the door behind us and was gone.

I looked back again at the guard. He was a brutal-looking fellow at the best, with a close-cropped head, bull neck, and repugnant features. Dressed only in a sleeveless vest and trousers, he revealed all the immense muscular power of his arms and chest. Obviously, from this physical development, and yet narrow, hair-bestrewn brow, he was composed of more brawn than brain. In his hand he carried a vicious-looking affair that was an improvement on the old-time cat-o'-nine-tails. Six tendrils of knife-edged metal strips swung from a thick butt, which he clutched in one powerful, hairy fist.

"Come!" he spat out at last, jerking his thumb over his shoulder.

I glanced behind me; the guard who had been with Jelfel had also disappeared. With an inward feeling of resignation, I took Elna's arm and together we slowly descended the twenty broad steps to the floor of this devil's workshop.

As we passed down the central aisle, the guard a trifle in front of us, I caught glimpses of worn and emaciated faces peering at us, with a dull inquisitiveness, over the various machines, Lack-lustre eyes that gazed, with a mingled feeling of sympathy and curiosity, across whirling, nerve-distracting gears; men with lantern jaws and cold eyes that watched, with almost pitiable intensity, the movements of incomprehensible dials and quivering, delicately balanced needles.

To gaze upon the Age of Problems from the outside it would have been difficult to have thought that so much misery and suffering could have been contained within its core.

"I wonder if I shall ever look like these poor women?" Elns muttered in my ear, her grey eyes looking at them in mingled horror and sympathy.

I looked down at her youthful, athletic form and the strong set of the shoulders.

"Never!" I vowed, with the deepest emphasis. "I'll blow the whole stinking outfit to Hades before you shall ever look like that. You, with all your health and youth, transformed into a hag... By Heaven, *no!*"

"You seem—" Elna began, but she left her sentence unfinished. The guard had stopped and was looking at us malevolently.

Unconsciously, we had ceased to follow him in our interest in things about us, but it was obvious from his expression that he intended to quickly rectify the omission.

"What do you think this is? A tour?" he asked sourly, hands on hips, surveying us with his lower lip protruding.

I did not answer that. "I'm being lenient with you," he went on, spitting with startling force on the metal floor, "but that's only because you're new here. See? Any monkey tricks, once you're settled down, and may the gods protect you!" He slapped his whip in an anticipatory fashion, spat again with eye-opening vigour, and blew out a deep breath of bestial emphasis.

"You're threatening us, you mean?" I asked him in a grim voice.

His beady eyes shot from me to Elna, then back to me again. He tightened the belt about his middle with one hairy paw. "Just warnin' you," he said. "Come on!" Once again that dirty thumb jerked to regions unknown, and we followed him to the end of the aisle. At this point we stopped.

"Now," he said, "there's plenty of room for you two on that time-liner we're building over there. You'll have to change first. Follow me."

We obeyed, and at the entrance to another aisle that led into gloomy regions unknown, we paused again. An iron-faced woman in forbidding costume came out of the gloom.

"Woman here for overalls," the guard said curtly. "I'll take charge of the man."

I tried to say a word to Elna, but it was useless. The woman seized her by the arm in a grip of steel, and half-dragged her into the gloom and darkness. I, for my part, shook loose my guard's grip as he endeavoured to do the same.

"I shan't run away," I said coldly. "Carry on, and get on with it!"

He sniffed unpleasantly and led the way through devious routes to a small, dimly-lighted place lined with shelves of overalls. Taking a swift measurement of my form, he searched amongst them until presently he hurled one at me.

"You won't want those clothes you've got on," he said with a grim smile. "Take 'em off and put these on. You're a worker now..." And he leered into my face in such a repulsive manner that I felt very much tempted to smash my fist into it.

The change occupied about ten minutes, and I did not feel particularly comfortable in my new outfit. The cloth was rough and coarse, more like sacking than anything else, and of a drab grey shade. It completely enveloped the form from ankles to neck. Upon my head I perched a small, circular cap.

"That's your number," my guard said cynically, and pointed to the figures 42,789 sewn in white upon my chest; then as I looked down at them with a twisted smile he spoke again. "Time to get movin'. Come on."

We returned to the doorway of the Machine Department again, and found Elna and the iron-faced woman already there. I could have wept at the vision of Elna in that awful sacking stuff, completely covered by the coarse material, with only her bright face and quick hands protruding.

"Now—work!" the guard said, before we had a chance to speak, and we were piloted along various aisles until presently we reached what was presumably a half-completed time-liner—a massive, cigar-shaped affair reposing in an iralium cradle and extending for quite five hundred feet down the immense hall.

At length we joined a party of similarly-garbed workers, busy upon the construction of this monster of Time. Men and women were everywhere, riveting, sawing, chiselling, and hammering. Nearby, a machine that emanated pure heat by a system of rays through narrow lenses, was melting solid metal into liquid. The heat of this brutal apparatus nearly turned me sick for a moment, then I fought against it and conquered.

"You need know nothing of what you are doing," the guard said. "That man there—Kariso—will tell you what to do. Do it, and ask no questions." With that he turned away about his normal business and Elna and I approached the short, bloated individual standing in the centre of the activity, watching the proceedings, and referring ever and again to a blueprint and chart. He turned as I tapped him on the shoulder and revealed a purply-red, beefy face and protruding, curiously brilliant blue eyes.

"Well?" he barked out, with such impatience that even I was startled. "What is it?"

"We are here for work," I said coldly, motioning to Elna.

"Well!" He put his arms akimbo and surveyed us from head to foot with a contemptuous grin. "Isn't that nice!" He made a note on a greasy-looking piece of paper. "Numbers 42,789 and 66,798. All right"—he looked up—"get busy with those workers over there. And when I say busy, I mean *busy!*"

We obeyed without a word, and in a moment were among the dull-eyed individuals, assisting them to erect a square contrivance of metal against the enormous side of the time-liner.

Our struggles had commenced in real earnest at last.

# CHAPTER XIII

## *A Remarkable Discovery*

Now that the preliminaries connected with our initiation into the hellishness of Jelfel's workshops were over, I began to exert my mentality as I worked on steadily, deliberately doing nothing to incur the wrath of the brutal Kariso. I had no desire to court disaster at the moment, or even move from this particular work I was engaged upon…

And the reason for this was because I was commencing to notice many peculiar things. I doubt if in my former mental state I should have detected anything unusual, but, now my brain was once again on the upward movement, and improved beyond all former efforts, I began to apprehend certain things. Elna, I think, noticed as well.

We were not at work upon a time-liner at all!

I was sufficiently acquainted with the construction and interior workings of a time-liner to know almost to an inch what would be required to make it up—and yet this five-hundred-foot monstrosity had none of these things! For one thing, the metal was not that which would float in the Correnium gas, and for another the all-important lead sheathings were missing! What the metal was I could not quite make out.

The assembling of the various parts was anything but in keeping with a time-liner. The control-room was being placed at the centre of the thing, and the other rooms at the two ends. And again, there were only six rooms in all. If this was the full accommodation of the ship, how on earth did Jelfel expect to move all his surplus population? Again I felt that growing conviction that he had been lying.

Elna was mostly engaged in assisting three other women to raise the metal sheets up to roughly-constructed platforms, where the plates were welded into position by electricity. For my own part I was busily engaged on helping in the construction of the control-board—just the work I needed if I was to solve the problem that confronted me. I thanked my lucky stars that I had the super-keen intelligence to comprehend not only what I was doing, but everything connected with it…

Presently I managed unobtrusively to work my way close to Elna, and talked to her as I went on with my work.

"Notice anything peculiar about this liner?" I muttered.

"Yes. It isn't a time-liner at all."

"Any idea what it is?"

"None at all. Have you?"

I shook my head. "Not yet; but a vague idea is forming."

She nodded and went on hauling the sheets of metal.

As I went on with my work I began to take stock of those about me. The man nearest me was young—not more than twenty-five, I felt sure, with a lean but clever face, and lank hair. He caught my look and turned a face that shone with perspiration towards me.

"What brings you here?" he asked, from the side of his mouth, as we struggled with the corner of the switchboard to get it into position.

"Revenge," I answered in a low voice. "I intend to destroy Elnek Jelfel."

"Then you're mad," he said cryptically. "Men have died in this Age for less than that."

"In other Ages, men live to accomplish," I answered him. "I belong to 2000, and this girl over to my left with the fair hair is my closest friend. She belongs to 20,000. She's Elna Folson, daughter of the Time Corporation President—now dead."

He looked at her and shrugged his shoulders slightly. "It's hell here—especially for the women. Keep your eye skinned for this pig, Kariso. He's death on us! One day I'm going to kill him!" The fellow's bony hand clenched fiercely on the metal he was holding.

"How do you propose doing it?" I asked.

"I don't know—but I'm going to! What's your name?"

"Sandford Lee."

"Mine's Lan Ronnit. I hope we will be friends?"

"Of course," I assured him, and at that our conversation ceased, for the brilliant eyes of Kariso had turned towards us in vague suspicion.

Our work continued for a space, then suddenly Kariso called a halt. I stopped, expecting him to say something to me for talking; but evidently he was not concerned with my remarks. Instead, he motioned to four men standing on a platform on the exterior of the half-completed machine. Grouped before the quartet were black box-like affairs, from which depended tough, heavily-insulated cables.

"Stand clear whilst the metal is tested!" Kariso snapped. "Hurry!"

We all stood back, grateful for the respite. I stood between Elna and the young man Ronnit, watching the proceedings with interest.

There was a sudden roar, and from the black boxes there sprang a pale yellow beam that struck the metal and enveloped it in yellow effulgence. The workers blinked, but continued watching through half-closed eyes. Every sheet that had been assembled was carefully tested; then again Kariso called a halt.

"Well, what's the reading?" he bawled, above the frightful din.

The operator of the centrally situated machine surveyed something on the top of the various boxes.

"Pressure, 460. Resistance, 990. Temperature resistance, minus 273.1, Centrigrade," he answered.

"Right!" Kariso snapped. "That'll do. Get back to work, the lot of you."

We returned to our tasks, but something was sticking in the back of my mind, trying to see the light. As yet it had not formed clearly, but I spared no mental effort to bring it into being.

"I'm an inventor," said Lan Ronnit presently, leaning towards me. "I got shoved in this place because I accidentally shot one of Jelfel's guards. I'm here for life—unless a miracle happens. If that miracle ever does happen, I know the way out to the surface. We're underground here, you know."

Silently we worked on. "What have you invented?" I asked presently.

He placed his ear close to mine as we drove home a rivet together. "I know how to make all organic substances invisible."

I felt a little thrill at that and looked into his lean face and dark eyes.

"You actually mean you have found it?" I insisted. "Not only in theory?"

"No—absolutely in practice."

"But how do you—" I stopped dead. Kariso was advancing towards us, his brutal face anything but reassuring.

"You two have got a lot to say, haven't you?" he asked sourly. "What's it all about?"

We neither of us replied, and at that silence Kariso's powerful arm shot out and his hand closed upon the collar of Lan Ronnit's overalls. He jerked him round with a single irresistible muscular movement.

"Trying to spread trouble again, eh, Ronnit?" he asked with a coarse laugh. "I got you once for doing that, and I'll do it again, if necessary!"

Ronnit did not speak. I, too, stood silent, my fists clenched. The rest of the workers looked on in mute consternation.

"You've done nothing yet," Kariso resumed, "but I may as well warn you not to go any further. My temper's short! Now get busy!" He released Ronnit with a vicious thrust that flung him sideways against the metal of the switchboard.

I looked sideways at his face and saw it set in hard lines in the glaring light of the arcs. He bit his lower lip tenaciously.

"The swine! The misbegotten snake!" he breathed venomously. "One day I'm going to make him pay, the spawn of Belial..."

He said no more than that; it was not safe. Kariso never relaxed his vigilance for a moment, and throughout the long night the work went on. By the time the shift was finished, in the early hours of the new day, I was about ready to drop from exhaustion. All the workers were the same. True, the work on the time-liner—I call it such at this stage purely for convenience—had progressed enormously, but at the cost of much human suffering and energy. I turned weary eyes to behold Elna nearby, drooping from fatigue, her face smothered in sticky dust and metal filings. She flung up a lazy arm and wiped the streaming perspiration from her forehead as I looked at her.

"Halt!" Kariso snapped—the energy of the man was phenomenal. Instantly work ceased. With that, Kariso departed to his own unknown quarters, and the day overseer took charge. Elna and I, along with the workers, were led from the Machine Department, down numberless passages until we came to what were evidently the sleeping and eating quarters. Four vast rooms, two lined with tables, and two lined with small, hard beds. One department for the men, and one for the women.

At the main doorway I took leave of Elna for the time being and went in with Lan Ronnit for a meal. This proved to be some abominable stuff like thin glue, which, although revolting to my refined palate, was consumed with avidity by my fellows. However, I was desperately hungry, so I ate it, and curiously enough, enjoyed it...

Then, like so many cattle, we were herded into the sleeping-room. By a little wangling among ourselves I managed to get the bed next to Ronnit. I felt that, if what he had told me was correct, he might prove very useful somewhere in my plans. Imagine my utter disgust, therefore, when he went straight to sleep without uttering a word!

Worn out in body and mind, I stretched myself on the bed and began to fall asleep; then suddenly I was awake again, in that curious fashion that sometimes precedes genuine sleep. I sat up, my mind cannily clear for an instant. I spoke aloud:

"Minus 273.1 degrees Centigrade! The temperature of absolute zero—of space! Elnek Jelfel is building a spaceship!"

For an instant I knew that fact quite clearly; then I fell back again on the bed and dropped into a deep sleep, worried nevertheless by distracting and distorting dreams. But from those dreams I followed up the absolutely true fact that had been borne to my brain, sharpened by that brief "false sleep."

Jelfel was not building a time-liner, but a spaceship. Why?

# CHAPTER IV

## *Escape*

I awoke to the insistent, violent clanging of a bell. A hard boot kicked me on the shin, and I became conscious of my bull-necked guard of the day—or rather the night—before, clutching my shoulder and shaking me vigorously.

"Like a cup of tea before you start?" he asked sourly. "Get up—and quick!"

I glanced at the massive pulsating clock situated high up on the far wall. The hour was five p.m. Time to get ready for the night shift once again. I fell out of the bed and scrambled into my uniform. As I sat at breakfast—once again that glue-like stuff—my mind went over what I had thought of in that transient waking moment the morning before. "Minus 273.1 degrees Centigrade." The metal of the supposed time-liner was made to stand the temperature of absolute zero—of space. No time-machine needed to stand that, except in rare cases—such as the experience of Elna and myself during our flight into futurity.

"Thinking?" asked a voice, and I looked round to behold the cadaverous face of Lan Ronnit.

"Ronnit, do you know what Jelfel is building?" I asked him. "Do you know what we're working upon?"

"Of course. A time-liner, similar to those owned by the Time Corporation, which Jelfel destroyed."

"No, we're not," I said quietly. "It's a spaceship."

"A spaceship!" Ronnit's jaw dropped. "You don't mean that? What on earth should Jelfel want a spaceship for? How do you know, anyhow?"

"Merely by the metal being of such a quality as to resist a Centigrade temperature of minus 273.1 degrees—outer space temperature. I just wonder what that devil is getting at?" I murmured to myself. "All the time I've known him, he's something different at the back of schemes to what he reveals openly."

"Space travel is impossible," Ronnit murmured. "Gravitational forces—law of acceleration. All that has been proved inimical to human life flying through space. Even Jelfel couldn't overcome that, clever though he is."

"Nothing is impossible to science," I said quietly. "I am not altogether sure that Jelfel *did* find out how to navigate space." And I freely admit that I had no conception in my mind at that time of any other theory. In any case I had no chance to say anything further, for Bull-Neck ordered us out to work.

I gripped Elna's hand reassuringly as I met her, and she returned me a steady, courageous gaze. I wished I could communicate my knowledge to her, but the guard was too heavy and too alert. Perhaps later on, I promised myself.

My mind on this shift was far improved upon the preceding one. Evidently the full power of that curious brain operation was commencing to take effect. I found, as I worked, that my conceptions were very clear and alert. My reasoning powers, also, were extremely astute.

As I worked, I asked myself once again the same question I had asked so many times before. Why should Jelfel go such enormous lengths merely to transfer his surplus population to another Age? Why such marvellous inventions? Why such merciless tenacity of purpose? The whole scheme seemed to me to sideslip somewhere; there was no *reason* for it all. The whole thing revolved around a completely pointless plot. Jelfel was in many ways no ordinary man; his powers of reasoning and capacity for scientific invention were almost unequalled in earthly records... He had come apparently from nowhere and mastered and subjected this Age of Problems. His motives were wrapped about in the deepest mystery. His Age was shielded from outside interference by etheric screens. What *was* he driving at...?

I knew that, despite his amazing ability, he had not the powers necessary to conceive entirely by his own initiative the immensely complicated details of a spaceship. Scientists had proved space-travel to be impossible, in so far that no human being could stand the strain. And yet here was Jelfel constructing a spaceship! And nobody, save I, had had the mental keenness to note the fact. Either Jelfel had had a staggeringly brilliant brain storm, or else a higher intelligence than his own was governing his movements. This latter possibility took quite a hold on my imagination.

"Say, what do you think you're here for? A rest cure?"

That rasping voice broke into my train of thought and disturbed me. I turned, expecting to find myself addressed, but rather to my surprise it was Lan Ronnit once again. He had been standing motionless, completely lost in thought, until Kariso's voice had guiltily awakened him into activity.

"I warned you yesterday, Ronnit, and I warned you a day or two before. I'm about sick of warning you. See!"

Ronnit turned slowly. "Can't a man think?" he demanded in a low, fierce voice.

Kariso stared in astonishment for a moment, then his lips projected in a fierce pout.

"You insolent hound! You dare to say that?"

"Why not?" Ronnit snapped, with growing warmth, encouraged by the silently approving workers about him, who had stopped work to listen and, if necessary, act. "Who in hell are you to say whether I shall think or not? You're only one of the little-brained community in any case. If you weren't, you wouldn't be just a bullying overseer!"

I held my breath at that statement. I really felt certain that Kariso would be stricken with apoplexy, so red did his face become. Then, whipping out one of the customary metal "cats" from his belt, he swung it around with all his strength, and struck Ronnit across the face. Instantly blood began to seep from deep weals in his cheeks.

"Shame!" came a low murmur.

"Down him!"

"Knock him down, Ronnit!"

"Silence!" Kariso thundered. "Back to your work, you scum! Back—and quick—or by heaven you'll all get a taste!" He wheeled round again on the still, silent, set-faced Ronnit.

"I'll teach you to defy orders. Take that!" He retracted his powerful arm for another mighty sweeping cut, and I saw the light of fear spring into Ronnit's face. He ducked in readiness for the blow… But the blow never fell.

I intervened instead, almost involuntarily. With a strength that astonished me—as it had often done since that brain operation—I sprang forward and seized Kariso's forearm, twisting it with all my strength. To my amazement there was a sharp crack as the bone snapped beneath my single-handed clutch.

A low roaring of approval began to come from the workers. Shouts of derision made themselves heard above the din of the machinery. A torrent of the vilest, filthiest expletives were hurled at the now cursing, groaning Kariso. Even so, despite his injury, he flung himself forward upon me like a wild beast.

I waited for his spring, then reaching forward I clutched him by the shoulder and trousers-belt, lifted him on high, and flung him with incredible force over the heads of the workers. He landed with a crash upon some metal-work in the far corner, and instantly uttered a piercing scream.

From beneath him there came a blinding flash and a puff of blue smoke. Flames began to envelop his form and reach up to the roof with alarming speed. I stood appalled.

"That's done it!" Ronnit breathed, clutching my arm. "You've thrown him on that machine we use for smelting metal. It projects rays of pure heat through those lenses. See—the weight of his body has short-circuited the thing. The place is catching fire! Don't let any of those rays strike you, if you value your life…!"

I stared at the melting machine like one in a dream. I remembered having seen it when I commenced work in this place, had felt its awful heat. Now, by some curious short-circuit, the thing was radiating rays in all directions, and everywhere the rays touched, metal or otherwise, flames began to spring forth.

The din of voices rose to a mighty, swelling roar. Smoke filled the great workshop.

"Fire! *Fire!*"

"This is our chance," Ronnit muttered, clutching my arm. "We'll never be seen in this confusion. I owe you a big debt for killing Kariso, and I'm going to repay it. Come with me."

"Elna—quickly!" I panted, clutching her arm and whirling her to me. "Keep with me… Right, Ronnit; lead on!"

# CHAPTER XV

## *Invisibility*

I do not clearly remember to this day how Lan Ronnit succeeded in getting the three of us out of the blazing workroom. I have a dim memory of desperate fighting with panic-stricken workers, of mighty blows and shoving, of struggling through jammed doorways, heaving and pushing through a maze of passages, floundering up steps and down slopes, until at last we had shaken off the greater number of the workers and were standing, the three of us, beneath the stars, with the glowing lights of the movable city to our left.

Lan Ronnit blew hard and wiped his cuff across his blood and sweat streaked face.

"Well, we did it," he said. "You all right?"

A brief examination proved that neither Elna or I were hurt much, save for a matter of bruises and contusions.

"You helped me, Lee," Ronnit said gratefully, taking my hand. "For that, my eternal thanks. I shall help you in return. I have been in this city since birth, whereas you two have only just arrived. There is nothing I do not know about the place. If we are careful we can reach my home. Come."

We followed him once again by a wide detour of the city. We went over open fields, beneath the Emanation Towers of Jelfel's shield of vibrations, across a small river—by way of a bridge, the river being used for electric power—and finally gained the outermost of the movable houses. After a brief look around Ronnit made some dexterous movements with the lock, and flung open the door.

"Quickly!" he breathed, and Elna and I hopped inside and stood waiting in the dark.

"I'm not putting the lights on just at the moment," Ronnit explained. "We'll move to a special secret place of mine before we do that. Just stay here a moment and wait."

His footsteps receded down a metal passage, and then we heard him busy with what sounded to be catches and switches. Presently there came a low whirring. In a moment I recognized it as the atomic motor affixed to the building itself.

Almost immediately afterwards the entire house began to move, and slowly gathered speed.

"Hang on!" Ronnit's voice came from somewhere up the passage. "We'll be all right in a moment…"

I held Elna tightly in the darkness as the moving edifice lurched from left to right and dipped up and down in the most giddy fashion. Then I fancied I heard a low gurgling sound, very much like flowing water. The speed of the "house-motor" began to decrease and at last ceased altogether. A light snapped on, and I beheld a vision of a short metal passage, with a neat little, combined living- and control-room beyond.

Ronnit turned from his switches with a faint grin on his lean face.

"Welcome!" he said, with a flourish. "This is just a portion of my humble abode—but you are more than welcome to it. Nor need you fear molestation."

"Where are we?" Elna asked curiously.

"At the bottom of the very river which Jelfel uses for his power-house! You know, there's a delicious irony in doing it!"

"The bottom of the river," I repeated. "But I didn't think these things were capable of going under water?"

"They're not as a rule," Ronnit calmly answered. "I have already told you that I am an inventor. Not only have I so sheathed my home that it can be subterranean whenever necessary, but it can also stay under water indefinitely, there being a perfect air regulating system. I also have it equipped with tractors, so that, if necessary, it can travel over any sort of land. I have found it most useful in the past to be able to go under water when making experiments… But please come into the living-room," and he led us away from the combined control and general room into an adjacent, beautifully neat apartment, switched on the heater, and motioned us to easy chairs.

"Make yourselves comfortable. I'll just bathe this cut face of mine, then I'll bring in some food. And it *will* be food!"

The meal was distinctly enjoyable, and it was remarkable how much more active we all felt after we had disposed of it... After its conclusion we sat round the heater beneath a diffused electric light, and Lan Ronnit expanded from the cowed, weary worker into a young man of remarkable theories and propositions.

"I didn't think when I told you last of my invisibility discovery that I should so soon be able to prove it," he remarked with a faint smile. "That, however, is by the way. I have solved it, and as I know you both to be firm friends of mine from now on, I'm going to explain it to you. It may be useful in overcoming this devil of a Jelfel—for, God knows, he needs wiping out! I was planning to have a try myself in any case, but your aid will make it easier. But, to my point. Nothing is visible—actual source of light excluded—except by the amount of light radiated or reflected from the object we view. That's so, isn't it?"

"As I understand it, light is a wave motion in the ether, assimilated to heat, electricity, and X-rays. A sort of to-and-fro variation of electrical force, accompanied by one of magnetic force. The two variations are inseparable, therefore the presence of one must imply the other," said I.

Ronnit laughed slightly.

"Just the old school of physics, eh?" he exclaimed. "I said *reflected* light, Lee—not the actual source of light. I suppose you'll be telling me next what is already known about *actual* light, and that is that wavelengths from one forty thousandth to one eighty thousandth of an inch are visible to the eye? Well, it's not that that I am concerned with. Stopping light at its source is too big a problem. But this is how I worked out my problem.

"Light, upon striking a material object, generates heat. That, of course, you know. Radiant heat and light—and electric waves—are all allied to each other, and move at the same speed of 186,000 miles a second... Now, we come to my point. When we look at an object—say you yourself for example, and forgive me calling you an 'object'—I only see you because you are reflecting light *and* radiant heat or energy back to me. You are not the source of light, you are the medium by which it is reflecting itself. If you were in dead black, completely enveloped, I should have much greater difficulty in seeing you than if you were in snow white from head to toe. Everything in the whole earth that we see, we merely see by reflection from either stellar or artificial light. That correct?"

"Quite," I assented. "I see you have studied the idea of reflection closely."

"Radiation is the correct word, Lee. Radiant energy is not heat, of course. Heat is purely the kinetic energy of molecules. Radiant energy constitutes a form of light, after the light has struck the body concerned, but in dealing with ordinary radiant energy we have to ascend to temperatures which no human could stand. Ordinarily, radiant energy constitutes the heat energy of a hot body, which is transformed into a kind of undulatory energy. This, at incidence with a material body is partly absorbed and re-transformed into heat, partially reflected, and, unless the body happens to be quite opaque, is partly transmitted as well. So far, so good.

"Now, the higher the temperature of a body the shorter is the wavelength of its radiation. That is the basis of my work. Radiant heat, energy, electricity, everything is directly due to the action of light; I don't need any calculation to prove that. Now, I have found that by projecting a given wavelength I can cut out the heat waves that make a human being—or anything organic—visible to the eye. A human being, with an average temperature of 98 degrees F. has scarcely any heat radiation when you compare it with solar heat waves, electric arcs, and what not. *But,* and this is my point, nothing organic would be visible to us at all, if it wasn't for this particular radiation of radiant energy. Light alone couldn't do it. Now, once again. Both light reflection and radiant energy reflection from a human being move in a transverse direction—that is, the direction of movement is perpendicular to the direction of vibration…

"You have followed me so far. Now let me revert to an instance which in essence is the secret of my invisibility wave length. If one takes a crystal of tourmaline it will split up a beam of light into two beams, which travel with different velocities, and are hence unequally refracted. Each beam is, of course, plane-polarized. Tourmaline crystal has the odd property of absorbing one of these beams so that the light transmitted is plane-polarized. Now, here's the point. Two tourmaline crystals placed with their axes parallel will allow light to pass through; but if they are crossed the light is completely cut out, since the plane-polarized beam which the first will allow to pass is immediately plane-polarized by the second…

"Now you have it. That curious quality which is supposed to be absorption of light is actually *radiation* of a wavelength. It is infinitesimally small, but it has the power of turning light, if we can regard it for a moment as a *positive* state—like electricity—into a similar positive state. Hence, the one repels the other, and the result is no light at all! Like repels like, of course. Now, likewise it repels the radiant energy of any body, which is embodied in light, and is the *necessary addition* to light if light is to be made visible at all... Thus, by finding the frequency of this particular and entirely unknown wavelength of tourmaline, I have succeeded, by the emanation of a compound of various crystals amongst which tourmaline is predominant, in producing an invisible wavelength that stops light from ever emanating from an organic body. I haven't yet attempted inorganic substances because they radiate no appreciable energy. The radiation from a human being is slight enough in all conscience, but it is enough to enable me to block it... Of course, the more powerful a radiant energy there is—take the boiling point of helium, 268.7° C., for instance—the more strength my wavelength has to have. I'll perfect that, later, however. For the time being I'm satisfied with having solved how to make a human being invisible..."

"I must congratulate you, Ronnit," I said heartily. "You've made a great achievement. But there is one thing I don't quite see."

"Well?" His lean face was eager to answer.

"I can follow your making a human being invisible—but what about the clothes they wear? They're organic, and have no heat."

"No heat? Come, come! Bodily radiation keeps clothes warm whilst you wear them, though not so warm as the body inside them, of course. Being of a lower radiation than the body itself they are, if anything, more easy to make invisible than the body itself, for my wavelength can incorporate lower radiations where it has not the strength as yet to tackle the higher."

"I see," I said thoughtfully. "And does this wavelength go through solids?"

"Believe me, it's perfect!" Ronnit said, slapping his knee emphatically. "Of course, it goes through solids—just the same as radio waves. And there is another thing that happens. Some curious magnetism in the body causes the invisible wavelength to follow the body upon which it is trained, no matter where it may go, just the same as radio waves follow a wireless set—only that radio waves are everywhere, whereas my own wave length only magnetizes itself to the particular object upon which it is focused. My limit of wave length is 12 miles. Past that distance it has no effect."

"Like the wavelength of a remote wireless station being unheard at all," I nodded. "It seems to me, though, Ronnit, as though other people who happen to unconsciously intercept the wavelength, would also become invisible."

"No, I've even guarded against that. For every human being there is a particular fixed rate of light and radiant energy emanation, highest in animals as they are hotter than a human being. Now, by determining with perfect accuracy beforehand—I will show you my instrument later, which works pretty much on the same idea as a compass—the radiation of the subject to be made invisible and attuning the wavelength to that absolute degree, nobody else can be affected because they are not in 'sympathy' with that length. Just the same, once again, as tuning-in a radio set. You wouldn't expect to hear Jelfel speaking on a wavelength of 1,600 metres if you tuned in to say, Polar City in 2000 with a wavelength of 280, would you? Of course not. The two are different frequencies. So are human beings. No two are alike... Anything else?"

"No," I said, taking a deep breath. "You've thought of everything Ronnit."

"Come and see for yourselves," he invited, and led the way through the living-room into another apartment; this time a remarkably well-equipped laboratory. Apart from countless beakers and test-tubes I noticed a considerable amount of electrical apparatus lining the walls. The benches themselves were composed of such a queer-looking metal, dull slatey blue in shade, that I asked Ronnit what it was. Once again he gave that queer little smile that seemed to be the shield of a mind of genius.

"Junison," he said calmly. "An isotope. Found it myself, and I have an idea that it's better than Jelfel's beloved iralium, junison is Atomic Number 140—atomic weight 280. The atoms are of course of two kinds, to form the isotope, and I think the atoms are those of iralium and calcinium, the latter my own invention. However, there's no time to go into the details, beyond the fact that junison blocks, completely and effectually, all forms of vibration—even radio waves. My invisibility wavelength won't even pass through it, that's why I have to project my beam through these iralium walls, which permit of the passage of anything. One of these days I'm going to use junison as a safeguard against eavesdropping radio, disintegrators, ray-guns, and the like!" He laughed, and turning, waved his hand to two instruments resembling cameras perched upon tripods, six neat wires in all leading back to a switchboard and complicated contrivance on the junison bench itself.

"These are the invisibility machines. You notice the actual wavelength transmitter is on a bench of junison, so that, apart from other things, it will not absorb any of the power into itself. Now, I'll switch it on."

He moved a button and a low, steady humming emanated from the curious apparatus.

"Now, Miss Folson," Ronnit said, "perhaps you would like to try? You will come to no harm."

"Willingly," Elna assented, and under Ronnit's direction walked forward to a spot in front of the nearest invisibility "camera." I stared, astonished. As she moved forward she suddenly became transparent, then at another step she had disappeared completely. The space was empty! Ronnit grinned at my amazement.

"That's effective enough for you?" he asked. "Now, if this mechanism were not switched off, that wavelength would continue to keep Miss Folson invisible no matter where she went, providing she didn't exceed the twelve mile limit. It will follow her and keep to her through solid metal, through everything but junison. I determined her emanation of radiation before I switched the thing on her. She's 1,600. Always rather higher in a woman than a man, you know."

I reached out my hand, and instantly it came into contact with something I couldn't see. I pulled at it, and I must confess I felt a trifle foolish when I heard Elna's voice exclaim:

"When you've quite finished trying to pull the sleeve out of my overall, Sandy, I'll be much obliged!"

Ronnit switched the mechanism off and Elna slowly reappeared.

"Naturally," she said, walking forward, "the object is still there—must take up the same amount of space. The only thing different is that it isn't seen. Of course, nobody could walk *through* it; it would mean another dimension to do that."

Ronnit nodded, and I looked at the universal bearings of the wavelength instrument, which permitted it to turn in any direction.

"Ronnit," I said, "you've discovered one of the most powerful weapons with which to outwit Jelfel that has yet been devised. Good wotk! You're only a young man yet; by middle age Jelfel won't have a look in."

"He'll be gone long before I'm middle aged!" Ronnit replied, setting his jaw. Then, relaxing again. "There's something else I want to tell you. Somewhere, deep under the earth, under this very city maybe, is the secret of eternal life!"

I looked at him sharply. "That savours of a medieval alchemist, Ronnit."

"Maybe it does, but it's true all the same. I had some records once, before my unfortunate escapade with Jelfel's guard that landed me in prison, in which it related the story of one explorer, Jansen, who penetrated, quite by accident the monstrous underground caverns beneath our feet, left from the atomic bomb war of 2468. You will know of it. However, he found that strange trees had evolved underground, utterly unknown to botany—products of the intensely electrified, magnetic soil. These trees, he found, have the property of instant propagation, both in themselves and other objects. Unfortunately, there the record ends, because he was killed shortly after—Jansen, I mean. But I've never given up hope of finding those trees—they will promote life for ever if properly handled. Just think of that!"

"One might not find it so wonderful to have life indefinitely prolonged," I said quietly. "After all, the allotted life span of Man is enough, packed with troubles and vicissitudes as it is… However, it's only a story, after all. We have more important matters to deal with at the moment. Come back into the dining-room—or drawing-room—and let's discuss matters. I want to decide on a plan of action."

We returned to our chairs before the radiator.

"For some reason," I said, "Jelfel has led everybody astray by his time-liner stories. True, he has—or believes he has—destroyed everything in preceding Ages; he has also wrecked every time-liner. But also, besides getting the secret of time-travel he is building spaceships! We have got to find out why, and stop it! Jelfel is the sort of man who will do anything, unless we check him. I am still wondering, too, why it is that this Age at some future point is to be seen as a blackened and charred wilderness. It would seem that same deadly fire is to happen, something world-devouring and destroying, that will blast Jelfel and all his perpetrations off the face of the earth. I just wonder what!"

I strained my mentality in a tremendous effort, and for an instant I caught a glimpse of devouring flame, blue-white and ruthless. Then the vision went, and I relaxed with a sigh. The answer still evaded me.

"There is only one thing to do," Elna said, practical as usual, "and that is to carry the business now right into the enemy's camp. Surely, if invisible, we ought to be able to accomplish something?"

"Most certainly," I assented, and rose to my feet in sudden decision. "The sooner we get moving the sooner we will avert whatever disaster is coming. Ronnit, I'm going to hear what Jelfel has to say."

He nodded. "All right; it's safe enough with my invisibility system. Come into the lab and I'll fix you up."

Once there it did not take long to make me invisible, and as I moved about the instrument turned in its universal bearings and followed me.

"I'll just lift the house up to the bank," Ronnit said, and disappeared to the controls. Within a few moments we were upon the river bank, with the door open to the now somewhat distant, winking lights of the movable city.

"Shan't be long," I said. "And for heaven's sake keep your eye on that invisibility wavelength of yours. It'll be all up if I'm landed in full view."

"Don't worry. Nothing will go wrong."

I turned away and commenced to walk across the stretch of dark land separating me from the city. I turned once and saw the darkened house of Ronnit's against the grey skyline; then I went on again steadily. It amused me immensely when I reached the main stretch leading to Jelfel's headquarters, to behold workers and ordinary individuals moving to and fro and never once seeing me. I felt astoundingly secure.

With perfect calmness I went to the door at the base of the observation tower, found that it opened, fortunately, to my touch, and slipped inside. Jelfel was there, amongst his instruments, so absorbed that he had not heard my entry (for, of course, sound was not blocked in any way) nor had he seen the door open and shut. I stood contemplating him from a distance for a while, then the nature of his work began to impress me.

He was seated at a desk, a pair of head-phones clamped over his ears, reaching behind him ever and again to twist carefully numbered dials or shift coils of wire to different positions. From somewhere came the buzzing of a powerful generator. I noted, too, that slung over the desk on a level with his mouth was a microphone.

Presently, after much alteration of his dials and coils he turned to the array of buttons and different-coloured bulbs on the desk itself—which looked for all the world like a very complicated type of old-fashioned typewriter. Beyond question there were quite as many keys and intricacies.

A blue bulb lit up amongst its extinguished neighbours, and with that Jelfel spoke. The words he uttered nearly caused me to betray my presence with a gasp.

"This is Station JLB. Earth calling to Jupiter! Elnek Jelfel speaking… This is earth calling to Jupiter! Earth—calling—to—Jupiter… Hello! Hello!" His words dinned into my brain. Earth calling Jupiter! What astounding thing was the man up to? Talking by apparently ordinary radio to the giant planet.

I stared at him intensely, so intensely indeed that that remarkable quality within my brain, the power of exerting an almost X-ray eyesight, suddenly began to operate! I was interested in the resumption of this practically forgotten faculty, and allowed it to have full play, gazing at Jelfel so intensely that I felt sure he would look up and see me—although of course this was impossible. He was, however, too absorbed in his task for that.

# CHAPTER XVI

## *The Jovian Ambassador*

How am I to describe my sensations at what my super-vision re-vealed? My gaze penetrated clean through Jelfel's black clothing and I beheld his skeleton form... But it was not the form of a human being, as we know it! I felt I must clutch something for support, so astounding and revolting was the shock.

The skeleton of his head was perfectly visible, and also a formation that corresponded very favourably with a human spine, chest bones, and ribs—but at the base of the ribs were six joints like small legs neatly curled out of position. The arms were likewise. Normal to the elbow—then they branched out into three sets of hands! The real Jelfel ended at his waist in six small legs—the rest of him was nothing more or less than pure artificiality, wonderfully constructed by some brilliant scientific mind to meet his natural figure. The normal legs were neatly couched inside an artificial waist of some unknown and extremely light metal, and then were added the artificial legs—evidently so constructed that he could maintain his balance faultlessly—the false forearms and hands. I remembered for a moment that day long ago, when I had shaken hands with him at the outset of these extraordinary experiences—how cold his hand had felt; how hard and metallic his voice had always seemed. As I saw him in that moment I realized that Elnek Jelfel was a creature of only about two feet in height, with six small centripetal legs, two small arms, six hands, and an earthly-looking trunk, head and face.

I wondered if I was dreaming, even though I knew I was perfectly wide awake and viewing not an exceptionally clever earth man, but a being from some other planet, so cleverly disguised in his formation by some super-surgical knowledge of an unknown world, that he would, and did, pass for an Earthling anywhere. I closed my eyes for an instant, and when I looked again their X-ray power had gone. I saw the Jelfel I had always known, seated at his complicated desk, sideways to my view.

I reflected. Of course, most creatures would carry their brain-cases upright. Was it after all so extraordinary that Jelfel should resemble an Earthling in facial features? His eyes were the most unusual part, for, as I have described before now, they were a pure sea green, possessing such a cold and icy quality in their wintry depths, that they seemed to be mirrors of a mind without a soul that could sink to unnamed and fright-ful cruelties if it were ever necessary to do so. The cold bleakness of an

Arctic dawn was far more friendly and offered far more hope than did those two round orbs of soul-freezing green. Yes, in those he was apart from an Earthling.

His body, obviously, in its normal state, was adapted for colossal gravitation. The six legs were intended to carry the weight of the trunk. Where else then but on Jupiter, the giant planet? I felt utterly astounded. Small wonder that he was so clever! Small wonder that he had risen to scientific genius beyond the reach of any Earthling; small wonder that he had appeared from apparently nowhere and subdued and controlled this Age of Problems with such iron ruthlessness that his very name inspired awe and terror.

He was nothing more or less than a Jovian! I felt it now—I was convinced.

More than ever I realized the imperative need of obliterating him—of ridding earth of his evil menace. And clearly, too, I now saw why he had been so ruthless in his destruction of time-machines. He had some plan of his own that would undoubtedly bode ill for Earthlings if it were not nipped in the bud pretty quickly.

I took a step closer to him. He was still operating his various buttons and bulbs. Then abruptly a red bulb glowed into life beside the blue one. A tube of orange light poured forth its radiance from some concealed point behind his coils and numbered dials.

"Earth calling!" he said again. "You will have to take this message in the earth language. I can't give it in our own tongue because of these vocal chords of mine. That Station Zagribud?"

In the head-phones I fancied I detected an answer in a high-pitched treble voice.

"Yes, this is Elnek Jelfel. Take this down and give it to His Serenity. Work is progressing rapidly with the spaceship; have destroyed all the Ages preceding this one. As soon as the first fleet of spaceships is ready I will dispatch the first load of humans for vivisection, so you may find out how to adapt our own organisms to life upon this planet."

I caught my breath and stared in dazed horror. Vivisection! Earthlings, to be torn asunder by these Jovian monsters, so that they could study earthly formation at leisure! Good God! The man was a fiend incarnate—unless he was acting under orders.

"I have them all in the hollow of my hand," he answered, in reply to some unknown question. "There has been trouble at one of the workshops—a fire, but as it destroyed my most dangerous enemy, a master pilot of the Time-Liner Corporation, who knew far more than was good for him, it has proved a better thing than I expected. Station JLB closing down now, with my humblest respects and obeisances to His Serenity.

May he continue to exercise his All Wise counsel over Zagribud… I will call tomorrow night at the same time—21.0 hrs. Earth Time Positive Meridian."

Jelfel removed his head-phones, sat looking at me without seeing me, and then snapped out the bulbs and stopped the generator that had made possible this astounding speech over four hundred-odd million miles of void. How it was done I did not find out until a little later.

I confess I felt very strongly tempted to obliterate him there and then with his own ray-gun, tucked so invitingly in his belt. I stayed the impulse for only one reason: when I did strike it must be effectual, I must first find out with whom he was communicating, and what the secret was behind his nefarious endeavours.

I continued watching him for a space, then as he crossed over to instruments of no vital importance I took the opportunity more closely to examine the battery of coils and numbered dials with which he had bus-ied himself during his astounding communication with Jupiter. Thanks once again to my sharpened mind, I began to comprehend the system he had used—a system so involved, so intricate, that I doubt if an ordinary Earth-man could have understood it, unless he had been an Einstein or a Clerk Maxwell.

The basis of the transmission was electrical, of course—converted solar energy once again, I had reason to think. Behind the massive panel with the tuning dials I beheld what was purely a complicated form of radio transmitter. I noticed that the receiving apparatus was slightly dif-ferent, in so far that from the tuning aerial coil there projected two bars—two black pencils—not unlike the carbons of an arc-light. These pencils pointed directly at a silver-coloured screen fixed to the wall itself. Closer inspection revealed to me that platinum wires were fused through this screen, and evidently went to some point outside. Having got so far there was nothing more to learn here; the exterior of the building would pro-vide the remainder.

I left Jelfel brooding over his various machines, and cautiously de-parted.

A close examination of the wall without very soon revealed the two wires I sought. These led to the summit of the observation tower. With-out any hesitation I set to work to climb the tower's latticed metal-work, and presently gained the upward flight of steps. Within ten minutes I was once again upon that circular platform, commanding a view of the entire, glittering, movable city.

A short search revealed the two thick, insulated platinum wires once again, leading to an object resembling a searchlight—which certainly had been put there since my last visit to this tower. The exact centre of this "searchlight" was composed of metal, wafer-thin, a metal entirely unknown to me. What was inside the instrument itself I had not the vaguest idea at that time. I only knew the entire "searchlight" was connected by wires and cables to three boxes, with more covered switches and coils, all evidently essential to the control of the curious device.

I felt I was on the borders of the solution. The "searchlight" was pointed skywards, to a spot mid-way between horizon and zenith. I looked above through the transfiguring, semi-translucent glow of the etheric vibration screen and beheld the stars—and Jupiter. He hung there, pale orange by reason of the intervening screen, almost directly in line with the "searchlight." With a sudden effort of concentration I comprehended the entire device—the receiving apparatus at least. There was much about the transmitter, involving as it did waves of such frequency as to both penetrate the etheric vibration and the Heaviside Layer, and lose nothing of their power during the trip through space, that even up to the time of my writing this narrative has not been thoroughly solved by our most brilliant radio experts and electricians.

However, to return to the receiving apparatus. The system used was magnetized radio waves, far different from our own painfully infantile system of ordinary radio waves. These outflowing magnetized radio waves from Jupiter (I piece this together in the light of recent discoveries on the matter, also) were drawn through trackless space to this spot on the earth, and then converted into their original sounds. Instead of the radiated waves of radio failing after they had proceeded some distance from Jupiter, the tremendous magnetic force, contained within this searchlight device, drew them through the void, protecting them, saving them from distortion, and bringing them ta the receiver with hardly any depreciation in their original value.

I felt that the Jovian scientists, and Jelfel in particular, were taking a leaf out of the sun's book. In some way they had duplicated the power that is the sun's patent—the harnessing of electrical particles, and the conversion of that energy into practical fundamentals upon which to work. In this case, radio.

I felt very small and insignificant for a moment as I stood there and comprehended all this. Yet I had not the least shadow of doubt in my mind that it was the truth. And, somehow, I had once again that strange feeling in the back of my mind that something could be done with what I had discovered. Somehow that magnetism could be utilized... For the moment, however, I could not see my way clear.

I descended the tower and ruminated for a while when I reached the ground. I had seen the lay of the land and I knew some of Jelfel's innermost secrets. It was impossible to do anything further without mapping a decided course of action.

Therefore I turned back to Lan Ronnit's abode; I was a much wiser and much grimmer man.

# CHAPTER XVII

## *Trapped!*

It was daylight, and we had all rested and refreshed ourselves before I put the whole matter before Elna and Lan Ronnit. When I had concluded my story they sat for a space in dazed horror.

"Vivisection! Jupiter!" Ronnit breathed. "Phew!"

"It's—it's massacre!" Elna said tensely, gripping my arm. "Sandy, we've got to stop it at all costs."

"We're going to," I assured her grimly. "There is only one thing that worries me. Even the elimination of Jelfel and all his trappings won't stop the menace for good. The Jovians know how to cross space—witness Jelfel—and the death of Jelfel won't interfere with them in the least. There will come a brief respite—then the trouble will be back again, only far worse. We can't compete with minds such as the Jovians possess."

Elna sank into a gloomy silence at that. Ronnit sat with his square chin cupped in his hands.

"Wonder what their scheme is, outside of vivisection?" he said, looking at me. I shrugged.

"Power, I suppose. In every age, man in every form, intelligence in every aspect, desires dominance. The less sentimental the intelligence is, the more chance they stand of getting what they want. It is the law of progress—the survival of the fittest. Jelfel, I take it, is the Jovian Ambassador, and a brilliant one. None have ever known of his coming; they all take him for an Earthling, which is quite natural. Only my own peculiar power of X-ray eyesight ever proved the truth about him."

"That doesn't explain the reason for it all," Elna said.

"As I see it, the reason is simply conquest—or maybe overpopulation. The Jovians, for reasons of their own, desire the earth on which to spread their activities. Jelfel, their ambassador, has destroyed practically everybody in every Age from 2000 to this one—or at least it appears that he has. What few are left can be very soon subjected by such minds as the Jovians obviously possess. Time-travelling is evidently one thing that the Jovians do not know, and Jelfel has set out to discover the secret—thereby accomplishing the dual move of destroying those in past ages likely to hinder his activities, and also of learning the secret of time-travel at the same time."

"It's certainly a mighty problem," Ronnit muttered. "We can't stop the rest of the damnable Jovians even if we can stop Jelfel. Somehow, though, we've got to save the people of this Age from being sent to Jupiter just for examination by Jovian science. The whole thing's ghastly!"

"If science is correct, there cannot be a great deal of life on Jupiter," I said thoughtfully. "Jupiter is considered to be in a comparatively molten state, with the possible exception of the curious Great Red Spot; and there isn't room on that for a tremendous number of beings. I cannot imagine why such high intelligence comes to be upon a world still believed to be comparatively molten. The whole thing outrages the laws of Nature."

"The exact nature of the circumstances doesn't really interest us," Elna said. "Our task is to obliterate these devils—and quickly."

I spread my hands helplessly. "Easily said, Elna. But *how?*"

"I don't know—yet." She sank her head in her hands and thought deeply.

For a long time we sat thus, three beings against a planet. Then I rose to my feet.

"There's only one thing to do," I said grimly. "We must wipe out Jelfel and all his machinery first, then we must marshal all our forces for war against Jupiter. I cannot see any other way out—not yet... And yet, there is a far better idea at the back of my mind striving to see the light." I concentrated for a moment; then shrugged. "Well, no matter. I can't place it properly. For the time being we'll have to follow out the plan I've arranged—tonight."

"You are going to kill Jelfel?" Elna asked tensely.

I nodded. "With no more compunction than I would a rattlesnake. I'm going to blow him to atoms with his own ray-gun."

"And destroy his machinery?"

"With his own vibration machine."

Elna rose to her feet decisively. "Then I'm coming with you!"

"But, Elna, this is dangerous work!" I protested; but she brushed my objections right to one side.

"I've been in many a pickle with you before, Sandy, and I'm not stopping now. You needn't try and stop me, because I've not the slightest intention of listening."

"All right," I sighed. "You win—as usual."

"And what about me?" Lan Ronnit asked. "I want to do my share."

"Your share will be guarding those two invisibility projectors of yours—and for God's sake don't let anything happen to spoil their effect."

Ronnit chuckled slightly. "You needn't worry. Nothing will ever happen…"

\* \* \* \*

The coming of night once again found Elna and me making our way towards the city. Calculating from the previous night's time I knew it would be shortly time for Jelfel again to communicate with his Jovian allies. There was little doubt that we would find him in his usual place in the instrument-room.

The surmise was correct. We entered the vast hall, as his back was turned, holding each others' hands so that we might keep in touch. Being invisible to each other, the only system was actual physical contact.

For a while we stood looking at Jelfel, then he turned his face towards us. I fully expected that he was going to sit at his enigmatic desk and commence his radio communication. Instead, however, he strolled into the next great apartment. Following him, we found him busy with the Emanator—that remarkable instrument for detecting objects at a distance by their vibrations, and which I have outlined elsewhere in my narrative. I did not feel particularly comfortable at finding the Emanator to be the subject of his interest…

Going closer to him we heard him murmur "670." Then he turned about and strolled back into the main instrument-room. In a few minutes he was busy with the light-wave trap, and to my horror there appeared upon the ground-glass screen a picture of Lan Ronnit's movable house perched upon the river-bank. The view was not particularly clear owing to the only illumination being the lights from the city; but there was no mistaking it.

Jelfel studied it broodingly for a while, then he glanced down at a written sheet on the bench before him. In silence he made a few calculations, then crossed over to yet another of his infinite variety of apparatus. A switch shot into place, there was a momentary spark, then silence. I looked again at the screen, feeling Elna's hand tighten on my arm—but the house of Ronnit was still there unharmed.

Jelfel smiled strangely, switched off the light-wave trap and then seated himself, as though waiting for something to happen…

It happened almost immediately—and how am I to describe my horror and consternation? For, quite suddenly, Elna and I became fully visible! The shield of invisibility dropped from us like a cloak!

I remember we both stood staring in dumb amazement into Jelfel's faintly mocking, green eyes.

"A really unexpected pleasure," he said dryly, rising to his feet. "You know, Commander, it comes as a great pleasure to me to know that you are not dead after all; it comes as even greater pleasure too, to know that you are still opposing me—and Miss Folson... But I am discourteous. Won't you be seated?"

He drew forth chairs from under the desk and we mechanically obeyed his behest. My mind was a turmoil of unexplained thoughts. I shot a glance at the closed door, but Jelfel merely waved his hand.

"Useless, Commander, much as I regret to state it," he said, his tones now so soft and deadly courteous that I realized he was in his most dangerous mood.

"It would appear that you have the upper hand, Jelfel," I answered, with a quiet and determined grimness, determined to retaliate.

"I more than 'appear,' Commander—I *have*!" he replied, closing his thin lips into a merciless slit. Then, in words of ice: "For a long time both of you have been meddling in affairs that do not concern you. I may as well tell you that I am about tired of it—and I have no intention of tolerating it any longer! I thought you were killed in the fire in the workshop, but my scouts soon discovered that you were in hiding in the abode of Lan Ronnit—another meddler! My scouts discovered everything about you, all about the invisibility system—everything. The particulars are on that sheet of paper on the bench. I knew of your coming tonight from my scouts, of course. I have not destroyed Lan Ronnit's home because I desire the particulars of his invisibility system; it will be both interesting and instructive—but I have destroyed him! I have vibrated his body and his soul, granting he possessed one, into nothingness. He is dust! You saw me do that, after discovering the location with the Emanator. As regards the sudden disappearance of the invisibility wavelength—which details my scouts discovered with a remote control radio tuned to Lan Ronnit's abode—I have merely placed around Ronnit's abode an electrical barrier—a contrawise wavelength—which has, in effect, heterodyned it; at least intercepted it far enough to prevent you being invisible any longer... And now, Commander Lee, Miss Folson, what have you to say?" His cold green eyes bored at us with all the soulless malignancy of which they were capable.

"You have destroyed Lan Ronnit?" I asked in a low voice.

"I have already said so!"

"I came here to kill you, Jelfel," I said, consumed with inward fury. "For too long you have seen fit to slay and destroy without mercy or question. Lan Ronnit was a genius—a future prince of invention—and you *destroy* him! You damnable, crawling, filthy Jovian!"

I leapt to my feet in sudden uncontrollable rage, my arm retracted for a blow.

"Wait!" Jelfel commanded. "Sit down, and don't be a fool! You know what happened last time. I am at an end of my patience. *Sit down!"*

I obeyed, and dropped my arm hopelessly to my side.

"So you have discovered that I am a Jovian?" he said, in steely tones. "How?"

"By the aid of the brain that I once told you was superior to your own," I retorted savagely.

"This is no time for humour, Commander. The proper explanation at once, please!"

Briefly, having no alternative, I explained the circumstances. When I had finished his face was more set and hard than I had ever seen it.

"Commander, I have been mistaken in you," he said, somewhat to my surprise. "If you are capable of such power, you are capable of anything. Unquestionably your mind is greater than mine. You are dangerous! You must be destroyed—and this woman, too."

"That remark is becoming monotonous, Jelfel," I said coldly.

"I assure you the monotony now will be amply compensated for later on," he countered smoothly, his rapier-like sarcasm flourishing into bitter life. "Since you evidently know all about me—since you know that I'm a damnable, crawling, filthy Jovian, I will tell you that which you have been striving to know. The reason why I am on this ghastly planet at all—the reason for the Age of Problems. You shall know of the horror to come for the human race. The human race!"—he laughed harshly— "the most motley, bigoted collection of self-righteous, narrow-brained, non-intelligent idiots I have ever seen from cosmos to cosmos. What an interesting time my fellow beings will have during their vivisection operations on Jupiter." He laughed again, and the great hall echoed with the deadliness of it...

## CHAPTER XVIII

### *The Story of the Jovians*

Elnek Jelfel resumed his conversation in a condescending tone.

"You Earthlings have long been incorrect in your theories about Jupiter—or Ran, as we call it. I have seen from your records that you regard Jupiter as a planet of steaming, furious heat, with the Great Red Spot as the commencement of slowly forming solidity. You have even assumed from the planet's brightness that heat is the cause. You have deduced, with commendable brilliance that it cannot be the sun because it is so far away. Truly wonderful, I am sure! Heat, then, is the only cause... But no, you are all entirely wrong. The only part you have correct are the mathematical computations, to wit, that Jupiter is of 1400 times the earth's volume, that his equatorial diameter is 88,500 miles, and that his revolution round the sun occupies 11.86 earthly years. That is correct. We Jovians are exactly as you have seen me—squat creatures of many legs, to bear up under terrific gravitation. These attachments of mine make up the extra in gravity, besides helping me to pass as an Earthling... Not all my fellows are so earthly in face, however. I am an exception. A genuine, full-blooded Jovian is rather repulsive to judge from your standards... But that is by the way.

"Jupiter, or Ran, my friends, is not a boiling planet. Quite the reverse. It is a planet of ice, save for the Great Red Spot on the southern equatorial belt. Jupiter cooled many thousands of years ago, and being so far from the sun became a frozen world. Our race, up to that period, had been mainly an underground one—a brilliant and very intellectual race. Then came the time when our leading scientist, Krot, found that the contracting of the outer surface with the cold was causing dangerous subsidences within. He found a system of continuous heat, a system associated with radium emanation, of which element Jupiter has more than enough, and work was immediately commenced on the surface to make a portion of it habitable...

Be it understood that our race has never evolved to any great numbers. We are few in number, but colossal in intelligence. What I have accomplished on the earth with my inventions is but a fragment of what my master, Roth Granod, His Serenity, the All-Wise, has accomplished. However, we chose a certain stretch upon the ice on the equatorial belt, and the radium machines and synthetic air apparatuses were set to work. The outcome was that eventually we had a perfect spot of comfort, above ground, and yet surrounded, beyond given limits, by a world of void and merciless ice and cold. So much Krot and Rath Granod accomplished...

"I have seen from your records that scientists have not always recorded the presence of the Great Red Spot. It is only mentioned about the time we set to work, which of course is correct... Of late, however, our race has grown tired of confinement; we seek a world of youth, or least of maturity. A world where we can expand our intellect. The earth was chosen, and it was the will of the All-Wise that I come as Ambassador. So I came to earth in a spaceship, but by some mathematical complexity which will greatly interest the super-mind of the All-Wise, when I relate it to him, I arrived here many hundreds of years behind the time calculated. Where the time was lost I do not know—there are many mysteries in the cosmos. So I came into this Age, conquered it by superior intelligence, and made it the Age of Problems. I learned also a great secret—time-travel. My instructions were to destroy as many humans as I could without endangering myself. You know how I did that. The spaceships, by the way, are remote controlled from Jupiter itself, and need no pilot. That is how Earthlings will be sent back to Jupiter, for there will be no pilots to take them…"

"I cannot understand the necessity for altering your organisms," I said. "You stand earthly conditions quite well, apparently."

"Only because certain vital differences were made in my internal organs before I came to the earth. I took my life in my hands in coming here. Our scientists had only guessed at what sort of organs I would need, by study of the earth. As it happened they were near enough to correctness to enable me to live without much discomfort—except for these accoutrements. Needless to relate, our telescopes are far superior to yours. We can quite distinctly see your cities and people with our instruments… For the future, in order to be safe, my fellow beings wish carefully to study terrestrial organisms, so that they may make no mistakes when they commence the migration in real earnest…

"During my early visits to past ages I met Miss Folson here, and from her it was that I learned two things. One was the utter foolishness of Men, and the realization of what a mistake it was—and is—to let such little minds, unable to grasp anything beyond length, breadth, thickness, populate this fair young planet at all. The other thing I discovered was who possessed the secret of time travelling…"

Jelfel stopped and looked at us thoughtfully. "I have told you all this so that you may be saved the trouble of finding it out for yourselves," he said sardonically.

"There are one or two points you have not made clear," I remarked, shelving my intense hatred of the man for a moment. "For how long has Jupiter been really habitable?"

"Tens of thousands of years. At the time when earth was commencing to cool, Jupiter's interior race was at its pomp. The exterior of Jupiter at that time was beginning to freeze, because, as I have said, of its distance from the sun. Always we have lived in the lighted underworld of our planet, warmed by the internal fires, until, as I told you, we sought the surface. Our race was born inside the planet instead of outside, but born into such a world of radium warmth and light that we were not blind, helpless, insectile creatures, but sighted, intelligent beings, given odd bodies to bear with the pull of our ruthless planet, but compensated by great and far-reaching intellect."

"That rather upsets our theories," I said. "A large body must always take longer to cool than a small one."

"Quite correct," Jelfel said, "but the radiation from the surface of the body depends, you must admit, upon the conditions surrounding it. My planet has no warmth upon its surface because of the sun's distance. The earth is more fortunate—it is warmed both within and without. The exterior of Jupiter, cooled into ice long before the earth had passed even into the melting period, simply because of the absence of solar heat. Jupiter is still warm in its centre, of course. Jupiter's brightness in your heavens is the combined effect of two things—radium emanation and ice-reflection. This latter is so piled up that to Earthlings it looks like dense cloud... Yes, a queer world—but upon so lovely a young wold as earth our race can flourish."

"You will come to earth as Jovians, with centepedial legs?" Elna put in.

Jelfel looked at her. "No. We shall come to the earth in the bodies of the Earthlings that are sent to Jupiter! Our brains will be removed from our Jovian bodies, and after examination of the various organs of an earthly body, will be planted in bodies of the Earthlings, from which the original brains have been removed and laid aside for future examination. I fancy Rath Granod will find much of interest in the investigation of these human brains..."

"You'll never succeed in so vile, so ungodly a plan!" I said steadily.

Jelfel laughed slightly. "Still trying to put up resistance, eh, Commander? Why don't you and Miss Folson accept the inevitable? I have you both in the hollow of my hand—and you shall be my first subjects to be sent to Ran. That is a great honour, my friends..."

## CHAPTER XIX

### *To the Death!*

Even as Jelfel was speaking my mind was working at top speed. But Jelfel had more to say.

"To be sent to Ran, as my first subject, is a great honour, my friends. Your bodies will do better work than ever, when we have disposed of them. For Jovian brains, I believe that is your adjective for our mighty sphere, will inspire your earthly bodies to marvellous achievement. The brains of Jupiter, as you call it, and the bodies of earth will make a wonderful combination."

On the face of it the position was desperate enough, and yet... I had almost succeeded once by barbarous methods; perhaps this time I might manage it again successfully. I cannot explain to you why, with all the attributes of science about me, my super-mind always prompted me to methods of the brute. I can only think it is the force uppermost in Man that rises to the surface in an emergency.

So it was that I suddenly hooked out my left foot, as though by some agency other than my own nerves, and kicked Jelfel violently on the leg. Naturally, as the leg was artificial, he did not even wince, but beneath the force of my blow the delicate metal jointing came apart at the knee, and presented the fantastic appearance of the lower half of his leg swinging in the embrace of his black tights. Instantly he dropped his likewise artificial hands to set to work to remedy the defect, then almost immediately remembered me.

But it was too late then. I was upon him, and bore him backwards to the floor. Both of us crashed over with the metal chair on top of us. He opened his mouth to shout for a guard, but I clapped my hand across it. He lay still for a moment, looking up with those burning eyes of his.

"Once before, when I had you like this, I nearly killed you," I murmured. "I was a fool to have ever let you go. This time I shall not make the same mistake! I—"

I had no chance of finishing my sentence, for he suddenly heaved up his normal, short body with all his strength and rolled me from him. In an instant he had torn the ray-gun from his belt and levelled it full upon me. I lay in dazed terror, awaiting the inevitable… But it never came. Elna suddenly jumped into activity, seized Jelfel's artificial hand with all her strength and pulled backwards mightily. She more than succeeded. The terrific wrench she gave ripped the false arm clean off Jelfel's short upper arm and three normal hands. She went toppling backwards to the floor, with the metal limb still held in a fierce clutch. She at least had the ray-gun, and as she endeavoured to rise from the floor I flung myself forward to seize it. Jelfel did likewise, however, and our movement was simultaneous.

Elna was quicker than either of us as events transpired. For she tore it away from our clutching hands and hurled it to the far end of the great room.

For a moment there was silence. Then Jelfel suddenly commenced to tear off his artificial integuments, and presently we beheld him as he really was, with the trailing black remnants of his suit clinging about him like a skirt, draped about his oddly repulsive form.

He stood about two feet six, two powerful, incredibly short, unjointed arms (no elbow, that is to imply) each ending in the three tentaculate sets of hands, and no nails. The legs were not visible in the shrouds of the cloth, but occasionally I did glimpse an insectile-looking foot.

"Since you will be a barbarian, Commander, so will I," he said grimly. "I cannot call my guards—you are too wary of that. I cannot get at my instruments and reduce you to ash. Therefore, I will meet you on your own terms. So far you have fought with great courage for the good of your planet—I will grant you that much—but I have done likewise for mine. I warn you that you are now fighting Jelfel the Jovian, in all his natural strength, for the gravity of this little world appears slight, now that all those metal integuments have been removed. I am ready!"

And with the words he hurled himself at me. I was certainly not prepared for the terrific strength with which I suddenly had to cope, or for his curious methods of fighting.

The three pairs of hands to each arm—six in ail—were dangerous appendages to tackle. They were at my throat and vitals before I knew what was happening. I found myself flung to the metal floor, struggling desperately to free myself of this sudden two foot six of calculating, tigerish ferocity.

Once again it was Elna who saved me. She seized Jelfel's hair in both hands and pulled with all her power. So great was her muscular power, and so intense the pain, he was forced to release me, but I regretted it a moment later. Like some hideous dwarf, his face distorted with fury, he twisted himself out of her grip and flung himself upon her, banging her to the floor, amd seizing her throat in a terrific grip. It was an insane and terrible clutch he had upon her. I knew in a moment from her desperately threshing legs and arms that he was choking the life out of her. With a hoarse cry I seized him by the shoulders; failing in removing him I rained blow after blow into his unprotected face, but he only shook himself and tightened his grip. Elna looked up at me with her eyes starting from her head, her face ghastly, purplish red.

"Stop!" I shouted frantically, kicking and punching the devilish Jelfel with all the strength I could muster. "Stop, you fiend! You're killing her!" I emphasised every word with a blow to the face or repulsive body, but he still clung on, a deadly smile now curving his thin lips. Suddenly, as I watched in dazed horror, I saw Elna cease struggling. Her eyelids closed and her lips came together spasmodically. With a thud her head struck the metal floor as Jelfel suddenly released her, I stood rooted to the spot for a moment, my gaze chained to the brutal marks about the flesh of her neck.

"Elna!" I panted desperately, sweeping her up in my arm; "Elna! For God's sake! Elna…!" I clutched her, I shook her; then with a trembling hand I felt her heart. It had stopped!

"Dead!" I groaned hoarsely, in a sudden abyss of despair. "Dead! Merciful heaven above...!" My voice rose up to the mighty roof and became silent.

Then abruptly I came to myself. I laid her back on the floor with reverent tenderness, and turned very slowly as I rose to my feet, my fingers distended, to behold Jelfel with a sardonic smile on his face, a few paces behind me. His tentacle hands were also ready for action, his whole mien repulsive and menacing.

"Elna Folson has gone—you are next," he muttered. "You would dare to stand in my way? You would presume to hinder my plans—and the plans of Rath Granod, the All-Wise?"

I stood quite still, rocking gently on my toes. I looked back at Elna's still form, face upwards to the brilliant arc-lights, then again at this devil incarnate from Jupiter. This devil had robbed me of the one creature in the world to whom I was devoted... I don't quite know what happened to me then; something gave way somewhere in my being. I had been a strong man before, but now I was a superman—a Hercules, a muscled giant controlled only by deadly, vengeful hate.

I hurled myself at Jelfel with sudden abruptness, as though I were catapulted. I cannoned straight into him, bowled him over to the floor, and then picked him up, cursing and struggling, in my hands. I scarcely felt the sudden effort; I was in a blind, demoniacal rage. By nature I am a peaceable man, but if ever murder was in my heart it was in it then. The ruthless, inhuman slaughter of Elna had changed me completely; I felt an intense and gloating satisfaction at finding Jelfel afraid. I saw it in his eyes.

I flung him to the floor again with devastating force, and somewhere a bone cracked within him—I fancy it was one of his wrist. He yelled for his guards, but only got halfway because I struck him a terrific blow in the mouth that split his upper lip. He glared up at me like an animal and spat the blood from his mouth. I noted, too, that the blow had smashed three of his artificial teeth, and also gashed my knuckles pretty badly. Not that I particularly cared in the mood I was in.

"Get up, damn you!" I snarled fiercely. "Get up!"

Instead he made to scramble away, but I caught him up by one arm and whirled him aloft above my head. His body flew in a semi-circle, crashed into a bank of glass jars and test-tubes on the nearby bench, and fell bleeding to the ground. He was cut, terribly cut, but still very much alive.

He was anything but a pleasant spectacle. Apart from his revolting form, the blood upon his face and limbs presented a most nauseating sight (it was slightly pinker than an Earthling's). Yet, somehow, the sight of his injuries filled me with intense happiness. He had murdered Elna—would murder the whole human race if he had his way—but not if I knew anything about it!

He scrambled to his feet as I went towards him again, and jumped upwards to clutch me with those frightful tentacles of his. I met him halfway with a mighty uppercut. It struck him clean on the jaw, a smashing, bone-splintering blow that sent him reeling backwards drunkenly, clutching frantically at the wires of his machines to save himself as he did so. At the breakages occasioned by his fall short circuits exploded and detonated from different parts of the great hall. Something in the next instrument-room went off with a din like a cannon.

Like a demon I was upon him. A glorious thought was in my head. I clutched him like a vice, whirled him up on to my shoulder, and marched at full speed towards the stairs of the observation tower. I wrenched the door open and hurled him to the staircase.

"Get up there!" I thundered.

"You—" he began, then as I assisted him with a violent kick he commenced to claw his way upwards, dizzy with pain and fury, becoming weaker through continued loss of blood. I was not too steady myself, either. My mighty strength and temper were commencing to tell upon my normally quiet constitution. But still I held on, the memory of Elna's death ever before me.

Step by step I forced him up the full five hundred feet, stair by stair I punched and hammered him, until at last it was a gasping, bleeding wreck I dragged up on the observation tower platform. Below were the lights of the city, winking unmoved as ever.

"Now!" I panted hoarsely. "Even if I cannot stop the rest of your vile hordes I can at least stop you! On earth, Jelfel, there is a certain code, a law, which says—a life for a life! I am going to administer that law! I was going to kill you for your other murders in any case, but with a ray-gun—a swift and painless passing. Now it is different, for you killed Elna Folson!"

"You cannot kill a Jovian," he said in a strange voice. "Though you reduce my body to pulp the entity of Elnek Jelfel will live on—*and return.* You do not understand Jovian science, but when I come back, you will understand it as never before! Yes, I know you are going to kill me—at least you are going to kill this material body in which you believe is contained all my knowledge and power. Commander Lee, you are making the biggest mistake of your life. One day I shall repay—my fellows and I, no matter what you may do, I will return… You have fought worthily for your planet; I have fought for mine. For the time being, you win." He ceased to speak.

I looked at him closely, standing there, a bleeding wreck, before me. I clutched him by the shoulder, and to my astonishment he fell forward on his face.

Quickly I made an examination of him, found his heart on the *right* side of his chest, and was just in time to feel it stop beating. He was dead!

I felt confused. This was no ordinary death. He had just passed away, as completely and absolutely as though his real being had moved into another dimension and was even now watching me in sardonic superiority, laughing at my inability to understand.

Then I gave a snarling grunt. I picked his dead body up, raised it high above my head, and looked up at the dim orb of Jupiter.

"Here is your infernal ambassador!" I shouted in a cracked voice. "Fire a signal to his passing!" And with that I hurled his body over the platform railing.

With burning eyes I watched him fall through the city-lit darkness, saw his squat, many-legged body go hurtling down, tattered ends of garment flying in the wind. He struck the tower once in his fall and rebounded; then at last I saw him strike the ground below. If there was any doubt about him being dead before, there certainly was none now.

"Return!" I said, with a scoffing laugh, clutching the rail. "Bah!"

I laughed again harshly, then it seemed as though something clutched at my throat, and the sky whirled giddily. I staggered a pace backwards, and collapsed helplessly on the floor, a choking feeling in my throat.

## CHAPTER XX

### *From Beyond Death*

I was not unconscious for long; only a few moments. When I recovered my senses I was drenched in perspiration and very short of breath. I had a headache, and my mouth was dry. But that fury had left me; I was again normal—a bitter, but vaguely satisfied man.

I looked again over the tower edge to satisfy myself. The dark spot was still there undiscovered. At least the body of Jelfel was quite dead, but I was still puzzled at his assertions concerning his return, and his mysterious exit from life... I looked up once more at Jupiter, and compressed my lips. Now indeed I was alone! Lan Ronnit gone—and Elna! A choking lump rose in my throat. I turned away and stood looking absently at the rotundity of the radio magnetizer. Could it be possible that...

Suddenly, out of the blank emptiness of my innermost mind there came the idea I had so long striven to bring to light. Like a physical blow it hit me in all its vividness. I stood astounded, overwhelmed by the amazing possibilities… The immensity of it staggered me…

"Yet it could be done!" I breathed. "Yes, it could be done!"

I stood thinking for a moment, every detail clear in my mind. Then I shelved it for a space whilst I went downstairs again to the instrument-room. Wincing from countless cuts and bruises I descended the stairs and found Elna still lying where she had met her death. She seemed peaceful now—even happy, the ghost of a smile, it seemed, about her lips.

"Elna," I whispered gently, and for a while held her already stiffening body in my arms. "Elna… But you shall not stay here. At least you shall have a decent burial—the hosts of earth shall honour you." I picked her up in my arms and commenced to walk towards the door. As I did so, however, I stumbled over an uneven stretch on the floor. Looking down, I saw that a heavy cable, broken in half, was lying upon it. It was evidently one of the wires that had been broken when Jelfel had fallen and brought about so many short circuits. What sort of current that wire had carried I could not guess, but it must have been a disruptive power of some kind, in the light of what took place a moment afterwards.

I remarked that the metal floor was curiously discoloured for an area of about six feet around the broken ends of wire, as though a powerful corrosive acid had dropped upon it. Then, not inclined to investigate further, I continued walking across the stretch, but I had no sooner reached the centre than there was an alarming crack, like ice which has suddenly received more weight than it can bear.

I gave a hoarse shout and tried to jump backwards as I realized what was happening, but I was just a shade too late. The entire metal within the discoloured section suddenly gave way and plunged me into unknown depths below, jerking Elna's body from my clutch…

I fell a distance of perhaps twelve feet, endeavoured to stand up, and then fell again, rolling over and over helplessly, plunging downwards and ever downwards. When at last I came to rest I beheld the hole in the instrument-room floor far above me like a star. I computed I must have dropped about one hundred and fifty feet. My investigatory hands came into contact with loose soil and rubble. Painfully I got to my feet and looked about me in the darkness. Dimly I could perceive that I had rolled down a gentle incline that had the hole in the instrument-room floor fifteen feet above its upper end.

For a moment I was at a loss, then I bethought me of Elna, and immediately commenced to search, stumbling knee-deep in places in the surprisingly loose soil.

At last I found her, but not before I had retraced my way about fifty feet upwards. She was lying half buried, her body becoming more rigid.

Once again I gathered her into my arms, for she was rapidly stiffening into that position.

Do not ask me why I carried her corpse in such a ghoulish fashion. I only knew that something at the back of my mind urged me to do so, despite the fact that she was plainly stone dead. I had obeyed such mental impulses before, and had always found a substantiation for them at a later point.

I was about to turn and commence to fight my way upwards again to the summit of this underworld crater, when I caught a glimpse of something—not far away—glowing in the darkness, like some hazy, near-at-hand nebula in a pitch-black sky. I sat down with a thud in the soil and strained my eyes to look at it. It had a curiously evasive quality; but I judged its full area to be about two miles. Two miles of glowing fire-like phosphorescence. What was this new revelation of a strange Age?

I laid Elna down gently on the earth, and scrambled down again to the apparently level floor of the enormous pit. Feeling my way gingerly I went forward towards that strangely glowing region, and as I went strange thoughts sifted into my head. All this undermining—these colossal craters and pits—the upper-world only supported by the remaining portions of rock and earth that had escaped annihilation. Of course! The atomic-bomb war of 2468! Disintegration, that had at last ceased. Radio-active soil!

"The secret of life!" I breathed suddenly, and stopped to recall the almost forgotten words of Lan Ronnit—"Those trees have the power of instant propagation!"

At that thought I hurried on slightly, nevertheless keeping always in view that tiny hole that was my guide to the upper-world again... As I came to the edges of the queer phosphorescence I could quite distinctly make out the forms of trees—queer, octopus-like trees, glowering and shimmering like a fairy glade—products of the radio-active soil. I stood looking at them doubtfully wondering if any dangerous emanations came from them. And as I stood something nicked my ankle. There was something horribly nauseating about that touch. It came again, this time around my wrist. I turned with a start and saw that the nearest glowing tree had *bent over* and was extending its whip-like branches towards me. Indeed I was already in its grip!

The instant I comprehended this I flung myself backwards with all my power, digging my heels in the earth. I felt leaves that actually writhed under my clutching fingers. Farther back I forced myself, and farther, until suddenly there was a sharp snap and I fell on my back in the soil. I felt my body, and my hands come in contact with limp, broken tentacle-like branches, armed with powerful suckers, still clinging about me, and glowing eerily.

For a moment I was about to rip them off with unspeakable repulsion; then I stayed my hand. After all, they were not hurting me. Tempted to experiment, I tore off a tiny portion of tentacle and dropped it in the soil, peering very closely at it. To my utter amazement it wriggled like something alive, and then commenced to thrust forth a stem and tiny branches.

"Heavens!" I gasped, and simultaneously an intense delight and gratitude seized me. These, then, *were* the trees that the explorer Jansen had discovered. Only when separated from the parent tree, and affixed to a substance upon which they could not possibly take root, were the tree branches useless. Though apparently dead, they evidently had the power to restore themselves to life and propagate, once planted.

I determined upon an immediate analysis of their peculiarities, the thought of Elna's dead body drifting into my mind. Leaving the sucker-like branches clinging to me, and taking good care to avoid other trees, I began to make my way back, the distant hole in the roof as my guide.

I found Elna at last, lifted her once more in my arms, and commenced the upward climb.

It was hard going in that loose rubble; for every two feet I gained I fell back six inches, but at last I did manage, by dint of much pushing and jumping, to scramble over the edge of the broken metal floor back into the instrument-room.

I looked down at Elna's ashen face and silent form, and also at the pieces of tentacle tree-branch still clinging to me. In the white light they appeared greenish in hue, tapering to a point at the end, and armed, as I had noticed before, with countless powerful little suckers. The luminosity had, of course, vanished.

Only one thought was in my mind now—to return to the home of Lan Ronnit, which luckily Jelfel had not destroyed, and investigate this strange and evidently life-giving plant to the full.

Hope born anew in my breast, I lost no time in leaving the building, after some difficulty in dodging various guards, and made my way by a stealthy detour, through the sideways between the movable buildings. It was half an hour later when I reached Lan Ronnit's abode. Quietly I opened the door as he had taught me to do, and slipped inside, switching on the shaded light.

I stopped when I reached his laboratory. There he lay upon the floor, quite dead, his hand resting on the control of the invisibility mechanism. In his fall he had pulled the switch to "Off," so naturally the mechanism had ceased. There was only one thing that puzzled me. Jelfel had distinctly said that Ronnit had been reduced to dust. Yet here he was, perfectly intact, but quite dead.

Laying Elna carefully on one of the long tables I commenced an examination of the young inventor. It took me some little time to find why he had not been reduced to atoms. The solution lay in the bench by which Ronnit had been standing at the time he had met his death. The bench was, of course, junison, and impervious to all forms of vibration. Hence, whilst the force had been sufficient to kill Ronnit, it had not succeeded in destroying his body completely.

I felt very much like an undertaker as I picked him up and laid him beside Elna. Then I set to work to pull off the sucker branches clinging to my body. This done, I dropped them carefully into massive glass jars and sealed them down airtight, until I should commence operations.

This done I set the mechanism of the house to work and took it once again to the bed of the river. Then, washed and refreshed, I commenced work in the laboratory on a lone bench beneath a brilliant solar arc, with the two corpses for company. Yet, strangely enough, I could not credit that they were really dead, with what I had in mind for their future; if the experiments with the plant proved successful, they were merely asleep.

Taking forth my first branch specimen from the glass jar, I laid it on the table, and examined it beneath the high-power microscope. My first discovery was interesting, and a trifle unexpected. The suckers, in truth, were campanulate calyxes—leaves in embryo, which, it appeared, instead of forming into the leaf common to the upper parts of the finished tree, formed into intensely powerful suction cups instead. The stem of the branch seemed to have a rubbery consistency, possessing no brittleness whatever. I could tie it into knots and it would net break. It also had a curling tendency when lying fiat, the ends quivering up after the fashion of a newly plucked human hair. Unquestionably the thing was alive within itself, I reflected, even though severed from the main tree. As I went on, I did not wonder at my sudden astounding knowledge of botany; my mind was rising to superb heights with constant exercise. I knew things I would never have dreamt of in my normal state...

"I might sever a calyx and see what transpires," I murmured, and suiting the action to the word I took a sharp-bladed knife from amongst Ronnit's instruments and cut off one of the suckers. Nothing happened, save that a greenish sap oozed gently on to the bench. Struck by a sudden thought I placed the calyx in a glass jar containing water. Instantly things happened—alarmingly so!

With incredible speed the thing formed a root, a stem rose with similar bewildering rapidity, followed small branches armed with similar calyxes—upwards again and a corolla began to form. This was too much! I annihilated it with a charge of electricity from Ronnit's instruments and stood looking at the gently steaming bowl, from which the water had instantly evaporated.

There could only be one explanation for this abnormal exuberance of growth. The trees were products of radium in the first place, just as moss and fungus is a product of damp. By some curious process, the slight radium content of the soil in which they had been born had brought about this astounding speed of growth, and incontinent propagation from any portion of the plant. This, too, was probably the cause of its seemingly lifelike actions in seizing everything in its arms—or branches. I know now, however, that the plants had not a vestige of intelligent reason. They were merely attracted to anything having the minutest quantity of electricity, hence their undesirable attractions towards human beings—myself in particular... In my own mind I named these astounding specimens, electric trees.

The pistil of this curious thing was also contained in the calyx, and immediately beneath it I found the ovary, and the cell within it. This cell was crammed to the top and edges with minute, scarcely visible seeds, which explained to me how it was that, in water, the sucker had so suddenly started to grow. Those seeds had not been scattered. It had been the combined effect of all of them working simultaneously. Nor was this all. The branch itself was composed of seeds! Life within life! A botanical freak, and yet a natural plant, the outcome of radium and unknown to the botanical world.

I sat down to study the thing out. I knew of what it was composed; I knew what power of propagation and life it had. But how to apply it to restore life to a dead body? That was the problem.

I returned my specimens to the airtight jars and set myself to flog my increasingly brilliant mind to one of the most difficult tasks of its career.

I was still thinking it out, seated in the chair before the bench, when I must have fallen asleep. When I awoke, with a start, the whole thing was clear in my mind. I have mentioned before the ultra-sharp keenness of my perception when awakening from rest or unconsciousness. I have found it to be so in normal life; the effect was quadrupled in my peculiar mind-condition.

The tiling to do was to find how a solution of the stuff would work upon dead matter. By solution, I meant the very sap of the thing. That seemed to be the secret of its astounding activities. It also seemed a straightforward course of action, so I set to work to drain off a portion by crushing it between the plates of a small press. The resultant fluid I collected in a bottle.

As I looked at it, studied it, I reasoned. Death was due in Elna's case, not to slow decay of the tissues, as in old age, or poisoning of the blood stream, or organic disease. No, it was due to asphyxiation—stoppage of air, which had stopped the action of the heart, and killed her. Therefore, the only thing that could revive her, if it were at all possible, was... was...*energy!* I reasoned that the sap of this plant, containing as it did the energy of radium emanation, without its dangerous emanations of the three rays, ought surely to be able to do something?

I set to work immediately. I turned on the sun arcs to their full power and warmed Elna's cold body, externally. The *rigor mortis* that had set in I could not alter in the least. I felt like a madman as I filled a hypodermic syringe with the green stuff, and making a neat little incision in a vein of her arm, compressed the contents of the syringe within it. There being no active circulation taking place the stuff congealed. At any rate, the only success I got was a greenish splotch beneath the skin of her arm, and a slow dropping of greenish-red blood to the table from the puncture.

I sat down and cursed aloud. The stuff had failed then, after all!

"You must start the blood stream moving—you must start the organs working again," something seemed to say in my mind. "You must start the heart! You must start the heart! As you would a pendulum to start the works of a clock!"

"How?" I snarled, beside myself with grief and disappointment. "It is beyond Man to reincarnate!"

I got up and paced about in the profoundest thought. Then suddenly I got the idea! I jumped round like one possessed, seized the syringe again, and filled it once more. Tearing off Elna's blouse with reckless abandon I bared her chest and very slowly sank the long needle down directly above the heart, injecting the liquid with a steady pressure. Then I stood back to watch. If my calculations of anatomy were correct that sap had dropped directly upon her still heart. My only fear was that I might have punctured that vital organ. If so, recovery was impossible... But no!

Great heavens above!

I saw a greenish glow spread about the area of her heart. Her skin seemed to suddenly start to glow as though she were afire. The whole of her body on the left side of her chest was glowing as though with luminosity. I stood quite still, staring, and biting my nails agitatedly. Had I set her on fire inwardly? Had I, in my blundering, discovered some new form of cremation—something profane and blasphemous, to be relegated perhaps to the annals of a Frankenstein?

No. What had happened was this. The sap, upon reaching her heart—solid matter—had changed itself into energy and heat—had resolved into the form *from which it had been born!* It was delivering to her heart an energy and warmth that no electric current or arc-light could ever give. Was giving the warmth of life, because the sap itself *was* life, in a chemical, minute, cellular form…

I stood there, clutching the bench behind me, staring with dilated eyes. The luminosity had spread now, she was glowing from head to foot. It shone even through her clothing. I touched her, expecting almost to feel burned, but instead she was just pleasantly warm. And… I caught my breath in sharply. Her limbs suddenly relaxed; the *rigor mortis* of death vanished!

I whirled around, snatched a clinical thermometer from the wall and placed it under her tongue. It read eighty degrees F. and was slowly mounting. But there was no moisture on the tube of the bulb; she was not breathing. The heat was coming from inside.

"It mustn't fail!" I panted hoarsely. "It mustn't fail!"

I glued my eyes to that thermometer. The thread of mercury slowly rose, until at last it reached 98.4 degrees F. I watched, something clutching at my innermost vitals. Would it continue to soar, until it destroyed her completely, or would it resolve itself into its own form—life? Cold sweat poured down my face with nervous excitement and tension as I watched.

Ninety-eight point four degrees. How can I describe my unutterable gratitude? The mercury had ceased to rise. I snatched the thermometer up to make sure. I checked it by the temperature under her arm and it read the same. She was normal in temperature, but still she glowed strangely. I flung the thermometer away from me, and it splintered on the floor.

Then abruptly, through the awful, aching silence there came a deep, sonorous sigh. It was the slow intake of a deep breath. I clutched Elna's arms, and they were warm and supple, as they had always been. I stared into her face. It was no longer ashen. Tiny traces of colour were creeping into it. Tiny capillaries leapt into life before my very starting eyes. Then her lips parted again and breath, glorious, life-giving breath, was passing in and out between them. I felt her heart. It was beating steadily!

"You live!" I shouted hoarsely. "Oh, Elna, you live! Thank God!"

As she continued to breathe the luminosity began to disappear from her form. She became normal in appearance, her skin pink and healthy. Dimly I apprehended that the sap of the plant had promoted life within her. Instead of changing that life into itself, propagating upon itself, it had released that mysterious, chemical reaction that is the basis of life, into her blood stream. In the first place the energy had started her heart beating. That had started the circulation—and now! She was breathing steadily, like one in a deep sleep.

She lay thus for a solid hour, an hour that passed like a year for me. I began to think that she would never recover; then at last I was rewarded by movements of her eyelids, and beheld once again those beloved grey orbs looking at me in the deepest wonderment. For a space they were quite without recognition, and a deadly fear chilled my being. Had I just restored her body, and not her real self? Had Elna Folson herself passed into the beyond, and I had merely brought about a revived corpse that would live indefinitely? I began to fear... Then she spoke.

"Why, Sandy, what on earth has happened? Have I been asleep?"

"Elna!" I shouted in ecstasy. *"Elna!* You know me! You know me!"

I became undignified enough to execute a hornpipe round the laboratory, and when I got back, panting, to the bench she was in a sitting position, rubbing her chest very thoughtfully. With a sudden start of embarrassment she drew her blouse into position. "Sandy Lee, what have you been doing?" she asked suspiciously. "My chest feels as though you've been ramming needles in it. And look at my arm—it's bleeding."

"What do you remember last?" I demanded.

"Let me see? Oh yes, Jelfel tried to kill me, and I fainted."

I took her hand solemnly. "Elna, you have been dead foi nearly sixteen hours!"

"Dead!" she expostulated, her eyes round in enquiry and wonderment. "What sort of witchcraft are you dabbling in now?"

With quiet insistence I told her all that had happened, and of her gradual revival. When I had finished she smiled whimsically.

"That was wonderful of you, Sandy—I never knew you were a surgeon. I can't find any words to express my feelings, except that I know I feel quite alive. A trifle on the giddy side, otherwise all right. I thought I had been dreaming. I saw you and tried to get at you, but I couldn't. I saw rosy mists, I felt chilling cold, and wandered through a valley full of glorious flowers. I saw a lot of people I used to know—I saw my Father and he tried to speak to me, but I didn't hear him. Then I felt a great and glorious warmth, a beating of pulses, a realization of sounds, of vision— and here I am..." She stopped and looked at the silent Ronnit by her side. "And poor Ronnit? Is he beyond recovery?"

"No reason why he should be," I replied. "I am about to set to work on him now."

With Elna's assistance, my first efforts were easily surpassed. I made no useless injections or blunders. Lan Ronnit revived two hours after the injection, and our emotions were of such an order, our awe at the marvel we had perpetrated so profound, that I crave leave to abstain from further describing that astounding reunion from beyond death itself.

# CHAPTER XXI

## *I Take Command*

It was towards evening of the following day before we had settled down into something like normal. I remember clearly how we all three sat around the table in the small but cosy dining-room, discussing the final details in this curious drama of time and space.

"I got the idea of wiping out this Jovian menace when I recovered from the reaction of fighting Jelfel," I said. "It came to me quite clearly, but don't gasp at what the idea is, or what it involves. Briefly, we must destroy Jupiter itself! Jelfel swore that nothing we could do would stop him coming back, but we'll do all in our power, anyhow. We must destroy Jupiter."

"Easy," Ronnit said dryly. "We'll do it right away!"

"How on earth do you propose to do it?" Elna asked, furrowing her brow. "By a pretty tough mental strain I can grasp what you're driving at, but you'll have to explain fully to make it reasonable."

"Scientifically possible, you mean," Ronnit said.

"It *is* scientifically possible," I responded steadily. "I've worked it out to the last equation and geometrical value. We're up against all Jupiter now, and whatever may happen with regard to Jelfel's assertion that he would return, we must take every safeguard, so far as we can, from an earthly standpoint. That safeguard is to hurl Jupiter, and his multiple moons, clean into the sun!"

"What!" Elna and Ronnit exclaimed simultaneously, gazing at me blankly.

I nodded silently.

"But it's impossible," Ronnit protested. "You're talking absurdly, Lee."

"No; I am stating a scientific fact. Given sufficient power it is possible to hurl Jupiter into the sun. But before that can be done every preparation must be made for all the people of this Age to be transported to a future time, beyond all reach of the events that are to happen. Otherwise it means death. I see clearly now what is meant in Time by that vision of this Age as a blackened wilderness. Don't you see that when Jupiter is hurled into the sun a vast amount of outflowing gas and energy will be literally spewed into space. For a time the earth will be enveloped in devouring flame. When the fire subsides it will, for a time, be a charred world. But later on, as Time has shown, Life continues. We will transport these people to the Age of Intelligence, where they will be safe and cared for."

"How can you be sure of all this?" Ronnit muttered.

"For two reasons. One is that I have mathematically proved it—and the other is the charred world further on in Time, which cannot be disputed. We *shall* succeed!"

"An astounding feat," Elna muttered. "But what of the other planets, Sandy? Think of the frightful changes in gravitation, the shifting and the upsets."

"I have all that planned out," I answered quietly. "You will see later on. I got the idea of this Jupiter-hurling stunt from Jelfel's radio magnetizer."

"A polarizer of radio waves will not magnetize a solid body," said Ronnit, with the cold incisiveness of the true scientist.

"Maybe not, but it provides the fundamental of the idea," I said. "Jelfel's system is that of polarizing and attracting the electrical content of radio waves… Now, gravitation is the attraction of any body or mass, varying with the size and density of the object, is it not?"

"True," said Ronnit quietly.

"Very well, then. Gravitation, in cold truth, is reversed propulsion."

"In a sense, I suppose it is."

"Propulsion, as I see it, is the process of driving a body forward either by a momentum to start the object going, or else within the object. Now, that force of propulsion can be humanly made by reflecting back the sun's force of propulsion upon any given body."

"How?" Ronnit demanded.

"The sun emits force? You admit that?"

"Certainly, but in no way in which it can be used."

"Up to the present it hasn't been used except for such things as heaters, etc., but that force has incalculable strength, if you know how to use it. Jelfel's magnetizer gave me the idea. The metal of that diaphram of his is the secret, for what can have attraction can also have repulsion, for there is nothing that cannot be reversed in force if you know the formula. I should imagine that the real thing to reverse the action of the metal would be a magnetic current of some kind. However, we have that to find out."

"I understood you to say *reflect* the sun's force?"

"Precisely. Perhaps I haven't been very lucid. This solar force must act upon the metal concerned, but also it will have to be propelled outwards through space again. We must have the power in our metal to throw back the sun's force when we get it."

"I begin to see," Ronnit murmured. "Analyse that diaphram of Jelfel's magnetizer, find the correct metal, substance, or current to reverse its action, capture solar force upon it, and then find a means of reflecting the force back on Jupiter. But, even so, that won't counter-balance the sun's gravitation."

"That's just it," I chuckled. "Centrifugal force is holding our planets away from the sun, but what is to happen if there is a slight balance on the wrong side of that mathematically perfect union? The pressure of a finger, to use a metaphor, could wreck a universe, so slight is the dividing line. A beam of force hurled at Jupiter will push him forward. He will stumble, narrow his orbit, and at last fall into the sun. That is the plan."

"That's all right, but suppose that instead of shifting Jupiter's great bulk we only push the earth into the void? Like a man trying to push a time-liner?"

"We shan't, Ronnit. We will set to work to calculate how to use a field of gravitation that will, metaphorically, hook us to the sun. We will increase the sun's power of attraction, or else the earth's weight, in accordance with the force we hurl at Jupiter. Thuswise we'll remain steady and push Jupiter off the Universal map!"

Ronnit blew out his cheeks. "A tall order! Still, it might work. That brain of yours seems to be working overtime."

"This will be my last effort," I responded. "I feel it. I can't keep up the strain of contemplating all this data much longer. Once this task is done I shall begin to go back to the normal. Don't you think so, Elna?"

"You ought to!" she said, with a smile. "I'm doubtful if mine will reach as high as yours even as it is."

I rose to my feet. "We must tell the people of our plans. We must have them on our side. We'll want every available man for the construction of our machinery. I've little fear that they'll fall in with everything we suggest. Once they know of the menace they will assist…"

And my presumptions were correct. The finding of Elnek Jelfel's dead body—the discovery that he was not an Earthling like themselves—had wrought fear in the down-trodden folks of the Age of Problems. They turned to me, as I harangued with them from the door of the late Jelfel's Headquarters, and listened to all I had to say. At my request for trained scientists and mathematicians to aid me, a body of about six middle-aged men came forward to my side. The rest contented themselves with cheering, which veered off into wild revelry at the sudden emancipation from Jelfel's merciless rule.

"Work must go on!" I shouted in conclusion. "You must build time-machines—as quickly as you can. You will all start work tomorrow upon the orders I give you. You foremen will receive the plans."

The crowd roared its pleasure and shook grimy fists to the skies.

"Down with Jupiter!" somebody yelled, a trifle ludicrously; and the cry was taken up unrestrainedly.

I turned to my six new helpmates. "Come, gentlemen, I would like some discussion in private."

I led the way into Jelfel's instrument-room, and closed the door.

In accordance with pre-arrangement, Lan Ronnit and Elna were already there, awaiting me. It felt extraordinarily good to have this marvellous instrument-room under my control, to feel that everybody relied on me for deliverance. I might have trembled at the onus it entailed, had not my mind been so gloriously keen and prescient.

I turned to my new assistants, and mentally decided that they were an able-looking sextet of men—lean-faced, three of them, bald-headed, and with keen, discerning eyes.

"Gentlemen," I said, "we are now faced with an extraordinarily difficult problem, but there is no reason why our combined efforts should not solve it. We have several things to accomplish, and I will enumerate them. Please make notes. One: To find the correct substance for reversing the process of Elnek Jelfel's radio wave magnetizer. Two: To discover and determine the force necessary to hurl Jupiter and his moons into the sun. Three: To discover a field of attraction—artificial gravitation—capable of counter-balancing the weight of the thrust upon Jupiter. Four: To compute the speed of the reflected force through space. Five: How long it will take to shift Jupiter. Six: How long a life may be granted to earth, in this Age, after Jupiter has gone into the sun. Seven: What actually will be the outcome of hurling Jupiter into the sun. That is, what alteration will take place in the Solar System, and what will happen to sun and earth. The rest will be my work. Time-machines must be built with all speed to enable the people of this Age to be transported forward to the Age of Intelligence... Now, gentlemen, you understand your work?"

Anton Frot, the tallest of the group—lean and bald, with small veins pulsating at his temples—nodded.

"As a mathematician, I will personally conduct the investigation," he said in a deep voice. "You have my promise on that, Commander."

I clapped him warmly on the shoulder. "Splendid, Frot! That will do admirably... And now I must be getting about my own work. You know my abode when you have news."

I left the six in the instrument-room and went outside with Elna and Ronnit. The seething revelry was still continuing with unabated vigour. I looked at the people in the city light, and shook my head.

"Always the way!" I muttered. "As soon as a real crisis arrives, as soon as a man is face to face with disaster, he will not tackle danger there and then! First he must satisfy himself—afterwards duty. Save for a cherished few, such as our noble friends in the instrument-room... We'll leave them until tomorrow. Come on."

# CHAPTER XXII

## *Anton Frot Elucidates*

Anton Frot, the mathematician, arrived at our abode early the following morning. His face was drawn and tired, and his brow creased in furrows of concentration. In his thin hand he held a sheaf of papers. At my invitation to a chair and a drink he nodded a warm thanks, and a tired smile touched his lips.

We three gathered about him.

"Well," he said, placing his fingertips together and lying back in his chair, "we spent the night working on the figurative portion of your scheme. The conclusions we have reached are quite successful, but there will have to be amendments in your original idea. To start with, Jupiter will not be in a convenient position for us, in a dead line, for several years!"

"Good Lord!" I muttered in annoyance. "I never thought of that."

"It doesn't really matter, Commander," Frot said, unmoved. "The task can still be accomplished, but we shall have to throw Jupiter into the sun by a system that we might term—'pendulumatic.' Intermittent thrusts upon the planet which will be counter-balanced by the sun, and subsequently cause Jupiter to be entirely chained by his attraction, and hence hurled into our luminary."

"I don't follow," I said.

"I will make it clear. This solar force you propose reflecting upon Jupiter must be used periodically, not constantly, and must push Jupiter away, not towards, the sun. Then, when you remove your force, Jupiter will swing inwards again, drawn by the sun's attraction. Again you will do the same thing—a little longer each time. Thuswise, by gradual stages, you will get Jupiter to swing backwards and forwards like a pendulum, each time taking a bigger swing, until at last he passes over the line of attractive demarcation, and drops into the sun itself."

"I understand," I nodded. "Congratulations, Frot. You have the figures, of course?"

"On the table there, Commander. The swaying of Jupiter during this process would cause colossal strains upon the earth. Mainly tidal-waves and land-slides as the orbit and force of attraction is altered. All this can be prevented by the gravitational 'field.' By arranging it so that it balances the force flung at Jupiter, the earth will be held steady. How the other planets will fare, I have not determined, but I fear that the hurling of Jupiter into the sun will take along the other outer planets as well—Saturn, Uranus, Neptune, and Pluto. The inner planets, being, as it were, inside the disturbance, will not, I think, be affected. I can't guarantee it, however."

"Whatever happens, we must carry on," I said resolutely.

"Quite so, Commander—quite so. Well, Kenton, our astronomical colleague has pre-determined most of the other details. The hurling of Jupiter alone into the sun—excluding the possibility of other planets—will cause the sun to become a 'nova.' The body of Jupiter will cause what we might term a pocket in the sun's gaseous envelope. The sun, being a gas, will cause this tremendously heated pocket to explode, owing to the colossal centre of heat about the planet lying within the sun. It is very likely that the explosion of this pocket will blow the upper layers of the sun clean away, the force being so terrific that the sun's gravity could not possibly hold them. Hence, the sun will become a nova. The calculation is not altogether clear whether the sun will be burned out completely, or whether it will remain at a small percentage of its former power. From visits in the time-line, we may be assured that the latter will be the case, However, the outflung gas, hurtling through space at about seventeen hundred kilometres to the second, will reach earth in about twelve hours or so. The result will be that the entire surface of the earth will be burned to ashes. Such are Kenton's calculations upon the effect of hurling Jupiter into the sun."

I nodded. "I expected that. What else have you found?"

"Isaton has proved the most important thing of all. That is the gravitational field to hold us to the sun whilst we act upon Jupiter. Gravitation is, of course, caused by every particle of matter attracting every other particle, with a force exerted along the straight line joining the particles. This force is directly proportional to the product of the respective masses of the particles, and inversely proportional to the square of the distance between their centres of gravity. That being so, the force of attraction at the approximate centre of the earth will have to be increased mutually in conjunction with the force of propulsion expended upon Jupiter. Gravitation is caused by the body itself, by the electrical content of its atoms and the atomic aggregates, the molecules. Hence, Isaton has calculated, that the gravitation of a body depends upon the quantity of electricity contained within the atomic content of any given substance. Now, there is only one metal on earth that will stand an almost infinite increase in electricity in its fundamental atoms."

"And it is?" I asked.

"Iralium! By electric current, projected at a tremendous speed, it is possible to make iralium weigh almost anything up to infinity. There is an ultimate point, of course. I am merely speaking figuratively. However, iralium will solve our difficulties. Iralium atoms, and electric current. Iralium atoms are unknown to science so far as I know."

Frot ceased his scientific disquisition for a moment, and finished his drink.

"You've worked hard to sort all this out," I said.

"Interesting, but tiring, Commander. Now, regarding the speed of the reflected force through space. It is nearly that of light—178,000 miles a second, to be exact. That is, it will take it 40 minutes to reach Jupiter, at his present distance of 400,000,000 miles. Regarding the reversion of Jelfel's magnetizing plate. I have Landon working on that, and so far he hasn't reached the solution. He will acquaint you the moment he does so. The time required to shift Jupiter into the sun will be six weeks, so far as I can calculate. That, I think, is all for the moment. Here are the notes. You would perhaps care to look them over?"

"Thanks," I said; then as he rose to his feet: "You say iralium, by electricity being supplied to its atoms, will create a terrific gravitation. But how much iralium is it going to take to do it?"

Frot smiled faintly. "A plain, one mile square, on the side of the earth exactly opposite, and at the absolute Antipode, of where the propulsive force will be."

"I begin to see," I said. "Iralium, by the increase of gravity in the atoms—the increase of electrical mass—will cause the metal to assume almost any given weight, and so counterbalance the force of moving Jupiter?"

"Exactly."

"Isaton was a genius to find that," I murmured.

Frot nodded. "So I thought when he elucidated. Well, that's all for the moment, Commander. I'm going along to get a little sleep—I've earned it!"

I accompanied him to the door. "See you later," I smiled, and watched him stride away in the direction of his movable home. I returned to the lounge and surveyed the mass of notes. I felt rather puzzled at my seeming inability to fully grasp matters, as I had the night before. Had I but known it that extraordinary lucidity of reasoning was again on the downward grade. Very rapidly I was once more descending to the level of the normal.

"Well, that fellow certainly knows a thing or two," Ronnit commented "And to think I called myself a scientist! In future I'll dig trenches…"

"You are an inventor," I replied, clapping him on the back. "Trained reasoning, such as Frot has revealed, is purely the outcome of practise and logic. Ask him to conceive the secret of invisibility out of nothing, and he'd be floored. Don't you be misled, old man; you're the cleverer of the two by long chalks. What do you think, Elna?"

"Every time," she answered, without looking up from the notes on the table, in which she was absorbed...

* * * *

Landon kept his word and succeeded in solving the problem by midnight of the same day. He himself came to our abode. Expecting him to come we had not retired for a well-earned rest after our activities of the day.

"I've been rather a fool," he said apologetically as he entered, "The solution is fairly simple, Jelfel's system of magnetizing the radio waves lay in the plate—the diaphram—itself. I've analysed the plate, and it's made of three elements—one is pure copper, but the other two are absolutely unknown to the earth, but they're going to aid us enormously. For one is nothing more or less than *pure magnetism*, and absorbs and retains any known force, whilst the other is *pure repulsion*! Can you beat that? The effect of all these two and the copper combined was to produce just enough of both magnetism and repulsion to collect the radio waves and re-transmit them. But we will be different. The elements can be duplicated. The magnetism element will be made into metal sheets, and likewise with the repulsor. Hence, we will draw the solar force with the former, absorb it, and pass via cables to the propulsor—or repulsor, whichever you like to call it. Thus, both the artificial gravitation sheet or iralium, of what Frot told you, and the magnetizer of solar force, will be erected on the other side of the world, at our Antipodes. Cables will be brought round the earth from the magnetizer and transmitted to the propulsor. Thus, whilst the power is drawn from the sun at the Antipodes, we will project the power from the night-side on this side of the world..."

"That is all."

My eyes were gleaming.

"That completes everything," I said in satisfaction.

"Save for calculations upon the strain imposed, and other details of trifling nature," Landon said. "That can take its turn, however. For the time being, we know all we need to know…"

# CHAPTER XXIII

## *Into the Sun!*

The following day work commenced in real earnest. I had already made the first advances to the workers, but now I had definite details to work upon.

I spent the entire morning giving them instructions for the future, and arranging the necessary men for the individual tasks we had on hand. In all, in the Age of Problems, there were twenty thousand souls. I divided these into ten thousand each, and gave orders that all the other cities of the world were to do likewise. One section was to begin work immediately upon time-machines, the plans of which I had supplied from Jelfel's own notes.

Another section was despatched to the other side of the world to start building the square mile of iralium gravitator and the solar magnetizer, and also to arrange for the cabling to carry the power around the earth to this particular spot.

A man named Dil Yedson I placed in charge of the emigration movement, having already made arrangements with the Age of Intelligence to receive the peoples of this Age…

And so our plans went forward, week by week, with perfect smoothness. Under the direction of Landon and Anton Frot the mighty Propulsor was erected, a great, towering affair that reared its challenging bulk to a murky grey sky. The etheric shield had of course been retained, but its secret was preserved for future use. I also took charge of the secret plans of many of Jelfel's brilliant inventions, that they might be used if ever it was again necessary.

Reports from the Antipodes announced that the Gravitator was going ahead perfectly, and also the Magnetizer. Already the cabling was well ahead in construction, and radio had been established between the two opposite points of the world.

Night by night, Kenton, the astronomer, kept Jupiter forever in the range of Jelfel's own mighty reflector. I would sometimes find time to be with him, and would gaze down into the silvered mirror upon that equatorially bulging spheroid, with its plainly defined Red Spot. I wondered if the Jovians knew what we were about to do? Had they already departed to safety before we could wreck their world, and were waiting to wreak some horrible vengeance upon us; or were they all unaware of impending doom…?

So matters progressed until the fated night of December 19th. This was the night set for commencement of our activities. Everything was in order—instruments fully equipped, cables laid, radio connection between the two vital factors, and every computation and figure determined by the brilliant Anton Frot.

Fortunately the night was fine. Jupiter, by now, was setting later in the night, and so skilfully had Kenton calculated his figures, Jupiter was "southing" at the time we set to work.

Everything was ready. I felt a trifle nervous as I stood there at the top of the propulsor tower, with my eight companions, the winking lights of the city below me, and the walls of switches all about me. Through the observation window I beheld Jupiter in a cloudless sky, dead to the south. I lifted the radio transmitter to my mouth, and at the same time fingered the master-control of the Propulsor. I thought of those mighty cables reaching from the other side of the world, carrying that solar power to this engine of destruction…

"Go!" I said curtly, waited a second whilst the radio-wave hurtled round the earth, and flung in the switch. Nothing apparently happened. There was silence, save for the buzz of generators and impedimenta, which proved, anyhow, that the current was coming through all right.

Kenton was leaning forward, staring at Jupiter as though he expected it to vanish from the sky; then he excused himself and made with all haste to the observatory to take notes. Isaton stood silent and pensive. Anton Frot's keen eyes were upon the dials and chronometers…

For two hours the reflected solar force, guided to follow Jupiter by clockwork motors, entirely invisible, must have been hurtling through 400,000,000 miles of space, to impinge upon the sun's biggest child. The enormity of the task rather overawed me. With one hand I was deciding the destiny of a planet 1,400 times the earth's volume! Had I any real right to decide what should be done with such a monster! Yet, after all, I was doing it to save the earth. I felt comforted by the hand of Anton Frot placed reassuringly on my arm. His intense eyes were dominating in the bright light.

"Don't weaken, Commander!"

So at the end of two hours that 148,000 per second force was stopped, and after giving the necessary orders for stoppage at the Antipodes, we all hurried over to the observatory.

Kenton was peaing into the refractor mirror, staring with scarcely blinking eyes at Jupiter's huge bulk. In silence we grouped about him.

"Doesn't look much of a success," I said presently.

Kenton did not reply immediately; he was looking intently at the hair-line cross on the mirror. "Calculate 30 minutes for the light to reach us," he said curtly; then at last in a voice of ecstasy: "Look! He's moving! *Look!*"

We followed, quite needlessly, his fixed, pointing finger. With burning eyes we all stared at the great mirrored surface. Distinctly now we could see Jupiter moving slowly backwards along the mathematically perfect hair-line. The movement was slight, but it was obvious.

"Why so long afterwards?" Elna muttered.

"It took forty minutes for the force to reach Jupiter, and thirty minutes for the light to be transmitted back to us. Even now we are looking at a spot Jupiter no longer occupies. We are merely seeing the light image. Anyhow, we know our computations are correct. He is now swinging slightly backward out of his orbit; in time he will swing slightly *inside* this orbit. Then again the force—and so on, until at last...!"

* * * *

It was nearing dawn, and Jupiter was not far from setting, when the order came again for the second attack.

Once again, until the planet set, that force was hurled at it; once again, at the Antipodes, the Gravitator and Magnetizer functioned perfectly. Indeed, the controllers of the Gravitator and Magnetizer, had to work constantly, in shifts, to keep the lurching earth steady, for even the very commencement of the shifting of Jupiter was commencing to cause strange cosmic disturbances...

Once the business was started we were kept at it almost ceaselessly. I took to sleeping by day, and working by night. Even on cloudy nights our calculations were perfect enough to enable us to continue the attack on Jupiter without seeing him—and as the days and nights went on he swung farther and farther out of his orbit, pursuing a drunken, zigzag movement around the sun.

In a brief interval I made arrangements for televisors to be erected at both our own depot and at the Antipodes, so that, when the time came for us to depart, we might be able to view the proceedings from our time-machine, so long as the televisors stood. These became known as the Day (Antipodes) Televisor, and Night, our own, of course.

Emigration to the Age of Intelligence had been completed by the fifth week. The only souls remaining in the world, in the Age of Problems, were myself and comrades, and the band of workers at the Antipodes. All of us had time-machines ready and waiting for departure. Whilst the Antipodes unit would be going to the Age of Intelligence along after the others, I had decided to return to my own time, 2000, with Elna, Anton

Frot, and other scientists, mainly to satisfy myself on a final paradox of time which had long been bothering me.

At the close of the fifth week, Kenton was jubilant.

"Calculated perfectly!" he declared. "Eight more days and Jupiter will swing so far sunward out of his orbit that it spells disaster for him—and unless I'm very much mistaken, for the other planets too."

With unremitting zeal we kept to our task, until we came at last to the concluding night. Again the force was hurled forth, then, to the second by Anton Frot's chronometer, I shut off the mechanism and bawled into the radio transmitter: "Run! Leave the Gravitator on to counterbalance any disturbances."

There was really no need to run, for the danger was not immediate. Jupiter was in the sky as usual, apparently. But the fear of imminent happenings prompted us all to race for our time-machine as fast as we could go. The moment we were within Kenton slammed across and sheathed the manhole door. I jumped to the controls, threw in the repellers, and watched that deserted, machine-mad land warp into the fourth dimension and vanish. We were away in Time—safe—so far back as to be beyond all hint of destruction. And, somewhere else in Time, going forward, would be the machine from the Antipodes.

We turned our attention to the televisor screens, and beheld again, on the Night Visor, the deserted, darkened landscape we had left, with the star-ridden sky above. In the other Visor we beheld the sun, near to setting, with the dully gleaming square mile of the Gravitator, and the bellying bulk of the Magnetizer plainly visible…

In silence we watched the night view, then I felt Elna's hand tighten upon my arm. Subconsciously, I heard a sharp intaking of breath from the others grouped about us. How light travelled, or how time operated via a televisor in Time, I have no means of estimating. The fact remains that we saw Jupiter was moving, very slowly, towards the sun. We had been too late to see how far it had swung on the backward motion—"voidwards," to be precise—but now it was plainly gathering momentum on the sunward side of its orbit, too far away to recover itself. Again, I wondered. Was the planet empty? Had the Jovians beaten us to it? Or…?

Gradually the planet increased its speed, but even so it only seemed the veriest crawl. Actually, it must have been hurtling with terrific velocity towards the sun, its acceleration ever mounting…

Still in dead silence we watched it. The pace increased very slightly—it moved with an apparently steady speed amongst the stars. As we viewed it with the naked eye, we could not discern its moons, but undoubtedly they must have been following somewhere. Then Kenton gave a shout!

"The other planets! There they go!"

We watched tensely. Sure enough there was yellow Saturn and green Uranus. Neptune and Pluto were too distant for our observation, but it was logical to assume they were also making the sunward journey, helpless, careening through infinity… It chilled me a little.

Onwards—ever onwards! The pace increasing with every moment as the sun pulled triumphantly upon its erring children. A snail's pace from our viewpoint, yet actually a dizzying stupendous onrush. At last the planets vanished from view behind the horizon. We turned to the daylight televisor, regretting we could not behold the actual fall into the sun.

I don't know how long we waited before we saw the sun, near to setting completely, apparently bulge outward upon every hand. Astounding streamers and bolts of light were cascading through the desolations of the twilight heavens. The brilliance increased; we were forced to shut our eyes. I obtained one momentary glimpse of a blinding mass of flame hurtling from the skies to the earth—searing, sight-destroying. In the Night Visor, too, the sky became, in the east, a sudden boiling mass of swirling, death dealing incandescence… Jupiter had entered the sun. The televisors both went black, the transmitters destroyed.

We stood looking at each other in complete silence for a space—and strange it was indeed to behold through the time-machine's window, owing to our occupying an earlier time, the body of Jupiter still serene in the heavens! The words of Anton Frot seemed to sum the matter up beautifully:

"So be it!"


# CHAPTER XXIV

## *The Final Paradox*

So it came about that Elna and I, and our scientific colleagues, returned to 2000 A.D.

To the utter bewilderment of Elna, everything was as it had ever been. The only thing different was that, according to report, a "mirage earthquake" had taken place some weeks previously. This constituted the apparent wrecking of the entire city—and it had happened all along the time-line right up to 22,000—but immediately after the mirage earthquake, everything was as it had ever been. Such occurences, we were told, were not uncommon since the discovery of Time. Upsets in past or future times had brought about this queer effect, which reduced human beings to a comatose condition often resembling death, but not actually death. To Elna's intense delight we learned that President Folson was not dead. He had been injured during the mirage earthquake, had been robbed of plans by some agency during this condition, but was now quite well again... The same thing had happened to Templeton.

"First I must see Templeton," I said quietly, taking Elna's ann. "Then we'll go along to see your father."

"But Sandy, I don't understand it all. I—"

"I'll explain in a moment," I promised her. "Come along."

We entered, after the usual procedures, the Debating Chamber of the Time-Liner Corporation. The directors were there, but Templeton did not wait until I reached the table. Instead he came rushing forward, gripped my hand.

"Commander! Miss Folson! I have done you both a grave injustice. I learned the truth of your statements only recently. I have learned also of your wonderful brilliance in outwitting the Jovian menace. Congratulations! Congratulations! Here!" He removed a badge from a plush case and pinned it on my chest. Then he saluted and stood back—"Gentlemen—Commodore Commandant of the Time-Liner Corporation—Master Pilot and Chief Director of Time Ways, Sandford Lee...! That, Commandant, is the greatest honour we can bestow..."

"Thank goodness I'm fixed up again, anyhow," I said, as we went down the steps of the building. "I'm the Big Noise now, and I'm going to make a few improvements—but come along. Let's get ready for seeing your father. We must pack...."

"One moment," she said. "How do you explain this mirage earth-quake business? Did we dream it, after all?"

"No, Elna. I knew this would happen. It's just like I explained to you once before. You can't bridge 'blank' time, and you can't make the future coincide with the past... If you try it, as Jelfel did, it seems that disaster happens *during that time,* but afterwards everything reverts to normal... Just like a dream!"

She pushed a hand through his thick fair hair.

"There's only one thing to do, and that is quote Ecclesiastes," she said, ruminatively. "I know my Bible well, and in Chapter I, verses 9 to 11, he says: 'The thing which hath been is that which shall be, and that which is done is that which shall be done, and there is no new thing under the sun. Is there anything whereof it may be said, See, this is new? It hath already been of old time, which was before us. There is no remembrance of former things, neither shall there be any remembrance of things that are to come with those that shall come after.' That just sums it up..."

"Exactly," I assented, and taking her arm we went down the broad steps.

THE END

# INVADERS FROM TIME

Tom Lawton, electrical analyst, had turned his enormously industrious and fertile brain to the complicated and little-known science of Time.

For, once this all-embracing problem found access to his mind, he had no thought for anything outside it, and upon the problem he trained his twenty years of knowledge and ingenuity.

Of course, nobody credited his discoveries or experiments; nobody believed he had any real line of research in his hands—save one person, a staunch friend and unswerving confidant: Bob Ritchard, possessing no claims to actual brilliance, but nevertheless intensely practical and calculating.

In the workshop at the rear of Tom's unpretentious London house there had grown in odd hours, through the passage of many months, an accumulation and litter of strange and remarkable devices.

Generators lay in odd corners; wires snaked from them across the floor and stapled into the roof-beams. Three-foot glass tubes filled with purple liquid were poised upright against the wall. In the centre of the workshop stood a machine—a squat, vaguely cylindrical affair of struts and circular discs, the discs being capable of revolving in their well-lubricated bearings when necessary. And, linked to the whole, a switchboard of meters, plugs, and pole-switches.

"If my calculations are correct," said Tom thoughtfully, surveying all this mass of apparatus one Saturday afternoon, when he and his friend had concluded the actual assembling of the machinery, "we ought to be able to take something from a future time and bring it here. I believe it to be physically impossible for us to move ourselves in Time, but it ought to be possible to move something from the future and bring it here to us."

"So you've said before," Bob remarked. "The trouble is, you're so wrapped up in your theories, you don't explain yourself properly."

"Well, this can be explained quickly enough," the young analyst promptly replied. "Time, logically and clearly enough, is linked immovably to the phenomenon we call Speed, or Motion. For instance, the faster you go, the less time you take. Were you to reach the ultimate of speed you would never move, because you'd be back before you started. That would bring Motion and Time to zero. Understand?"

"Uh-huh," Bob assented doubtfully. "Sounds a bit Irish!"

"Irish be hanged! It's logic—scientific! That's the basis of the idea. Now, my system is the exact reversal of, shall we say, the ultimate of Speed. Since maximum velocity would result in no Time at all, it follows that great slowness of speed—that is, from the slowest possible rate—would result in Time going actually faster than Motion. Hence, Time would shoot onwards, whilst apparent Motion remains at Zero. Get it?"

"Well—vaguely. You mean, that this machines alters the normal law of Motion in relation to Time, by making Time faster than Motion, hence it must go forward millions of times faster than is natural. Is that it?"

"You've got it, absolutely! That's just it! And I do it by this special electricity of mine, which exactly reverses the law of Motion. That causes those discs there to rotate, and in rotating they send out invisible magnetism into Time, magnetism capable of bringing back to here any object it encounters. You see, the moment I shut the current off the magnetism returns to the machine here, which, as I calculate it, must result in any object in future time coming back as well."

"Men?" Bob queried dubiously.

"Possibly. But there are other things besides men, you know. Oh, I see what you mean! Yes, this magnetism attracts flesh and blood—anything. It isn't just limited to metal, like ordinary magnetism. You see, the magnetism will bring back whatever happens to be in its path in future time. That's why I think we ought to make some pretty interesting discoveries if the thing works."

"But, say, aren't you ignoring a factor of Time?" Bob broke in, calculating as ever. "You can't bring a thing back, because if you do it will be in a space, or Time, in which it never really existed or had being."

Tom growled and turned to his switchboard. "You've just repeating a supposedly unalterable law of science," he said. "I intend to prove it for myself. Why should it apply, anyhow? It's all supposition… We'll make a test and see, anyway."

Bob stood on one side and watched intently as his friend set to work with the controls of his remarkable device. Presently the generators began to hum; the purple liquid in the glass tubes boiled strangely. The air became heavy with the smell of ozone from electric discharges. Sparks flashed from the master-contacts. The whole affair took on an indescribable weirdness.

Tom's face glistened with the perspiration of excitement as he stared eagerly at the empty space beneath the now rapidly rotating discs of the "Time Investigator." With a quick movement he turned and swung the Time Pointer to the year A.D. 2534, six hundred years ahead of the present.

For perhaps ten minutes the humming and buzzing continued without abatement, then Tom cut out the master-switch. The droning stopped; the boiling liquids subsided.

There came a thud. Petrified, the two friends stared with goggling eyes at the floor beneath the Time Investigator—stared transfixed at a glittering box of some unknown, silvery metal.

"What—what is it?" Bob ventured at last, taking a step forward. "We'll soon find out, anyhow."

Stooping, Tom picked the box up—it was perhaps six inches square with a remarkably engraved lid—and placed it on the bench. A quick examination revealed no trace of a lock, yet, manifestly, the thing was not solid.

"A box—out of future time—out of 2534!" Tom breathed, fascinated. "Bob, do you begin to realise the wonder of the thing we've done?" His whole idealist's soul was momentarily overcome with futuristic visions, visions which the practical, mundane Bob quickly dispelled.

"Be hanged to that—let's get the thing open. Any suggestions?"

"Try an electric charge on it," Tom responded, and placed the box in the area of a force beam. The switch shot over, and almost instantly the box blew apart under the stream of high-tension energy. From its shining interior rolled a sheet of wafer-thin metal, rolled up in the fashion of an old-time parchment.

"H'm, the box seems to be of something like silver, and this scroll thing's the same," Tom commented, unfurling the roll with slightly shaking hands. "It appears—Great Scott! What is it all, anyhow?"

Puzzled, the two stared at the now unfurled two foot length of metal. Upon it were engraved columns upon columns of names and, apparently, addresses, with dates at the sides of the names. The lettering was understandable English, though the names at the top of the scroll assumed remarkable pronunciations. "Varkol, 2534; Mornas, 2533; Ramikal, 2434…" Tom looked up in amazement. "What in the name of wonder is it, Bob? See, the list goes right down through these names"

"I believe I've got it!" Bob exclaimed suddenly, after thinking for a moment. "In fact I'm sure of it! It's a pedigree!"

"A what? Don't be an ass! We're not dog-fanciers!"

"Well, an ancestral record, then. See, the name of the person in 1934 is quite sensible—Robert Halford, 42 Maryland Gate, London, E.C. The names are quite normal until 2134 is reached, then they assume weirdness. Don't you see? These names here, and numbers, are ancestors of these other people! Look carefully, Tom. At the top of the scroll are four names—Varkol, Ramor, Forjan, and Lanor. Those four chaps obviously exist in 2534, where we pinched this thing from. Their ancestors are shown on this list, and boil down finally to one man—Robert Halford, who is presumably alive at this very moment. Though he doesn't know it, he's the forefather of all these folk who will come in future generations. Understand?"

"Gosh—yes!" Tom whistled blankly. "After all, through the years, the number of people from one forefather would be tremendous... I believe you've hit it, Bob, though it does seem a dizzy sort of conception. Say, all this is too muddling to talk over here. Let's go in and have tea, and perhaps we'll straighten things out a bit..."

\* \* \* \*

Tea and conversation brought home the realisation to the two friends that they had indeed captured from 2534 a record of ancestry, engraven on unbreakable metal parchment.

"Well, what are we going to do about it?" Bob enquired, when they had discussed the matter from every angle.

Tom stroked his chin pensively. "I'm hanged if I know! The trouble is, we can never send anything back where we got it from. I'll tell you what we will do. I'll put this scroll in my own private section in Dad's safe, and we'll have another shot at probing 2534 tonight. The whole business is fascinating. Are you on?"

"Nothing could stop me. Let's get going."

In a few minutes they were back in the laboratory, and once more the Time Investigator got to work. For ten minutes it hurled its invisible magnetism into Time, then, as before, Tom cut the current off. A brief pause, then—

The two friends jumped back, overcome with shock. For, standing beneath the discs were four grim, square-faced men, attired in close-fitting uniforms, with instruments—six to each of them—in special holders in their leather belts.

For a while they stood in silence, gazing round the workshop with eyes of cold blue. Indeed, the four of them were so much alike in their blue eyes, square faces, and black-haired heads, barely covered with peaked caps, that they might have been brothers. Then, with a slow, faintly majestic tread, they walked out into the laboratory.

"We'd better run for it!" Bob breathed, sudden fear overwhelming him. Then he looked about him desperately as the ruthless eyes of the obvious leader of the quartet turned to him.

"You are responsible for the theft of our ancestral record?" he asked, in a hard, un-mellowed voice. "Answer me! Quickly!"

"That was my doing—an accident," Tom broke in quickly. "Tell me, who are you? Where do you belong to?"

The man considered for a moment, and glanced significantly at his rigid-faced companions. Then at length he turned back to Tom.

"I, my young friend, am Varkol, Master of Greater London in the year 2534. These three are my brothers, Ramor, Forjan, and Lanor. By a clever piece of trickery with Time and electricity you stole from us a valuable ancestral record!" The man brooded over that for a space, and looked at Tom's worried face thoughtfully. "You are clever for your age, my son. Very clever! Of course, we knew you would make this discovery, and we know it to be a practicable way of investigating Time."

"How did you know?" Bob asked in amazement.

"It is in our history records that in 1934 a young man named Thomas Lawton found how to explore Time. His invention was not used after the twentieth century because it proved of little use but it did provide the basis for a more thorough search into the mysteries of Time." Varkol smiled faintly. "You see, to me your history is past; to you, it lies in the future... After the accidental theft of our record of ancestry, we discovered the cause of the trouble, and decided to see if you made an attempt to investigate Time again. We placed ourselves in readiness in the same spot as our box was stolen from—and so we came here. Now we *are* here, there are many things we can do."

"Bu—but, we can't send you back again!" Tom cried despairingly.

"Let that not worry you," Varkol returned calmly. "We realise that. However we of 2534 are a scientific race; we give our lives for its progress. What better than that my brothers and I spend the remainder of our lives in studying the habits and ways of the Ancient Britons? Indeed, we might make a few improvements with our greater knowledge."

"What do you propose doing?" Bob demanded, gathering courage.

"Oh, who knows?" Varkol shrugged his massive shoulders. "Presumably we are in the Ancient London we read about, with its Trafalgar Square, and Thames, and Strand... We will change all of that. We have the knowledge of future time, and can turn it to advantage."

"But you can't go upsetting a city of eight million inhabitants like that—spoiling all law and order!" Tom protested. "You've no right, Varkol—"

The Master interrupted him with a bass chuckle. "Eight million inhabitants, all with the knowledge of medieval England! Don't you see what you could do if you went back six hundred years? You could perform miracles! So it is with us... You two, for you obviously possess fairly clever minds, shall be our ambassadors!"

"I refuse—and so does my friend!" Tom snapped hotly. "I—" He broke off suddenly as Varkol whipped one of his six instruments from his leather belt.

"You cannot refuse the wish of Varkol!" he retorted fiercely. "I can see you are both very fractious, but you shall obey! For the time being this will suffice."

He pressed a button upon the instrument and a pink pencil of fire leapt quickly at both men, each in turn. Instantly they sagged helplessly to the floor, all strength of bone and muscle curiously set at naught. They found they could not even speak, only watch and listen.

"Just electrically-induced paralysis," the Master explained coolly, replacing his weapon. "We have quick ways of dealing with the obstinate...."

He ceased to speak, and placing his hands on his hips and feet astride, surveyed the laboratory with studied care. Finally he nodded. "H'm, you two have enough stuff here for our purpose. Come—we will proceed." This last remark was addressed to his three brothers.

In the sixty minutes that followed, the helpless Tom and Bob became the amazed spectators of scientific wizardry on the part of the four men from Time. Using their various instruments they converted numerous electrical devices in the laboratory into one complete and complicated machine, a mass of wires and switches—the only predominant thing about it being a cylindrical projection possessing a concave lens, from which, upon tests being made, there sprang a beam of greenish-blue.

"A brain-transformer," Varkol commented at length, smiling grimly. "We have many of them in our own Time. They turn dolts into geniuses, and geniuses into supermen. You see, slow brain activity is merely occasioned by excessive brain-substance, which hampers the activity of the brain cells. This machine, rough though it is in design, acts on the same principle as our normal ones. Namely, it painlessly disrupts the encroaching brain tissue and leaves the cells clear and active. Also, by a slight alteration in frequency, we make a brain—your brain!—entirely subservient to ours. You will be brilliantly clever, as we are, but you will only do what we tell you. You call it hypnotism—but it isn't. It is electrically controlled brain-activity. Now you see how you will become our ambassadors!"

The two friends were roughly hauled to their feet and dumped on laboratory stools before the bench. Varkol surveyed them for a moment in amused silence, then flicked the main switch on the remarkable contrivance he had caused to be created.

The greenish-blue beam immediately played upon Tom's shock of fair hair, his brow and temples seemed to glow strangely. For himself, he experienced the most amazing mental metamorphosis he had ever known. His mind seemed suddenly capable of conceiving the most abstruse and astounding things. He found he could quite clearly understand that tremendous mathematical riddle==the calculus. Yet, despite this el-evation of thought, there was withal a sense of control. Dimly he realised it was the mind of the amazing Varkol dominating him.

So the brain-transformation continued, and finally the four men of 2534 had before them two super-geniuses, yet both under their dictates. The paralysis was removed, and the two friends abruptly found normal bodily vigour had resumed. No thought was in their minds of rebellion. They were machines—just controlled, flesh-and-blood machines.

"Excellent emissaries, indeed," commented Forjan, glancing at his Master. "We could wish for nothing better."

"Truly," Varkol conceded, complacently putting his various instru-ments in his belt once more. "This particular task is complete; now let us view the old city of London. You two will lead us to the centre of your London—your Trafalgar Square."

"This way, Master," said Tom mechanically, and, opening the labo-ratory door, he stepped out into the back garden of his home. He had no recollection of his parents inside the house, otherwise he would undoubt-edly have tried to summon their aid.

With the same measured tread, Bob by his side, he led the way through the wicket gate and out into the street beyond, dimly lit by gas lighting—for darkness had now fully come.

"Gas," grunted Farjon. "A system practised by the ancients, Master."

"Beyond question," Varkol agreed.

"We have electricity," Tom said quietly. "This is not a high-class, residential district you know. How would the Master prefer to reach Tra-falgar Square? It is twelve miles from here on foot—nearly four hours. Perhaps you would prefer a bus or trains?"

"Are those modes of progress?" the Master asked curtly.

"Yes."

Varkol shook his head. "No, then. We do not wish to excite the pub-lic curiosity. We will walk."

"As you wish, Master. I will lead you."

So the journey commenced—a journey which proved the utter tire-lessness of the brain-enslaved Tom and Bob, and the enduring powers of the men from Time. They walked with steady, rhythmical tread, draw-ing into the shadows as people passed, though it was obvious that their almost orthodox uniforms occasioned little curiosity. They could easily have been mistaken for seamen, or something similar.

Then eventually the bright lights of the city began to loom up, and progress by stealth was no longer possible. This being so, Varkol led the way forward with determined strides, but still no heed was paid to him or his three iron-faced brothers. True, glances were cast at the somewhat vacantly staring, hatless Tom and Bob, but that was all.

So, down the Strand, amidst the throngs of theatre-goers, across the traffic-jammed square, and to the centre of Trafalgar Square itself. Here Varkol called a halt, and stood for a while looking about him in apparent amusement at the teeming life, the sky-signs, and the black silhouette of Nelson's Column behind him.

The vision of—to him—old-world London seemed distinctly funny. He chuckled silently to himself at intervals. Then presently he turned and cast a suggestive look at his three brothers.

"An excellent spot for a base," he commented calmly. "The very heart of old London. There is indeed something wonderful in being back in history like this—right back in the core of an almost forgotten city. Yes—here will be our headquarters."

With that he turned slightly and surveyed Nelson's Column thoughtfully, right up to the dim summit where stood poised the one-eyed mariner. Quietly, he loosened from his belt yet another of his instruments, then, sighting it upon the one hundred and fifty foot length he pressed the button.

The result was astounding!

The column, time-honoured and almost sacred, suddenly split in twain, and came toppling downwards in a cloud of disintegrating chips of stone and dust. The figure of Nelson himself collapsed outwards into space and smashed into a thousand pieces.

Within the space of a few minutes, as it seemed, a startled dazed populace beheld Trafalgar Square littered with blocks of stone and thick black dust slowly dispersing in the night wind. Traffic came almost to a standstill; people came from all directions to stare and wonder.

"Stand back!" Varkol commanded, as the surging people pressed close about him. "To touch me means death! I have warned you!"

"What's all this about?" demanded a constable, striding through the crowd. "Hey, you! What do you think you're doing? You four are up to no good! Incendiarism, that's what it is! Come with me!"

"I've warned you—stand back!" Varkol grated out, whipping another weapon from his belt. "Take heed, you fool!"

"Aw—enough of this!" the constable began, seizing Varkol by the shoulder in a fierce clutch. Then he staggered backwards, gasping hoarsely, as a sudden beam of pure crimson enveloped him. Finally, he fell backwards into the arms of the crowd, shuddered, and became still.

"He's dead!" came an astounded shout.

"Yes—dead!" Varkol snapped. "I warned him. You others do as I tell you. Keep away! Come along,"—he turned to his brothers—"we have much to do."

Resolutely, the party pushed their way to the crumbled ruin of stone and dust that had been Nelson's Column. Then, with infinite calmness, ignoring the shouting people and screeching of police whistles, Varkol laid out four of his instruments on the stonework ready for use. His brothers did likewise.

"Granite," Farjon commented "This will be easy, Master. The transmutation of granite into maldelene steel will be simple, but we had better hurry—the crowd is in an ugly mood."

"Have no fear of them," Varkol returned, with his customary placidity. "They are nothing but fools; we can more than beat them with our brains and knowledge."

The vast crowd that had gathered became quieter, however, as they witnessed what followed, for, in the same manner as they had formed a brain transformer out of odds and ends of electrical apparatus in Tom's laboratory, the men from Time created a small but efficient metal abode out of the granite of the fallen column!

Four of their instruments, which emitted dull yellow beams, were capable of causing transmutation of elements, a science so perfected by their advanced time that they could—and did—form out of the granite a square metal dwelling. It became obvious for the first time when the dust and smoke from their satanic operations had subsided.

There it stood—an impregnable fortress in the exact position where Nelson's Column had been a few short hours before.

There seemed to be only one door in the tiny stronghold, and through this the four men entered the interior, Tom and Bob, still mentally controlled, accompanying them. The door shut, and a gaping populace realised for the first time that something had come into their ordered lives that was as apart and alien as anything they had ever known or dreamed of!

\* \* \* \*

Towards midnight, as nothing further happened and the metal stronghold remained as solid as ever, the populace drifted on its way and normal life returned.

The story, however, had reached the newshounds of Fleet Street, Scotland Yard and the Home Office. As a sequel, the following morning an attack was made on the stronghold by the home-defence corps, and Trafalgar Square became, for perhaps the first time in history, the scene of martial law.

High explosives were flung at the domain of the invaders; every known means of destruction was rained upon it, but still it remained an impregnable fortress. How were the Home Office to know that maldelene steel was the secret of 2534? That it was indestructible by all known forces and had a life of one million years?

Hostility failing, ultimatums were proceeded with. Men paraded before the dwelling with friendly messages on sandwich boards, hoping the inmates would see them somehow through the apparently solid walls—but still nothing happened. So finally, tiring of their efforts, the corps withdrew to await events.

In the stronghold itself Varkol chuckled with sardonic satisfaction. He was gazing through the wall, and on all sides it appeared as though the domain was of nothing stronger than glass—hopaque seen from outside; transparent from within.

"Wonderful stuff this maldelene steel," Varkol said presently. "Owing to its atomic constitution it is impenetrable when light falls upon it—in the sunlight outside, for instance. In here it is totally dark, the only opening at all being those ventilation holes in the roof—thus we are enabled to see through the walls. These people of old London are very amusing with their toys. We will change it all. Since we are doomed to stay in 1934 because we cannot return to our Time, we will at least have a city worth staying in. You two, my young friends, will now carry our message to the people. We will control your brains so that the right words are spoken. No harm will befall you. Now go...."

"It shall be done, Master," Tom assented quietly, and Bob nodded also.

In another moment the two friends were outside, and, under the mental dictates of the men from Time, made their way to St. James Park. People standing round Trafalgar Square followed at a safe distance, and by the time they had reached a deserted bandstand, a monstrous crowd had gathered round to listen.

"My friends," Tom shouted, using the words the distant Varkol was deliberately putting in his brain, "you are at the mercy of four men from the year A.D. 2534—men brought here by a scientific experiment. They mean you no harm; rather they seek to improve on your methods by using their enormously advanced knowledge—knowledge six hundred years ahead of you. They ask that you place yourselves unreservedly in their hands, and in return they will give you a super London, a dream of luxury. They cannot return to their own Time, so will improve this one instead, and, ultimately, London will be a city of super knowledge and power. It is for you all to decide. What is your answer?"

"If they mean no harm, let them carry on!" shouted one.

"We could do with improvements!" bawled another.

"Hear, hear!"

Such was the general tenor of the crowd's response. In no time the news spread until all London knew. There were many dissenters, but they were in the minority. Finally, it was agreed that the populace were willing to listen to schemes for improvement, and so the invaders from Time won their first point. This point achieved, the two ambassadors returned to the Trafalgar Square stronghold.

"All London unreservedly in our hands," commented Varkol with a grim smile. "It is excellent news indeed. Once we have London we can soon command the world. I am a lover of power, my young friends; in 2534 I was just the ruler of one city. Here, back in Time, I can master all the earth—a treasured dream fulfilled. So be it! The improvements will commence."

From then on improvements did commence. Four radio sets were obtained by Tom and Bob, and were converted by the invaders' remarkable instruments into one remarkable machine for radio television. Indeed, super radio-television, for the apparatus was capable of viewing and hearing anything without the necessity of a transmitter at the 'other end.' Also, it could, by alteration in its circuit pass through solid buildings and obtain clear-cut pictures of what was taking place within them.

With this machine, by issuing radio instructions to the B.B.C., which, in turn, were relayed to all London, the vast improvement scheme began. Aided by Varkol's uncanny knowledge of advanced machinery months of work were accomplished in one day.

So London became a slowly changing city. Buses disappeared, and in their stead appeared bullet-shaped machines that moved with demoniacal swiftness on almost hidden wheels. The streets underwent lightning changes—the Strand was widened; edifices appeared and disappeared, in a vast, magically changing mystery, as various elements were transmuted into different orders.

The Tower Bridge rose no longer by chain-system as time passed, but by small but incredibly powerful atomic force motors. The noisy, fussy tugs vanished and gave place to streamlined enigmas that piloted the oily waters with a swiftness and strength never deemed possible...

So the change went on, everywhere. The Underground became a world of hurtling, snub-nosed vehicles; above were the strange conveyances, the wide streets. A changing skyline and a changing city. In four months the invaders from Time had brought about a master-city in power and design.

In those four months they had emerged from their tiny stronghold in Trafalgar Square, and instead created a massive one on the same site. A six-story edifice with windows at the summit only—a building of maldelene steel equipped with every comfort and countless scientific devices the sole secret of the invaders themselves.

The people of London had little cause to resent the presence of the invaders until one eventful, early spring day, when the tide began to turn.

Tom and Bob, still ambassadors, addressed an enormous meeting in St. James' Park once again.

"You have seen what the men from Time have done," Tom shouted, speaking, as ever under mental control. "They have given you a perfect city; now they propose to make very necessary alterations in the populace itself. In London there are eight million inhabitants—four million *too many* for comfort!"

The multitude remained significantly silent, waiting for the next. "Varkol, the man who has given you so much comfort and progress, has decided that for equal social footing four million inhabitants is quite enough. He therefore proposes to destroy the remaining four million! Briefly, my friends, half the population of London will painlessly die at sundown tomorrow night—six o'clock. That is Varkol's edict. This he will do with his asphyxiation machine, which he has in his stronghold. He—"

Tom proceeded no further. The multitude, at first overcome with horror at the ruthless announcement, were too astounded to speak, then their rage became abruptly unleashed. They surged towards the bandstand in a furiously shouting sea. Stones began to sail through the air. Dust rose in clouds, and, obeying mental commands, Bob suddenly turned, descended the band-stand steps, and raced with more than human speed back towards Trafalgar Square.

Tom, however, was not so lucky. A flying stone caught him full in the forehead, he reeled dizzily, toppled over the rail of the stand, and into the midst of the crowd. Immediately they bore him down to earth.

"Hey, wait a minute!" shouted one, "The kid hasn't anything to do with these dirty invaders. He's somehow hypnotised by them, or something. Give him a chance."

"Yes—stand back there! Give him air!"

Gradually, the incensed people began to cool down, and one member made a cup from a sheet of paper and brought water from a nearby drinking fountain. Under its influence Tom began to revive.

"What—what happened?" he asked dazedly, at last, looking at the sea of faces about him. "I—Good heavens, yes—I remember!" He sat up with a sudden jerk, wiping a smear of blood from his forehead.

"Take it easy, kid—you'll be all right," counselled someone.

"I'm all right—just a bit dazed," Tom answered, staggering to his feet. "A most amazing thing has happened!" He stood quite still for a moment in something like silent awe, then he turned to face the crowd again. "Friends, up to now I have been controlled by Varkol—you probably know that—but that blow on the head has broken that mental control somehow! I am master of my own will again. But, if it has broken the enslavement, it hasn't spoilt the genius which Varkol gave to me. I am nearly as clever as he is! He made me that way. Listen…"

Completely recovered, Tom climbed actively to the stand again.

"This monster from Time has spoken to you, through me, in honeyed terms. What he really aims at is control of the world, through bloodshed and ruthless destruction! My powers of memory are not impaired, I can remember everything he plans to do. At sundown tomorrow half London's inhabitants will die. Somehow, we've got to stop it! We must attack—and I, only I can lead you. My friend, too—he must be rescued!"

"What do you propose doing?" somebody shouted.

"Make weapons—commandeer the assistance of everybody we can. The only known government at the moment is Varkol himself so we'll take the law into our own hands. In my mentally improved condition I can think out the weapons necessary. It means war against the Invaders—rout them out, destroy them before they destroy us!"

"He's right! Down with the invaders!"

"Death to Varkol!"

And the shouts echoed, as it seemed, over the vast mass of newly-made London.

* * * *

Varkol scowled heavily as he studied Bob Ritchard standing before him.

"Your friend got away; I can't find him by my televisor system. Where is he?" he demanded grimly. "It is better that you speak!"

Bob's face remained a blank; he shook his head slowly. "No use that way, Master," remarked Farjon. "His mind is only controlled by your own. Even if he knows anything, his mind is not capable of letting him tell it."

Varkol started at that. "Of course, Farjon! That had not occurred to me. Very well, stand him before the brain-neutraliser and we will break the enslavement of his mind. A pity, for it means we can never resume it. However, we must know where Tom is. We cannot have a missing ambassador."

Accordingly, the machine for neutralising the brain-enslavement was switched on, and in another moment Bob was again the master of himself—but, unlike Tom, he no longer retained genius. He was simply back to his normal self. With clenched hands he stood facing the grim-faced men of 2534.

"Where is Tom?" demanded Varkol again, his pale blue eyes menacing.

"I don't know what happened to him—he's probably dead," Bob answered thickly. "The crowd were out to lynch him after he spoke those words of yours."

"You're lying! You know full well what happened to him. Speak, or it may be the worse for you!"

"I tell you I don't know! You've got to believe that, Varkol! One thing I do know, and it is that all your former friends are now bitter enemies."

"What does that matter to me? All fools incapable of doing anything, any more than an arrow from an old-time bow could penetrate one of your modern tanks. Don't forget our stupendous knowledge—and this controlling building is proof against anything!"

Bob shrugged hopelessly. "All right; I've said I know nothing. What are you going to do about it?"

"Be rid of you, ultimately," Varkol snapped. "For the time being you will be imprisoned in the adjoining room whilst we arrive at some decision."

Unable to help himself, Bob was roughly seized and pushed into the contiguous apartment. The door, possessing a strange and puzzling lock, closed.

In moody silence Bob wandered about the great apartment, gazing at the scientific machinery stacked against the walls in the sunlight streaming through the windows. He did not attempt to find a way out, he knew from past experience it was impossible. The windows, of which there were three, were equally useless exits, being such a vast height from the ground.

For a while he stood by one of the windows looking down on an almost suspiciously quiet London. Then presently he turned to the wall of instruments again, and began to finger the various apparatus thoughtfully. It was as he was doing this that the door suddenly softly opened again, and Varkol and Farjon were standing on the threshold.

"Leave that machinery alone!" the Master snapped savagely. "You may do some damage. That is the machine to asphyxiate half of London's population tomorrow night!"

Bob wheeled round. He had forgotten the Master's villainous plan, but now it returned to him with vivid recollection. Quite suddenly, almost by instinct, he drew up his right fist and struck the Master a terrible blow on the jaw. Unprepared for the assault, he staggered backwards and collapsed against the metal wall, striking his head with numbing force. A short grunt escaped him, then he sagged sideways and became still, obviously stunned with the concussion.

Surprised and delighted at his victory, Bob swung around on Farjon. This worthy was desperately striving to rip his paralyser from his belt, but chance ordained that it stick in its holster. In another instant Bob was upon him, and it became increasingly obvious that, whilst the men from Time were great brain workers, they were anything but physically powerful. Against Bob's heavy frame and strong muscles the hapless Farjon stood little chance. In a few moments he was tethered to the unconscious Varkol by long lengths of metal wire, and firmly secured to the legs of one of the instrument boards.

Bob grinned as he rose to his feet.

"Think your way out of that!" he threw down to them. "It's time somebody else had a chance!"

With that he strode from the chamber, taking care to leave the door slightly ajar because he knew not how to operate the lock. Then, with quick strides, he moved to the radio-televisor machinery which he understood fairly well, hoping desperately that Ramor and Lanor, who evidently were elsewhere in the edifice, would not see fit to arrive.

Frantically operating the dials of the machine, he stared into the screen until St. James' Park came into view. The place was deserted, nor did any sounds of interest beyond the chirping of birds reach him through the loudspeaker. Disheartened, he searched London as circumspectly as he could, but nowhere could he find a trace of his missing friend. Tom had completely and mysteriously vanished.

At last he switched off, and sat for a moment in thought.

"Since I can't get out of here, the only thing I can do to help is to destroy that Asphyxiator," he muttered to himself. "An Asphyxiator, eh? Sends out a beam for ten miles, and, ten miles away—in a circular area—the air is sucked dry long enough for humans to choke. A bright idea! I'll stop that, anyhow."

Nodding with decision he returned to the adjoining apartment, to find that Varkol had recovered consciousness. He and Farjon glared fiendishly and struggled to release themselves from their bonds of wire as Bob calmly walked across to the Asphyxiator and surveyed its massive bulk, deciding upon the best method of destruction.

Presently be bent over it and examined the many wiring terminals, debating in his mind—to be suddenly brought to attention again as something hard prodded him in the back.

"Better not, young friend," commented a grim voice; and swinging round he beheld Ramor and Lanor immediately behind him, paralysers levelled. They had made no sound in entering owing to the thick pile carpet.

"Good work!" growled Varkol. "Tie the young traitor up, then release Farjon and I."

The instructions were duly carried out, and Bob, to his alarm and disgust, found himself in the same position as his former victims had been. Varkol nodded in silent complacency and led the way from the room with his three brothers, closing the door securely behind him.

"We will dispose of that awkward young man tomorrow night," he said grimly. "When we release the Asphyxiator we will place him in the area of the electric charges. That will mean he will be surrounded by the same energy we are proposing to spread over half London. As a result, he will die. A good idea, is it not?"

"Excellent," nodded Forjan in satisfaction. "And what of Tom?"

The Master shrugged. "We cannot do anything about him. He has disappeared, and London seems quiet enough. Until tomorrow night there is little we can do...."

\* \* \* \*

If, however, the egotistical Varkol expected perfect quietness and submissiveness to his grim plan to destroy half London's population he was mistaken.

For at five o'clock that same evening he was startled to behold his entire controlling edifice surrounded by a literal army of people, headed by one whom he instantly recognised as Tom himself! His square jaw set as he beheld strange machines in the people's midst, trained on the invincible building.

"Trouble coming, Forjan, from the look of things," he commented bitterly. "Tom must have somehow broken my will-power over him. All right, if they want trouble, they'll get it. Close all the windows with the shutters; we must have darkness in here, then we can see through the walls. After that the three of you will stand by the switchboards for the defensive weapons. I'll give orders. Get ready."

"Very well, Master," Forjan nodded—for, brother or no brother, Varkol was always the commander-in-chief.

Down in what had once been Trafalgar Square, at the foot of the great building—the building without visible doors—Tom was shouting to the army he had brought with him; an army equipped with hastily made machines, constructed from his own knowledge of Varkol's own complicated weapons, and aided by his electrically-given genius.

"My friends, this is our only chance to destroy the invaders. If we fail, you know the penalty at sundown tomorrow. Probably my friend is in here, too, but if he is we cannot discriminate. The invaders must be destroyed, no matter who goes with them. It is the only course. Now—open fire! Our very lives depend on this!"

Immediately there sprang from the machines of the remarkable civilian army rays of various colours—some heat-rays, some cold-rays, others disintegrators—which with one accord hurled a battering ram of destruction upon the grey walls of the Controlling Building. Nothing happened. The maldelene steel remained impervious...

Then came the answer.

From hitherto unnoticed apertures high up in the six-story building, there poured forth a death-dealing barrage of counter-rays, rays which carved a hideous arc of death and smoke wherever they touched. The people screamed and fell back. Those who were not quick enough vanished in clouds of fine ash! The very concrete of the ground was riven asunder by the nameless, terrifying force, and smoking, bottomless chasms and abysses appeared.

"Open war!" Tom thundered. "Let 'em have it! *All* your weapons!"

Under this order tractors, guided and driven by atomic motors, rumbled heavily through the smoke, bearing monster machines, from which sprang invisible radiations of electricity. The instant the radiations hit the walls they turned into cascading streams of blue and purple fire, crackling and flashing—yet still, to Tom's growing horror, the building remained untouched and hardly scratched by the frightful onslaught. In the meantime, the terrible weapons of the Time Invaders were wreaking death and destruction in all directions. People were vanishing by the dozen under the disintegrator and heat-beams, far greater in efficiency than anything Tom had devised—secret machines, of which Varkol had never spoken. Evidently he had deemed it wisest to keep warfare knowledge private.

"Only one last course," Tom muttered at length, to the man who was acting as his commander-in chief. "Try out that disruptive energy thing we brought along. It's loaded with two tons of pure copper. It seems to me that the instant disintegration of all that copper into pure energy ought to blow this building to the skies. We can but try. Tell the people to get back; there'll be danger."

Hurriedly, the news reaching them, the people pressed back and the tractor containing the copper-energy releaser moved forward, governed now by remote radio control, so that the operators could be well out of range. At length Tom nodded, and himself depressed the disruptive-current button.

An unearthly blaze of green fire hurled itself *en masse* at the edifice. The ground shook and quaked, the beams of the Time invaders were hidden for a while in the eye-paralysing glare, as the copper converted itself into pure energy. Smoke rose in dense, solid columns; an appalling din split the ears drums… Then the confusion began to subside, and with it sank the hearts of the brave little army who had fought so desperately for their liberty and freedom.

The building still stood—untouched!

"We're done!" Tom groaned hopelessly. "Oh, why did I ever experiment with Time! The disaster I've brought upon the world!"

"No use reproaching yourself now, son," muttered his commander-in-chief, "The damage is done. Varkol wins!"

So the defeated army began to retreat, and the rays of the invaders from Time were cut off as the fact became obvious. The building of maldelene steel was invincible!

At nightfall. Bob was released from his bonds and allowed to move about in comfort. The four rulers of London, complacent in their victory, spent the time strolling about the edifice and planning carefully for their intended future conquest. They took good care, however, to leave the room containing the Asphyxiator securely locked.

Having no need to guard Bob they left him to his own devices, seated deep in thought, and, talking amongst themselves, left the main control room.

"There must be a way, a mathematical way, to defeat these monsters!" Bob muttered to himself. "I wonder if… That pedigree of theirs! It seems it ought to be of use somewhere. I.... Good heavens!" He sat up with a jerk in his chair, astounded by a sudden conception. His face flushed with the audacity and yet scientific possibility of it. "Tom! If I can radio him!" he breathed. "It's a chance!"

In an instant he had crossed, for the second time that day, to the radio machines and began another careful search. This time, to his satisfaction, he met with luck, finding Tom where he expected—in St. James' Park. The place was floodlit with electric arcs, and, in the loudspeaker, which Bob kept muffled perchance the invaders might hear it, Tom was apparently sitting, listening to reports over a radio set from the new London broadcasting station.

Intently Bob searched the televisor screen and presently detected the radio set front which the voice was emanating—a few adjustments and he had Tom's face clear on the screen. Beyond doubt it was his friend, surrounded by a group of his immediate supporters. There was little doubt of the melancholy expressions on the faces of everybody.

Bob quickly adjusted the wavelength apparatus of the invaders' radio-televisor, issuing forth a heterodyning wavelength that immediately cut out the announcer's voice in the St. James' Park radio set. Tom and the others looked up in surprise—then became rigid in attention as Bob's own voice floated to them in place of that of the announcer.

"Tom! Tom! Listen! This is Bob speaking from the controlling building—and it's dangerous work, too. The invaders may be back at any moment. Listen carefully. The only way to save London is to get that pedigree from your safe back at home—your house was one of those which wasn't altered, as you know—and find the address that was given for Robert Halford. He's the ancestor of these four invaders. Find him, and explain to him that the only way to save London is for him to die, for by so doing he will destroy the ancestral line. At that rate the invaders should vanish from sight! It's Time logic, and the only chance. Can't say more now. Act!"

* * * *

The night passed quietly enough, and the following day until towards sundown. Then Bob was quietly but firmly placed in the area of the Asphyxiator and immovably secured to it. Varkol surveyed him with grim satisfaction.

"You have one hour, my young friend—then extinction."

Bob compressed his lips. He wondered what Tom was doing; certainly he had received the message—that much had been seen from the televisor. But what was happening in the interval? Bob's heart seemed to sink with the sun, until presently Varkol's voice jerked him into alertness again.

"Five minutes, my young friend." The master-scientist reached out his hand to the main lever for starting the generators, his eyes on his strange watch. "Four minutes! Three... Two...."

He clutched the lever tenaciously, preparatory to pulling it over, then, before Bob's very eyes, the four men mysteriously melted and vanished from sight!

The room was empty!

Sobbing with relief he found himself overcome with the strain and fainted clean away.

When he came to, Tom was leaning over him.

"Bob! Thank heaven you're not dead!" Tom whispered. "I could never have forgiven myself. Your idea has probably saved the world—just as mine nearly destroyed it!"

"You mean—you mean you found Robert Halford?" Bob asked, sitting up, alert again. "My idea worked?"

"To perfection. Yes, we tracked down Halford—the address was correct—and, fortunately for us, he was a scientific sort of chap who fully realised the position—really understood that he was the ancestor of the men from Time. But, by dying—which in the urgency of the case was done by an overdose of drug at his own wish—he destroyed the ancestral line by defeating Time itself. Hence, all those who really came after him never really existed once he died. So, our four enemies from Time evaporated into thin air. Halford died at one minute to six exactly."

"Yes—yes. The invaders vanished at the same second," Bob nodded. "I thought my idea was right, and thank goodness for that pedigree we stole, otherwise we'd never have been able to do it. But, Tom, if Halford killed himself how did the ancestral line ever come to be in existence at all? As I see it, the invaders never existed, because they were never even born! You can't cheat Time."

"It depends." Tom answered thoughtfully. "There are two states of consciousness, conscious and subconscious. In one, the invaders might be still existing; in the other, by what we've done, we caused them to lose—er—visible entity. Get it? It is all a paradox. What is Time but a paradox, anyhow? We've got rid of them, and I've become a genius through them; we've got a super city and everything—so why worry?"

"How did you get in here, anyhow?"

"Climbed up to one of the windows and smashed it through with a force-ray. Only ordinary glass, you know. Well, that about finishes our little adventure with Time, and thank goodness for it. What more can we ask?"

"I'll tell you. A good meal and a shave."

"Right on the nail! Let's be going!"

# ABOUT THE AUTHOR

British writer **JOHN RUSSELL FEARN** was born near Manchester, England, in 1908. As a child he devoured the science fiction of Wells and Verne, and was a voracious reader of the Boys' Story Papers. He was also fascinated by the cinema, and first broke into print in 1931 with a series of articles in *Film Weekly*.

He then quickly sold his first novel, *The Intelligence Gigantic*, to the American magazine, *Amazing Stories*. Over the next fifteen years, writing under several pseudonyms, Fearn became one of the most prolific contributors to all of the leading US science fiction pulps, including such legendary publications as *Astounding Stories*, *Startling Stories*, *Thrilling Wonder Stories*, and *Weird Tales*.

During the late 1940s he diversified into writing novels for the UK market, and also created his famous superwoman character, The Golden Amazon, for the prestigious Canadian magazine, the Toronto *Star Weekly*. In the early 1950s in the UK, his fifty-two novels as "Vargo Statten" were bestsellers, most notably his novelization of the film, *Creature from the Black Lagoon*.

Apart from science fiction, he had equal success with westerns, romances, and detective fiction, writing an amazing total of 180 novels—most of them in a period of just ten years—before his early death in 1960. His work has been translated into nine languages, and continues to be reprinted and read worldwide.

### THE ANJANI SERIES

*The Gold of Akada: A Jungle Adventure Novel*
*Anjani the Mighty: A Lost Race Novel*

### THE BLACK MARIA SERIES

*Black Maria, M.A.: A Classic Crime Novel*
*The Murdered Schoolgirl: A Classic Crime Novel*
*One Remained Seated: A Classic Crime Novel*
*Thy Arm Alone: A Classic Crime Novel*
*Death in Silhouette: A Classic Crime Novel*

### THE HERBERT THE DINOSAUR SERIES

*A Thing of the Past*
*The Genial Dinosaur*

### THE ADAM QUIRKE SERIES

*The Master Must Die: Impossible Crime Science Fiction Novel*
*The Lonely Astronomer: Impossible Crime Science Fiction Novel*

### OTHER BOOKS

*1,000-Year Voyage: A Science Fiction Novel*
*Account Settled: A Science Fiction Mystery*
*Before Earth Came: Classic Science Fiction Stories*
*Bury the Hatchet: A Crime Tale*
*A Case for Brutus Lloyd: A Science Fiction Mystery*
*The Crimson Rambler: A Crime Novel*
*Don't Touch Me: A Crime Novel*
*Dynasty of the Small: Classic Science Fiction Stories*
*The Empty Coffins: A Mystery of Horror*
*The Fourth Door: A Mystery Novel*
*From Afar: A Science Fiction Mystery*
*Fugitive of Time: A Classic Science Fiction Novel*
*The G-Bomb: A Science Fiction Novel*

*Here and Now: A Science Fiction Novel*
*Into the Unknown: A Science Fiction Tale*
*Last Conflict: Classic Science Fiction Stories*
*Legacy from Sirius: A Classic Science Fiction Novel*
*The Man from Hell: Classic Science Fiction Stories*
*The Man Who Was Not: A Crime Novel*
*Manton's World: A Classic Science Fiction Novel*
*Moon Magic: A Novel of Romance (as Elizabeth Rutland)*
*One Way Out: A Crime Novel (with Philip Harbottle)*
*Pattern of Murder: A Classic Crime Novel*
*Reflected Glory: A Dr. Castle Classic Crime Novel*
*Robbery Without Violence: Two Science Fiction Crime Stories*
*Rule of the Brains: Classic Science Fiction Stories*
*Shattering Glass: A Crime Novel*
*The Silvered Cage: A Scientific Murder Mystery*
*Slaves of Ijax: A Science Fiction Novel*
*Something from Mercury: Classic Science Fiction Stories*
*The Space Warp: A Science Fiction Novel*
*The Time Trap: A Science Fiction Novel*
*Valley of Pretenders: Classic Science Fiction Stories*
*Vision Sinister: A Scientific Detective Thriller*
*Voice of the Conqueror: A Classic Science Fiction Novel*
*What Happened to Hammond? A Scientific Mystery*
*Within That Room!: A Classic Crime Novel*
*World Without Chance: Classic Science Fiction Stories*

www.ingramcontent.com/pod-product-compliance
Lightning Source LLC
Chambersburg PA
CBHW022153260626
47155CB00018B/1867